Did she truly
who seemed so unfeeling?

Then again, suitors were not exactly lining up at
Glamorgan's gates. Ariana could scarcely afford to
be choosy about her husband. Her heart hammered
in her chest, as much from being caught skulking about
the door as from nervousness at meeting the knight.
Flustered hands straightened her surcoat as she cleared
her throat and strode forward. Heat rose in her cheeks.

Hope sparkled through her when the stranger turned
green eyes upon her. For one shining moment it seemed
as if the veil of the curse had lifted. His gaze penetrated
her with the intense scrutiny of a man seeking a mate,
and in that moment she connected with him on some
unspoken, fundamental level.

And then it vanished.

The curse still loomed, but by God, Roarke Barret had
seen through it for one incredible instant...!

* * *

The Knight's Redemption
Harlequin Historical #720—September 2004

Ch Br

Praise for Harlequin Historical author Joanne Rock

"Charming characters, a passionate sexual relationship and an engaging story—it's all here."
—*Romantic Times* on
Girl's Guide to Hunting and Kissing

"Saucy, smart and sexy, Rock's story rocks with a hero to die for, a classy heroine and a romance that will leave you breathless."
—*Romantic Times* on *Sex & the Single Girl*

"Joanne Rock's talent for writing passionate scenes and vivid characters really sizzles in this story. Even the hot secondary romance has chemistry!"
—*Romantic Times* on *Wild and Wicked*

The Wedding Knight
"*The Wedding Knight* is guaranteed to please! Joanne Rock brings a fresh, vibrant voice to this charming tale."
—*New York Times* bestselling author Teresa Medeiros

Joanne Rock

The Knight's Redemption

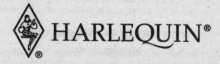
HARLEQUIN®

TORONTO • NEW YORK • LONDON
AMSTERDAM • PARIS • SYDNEY • HAMBURG
STOCKHOLM • ATHENS • TOKYO • MILAN • MADRID
PRAGUE • WARSAW • BUDAPEST • AUCKLAND

ISBN 0-373-29320-8

THE KNIGHT'S REDEMPTION

Copyright © 2004 by Joanne Rock

This edition published by arrangement with Harlequin Books S.A.

® and TM are trademarks of the publisher. Trademarks indicated with ® are registered in the United States Patent and Trademark Office, the Canadian Trade Marks Office and in other countries.

www.eHarlequin.com

Printed in U.S.A.

Please address questions and book requests to:
Harlequin Reader Service
U.S.: 3010 Walden Ave., P.O. Box 1325, Buffalo, NY 14269
Canadian: P.O. Box 609, Fort Erie, Ont. L2A 5X3

For Kim Hacking, who listened to the long version of the dream that inspired this book while we watched our little boys play at the beach. And while it wasn't always easy to attend to the real-life concerns of toddlers while still sharing pieces of ourselves, you somehow found time for Jungian psychology, world religions or Arthurian legends while we doled out peanut butter sandwiches.
Thank you for believing in me and my stories.

And to Cecil Wall, for being my first fan.
Thank you for making me feel like family during my time in Utah, because "I was a stranger, and you invited me in." I wish you all the best!

Prologue

Wales, 1260

"*The knight we have dreamed of enters the realm before nightfall. Do not let him escape you.*"

Though the whispered words emanated from the lips of a dazed old woman, they were of grave import to Ariana Glamorgan.

"A man?" Shifting closer to the drowsy figure on the hard wooden bench, Ariana touched the seer through the fog of hickory-scented smoke wafting from the stone hearth, hoping to gather more insight before the trance dissipated. "At Glamorgan?"

But the wisewoman's gray head drooped forward as if in sleep, and Ariana knew her mentor's revelations were finished for today.

"Arise, Eleanor." She shook the healer gently, frustrated she would learn no more about this mysterious newcomer and eager to test the truth of the woman's vision. "I must return to the keep."

Full blue skirts swirled around Ariana's feet as she stood and gathered her things from the small wooden cottage. The fustian gown was rich and obtrusive to wear while sneaking about the forest, but Lord Glamorgan insisted his daughter don nothing but the finest garments.

One of many ways he restricted his only daughter.

Impatiently, she pushed up the heavy lace sleeves and collected the herbs Eleanor had mixed before she took up her seat in front of the fire in a search for prophetic visions.

The old woman woke with a start, her gaze focused and penetrating as she peered into Ariana's eyes. "I have foreseen a foreigner's arrival, child. He may be your only chance to break the curse."

Ariana hesitated, gazing into the beloved older woman's eyes. Eleanor had been her nurse. Her mother's nurse. But that had been before her father banished the old woman from his keep when she failed to save his wife with her healing.

"You do want to free yourself from the Glamorgan legend, do you not, my dear?"

Desperately. She had endured her father's bitterness and the suffocating atmosphere of her doomed household long enough. Having given up any pastimes that would bring her pleasure within the confines of Glamorgan, Ariana still pursued her love of music in secret, retreating to the forest to sing and to seek out the wisewoman for her counsel and for lessons in the healing arts.

Now, she would give anything to break the cycle of unhappiness that held her and her nieces in thrall.

Whether the so-called curse of the Glamorgan women was real or imagined, the females of Ariana's line had certainly experienced more than their share of heartache for nearly one hundred years. 'Twas whispered that long ago a Glamorgan woman stole another woman's love. The spurned female cursed all the family's daughters to spinsterhood, a fate that had claimed all of Ariana's aunts ever since.

Twisting her fingers through the intricate adornment of her cuffs, she confided her biggest fear. "But what if this stranger is not well suited to me? 'Tis such a gamble to rest my future on the shoulders of a man I know nothing about."

Pacing the dirt floor, Ariana hummed away her nervousness in a halting rendition of a somber chant she'd heard at chapel, an ancient habit she'd never fully conquered.

"'Tis not as bad as all that, my girl." Eleanor cast her a stern look, the weathered furrows lining her face deepening. "The situation hardly warrants a funeral dirge."

Chastened, Ariana paused her song as well as her pacing.

"If you break the curse with a marriage, you will bless your brother's daughters with a bright future as prospective brides." Eleanor rose, her posture bent, but the tilt of her chin still proud despite her ancient years. She smoothed one leathery hand over upswept snowy locks. "Furthermore, you know your marriage was your mother's greatest wish. Her last wish."

Ariana chewed her lip in thought, needing no reminder of her final promise to her mother. "The girls deserve a happy fate." Nervous fingers worried the polished amethyst stones strung about her wrist. "How can our futures rest in the hands of one man? A stranger to Wales, no less."

Eleanor leaned close to whisper. "All of Cymru knows of the legend surrounding your family. Some of the locals even claim blood ties to the jilted lover who supposedly cursed your line when she was tossed aside for a Glamorgan bride. With that much history hanging over your head, no Welshman would ever dare to wed you even if he could see you for the fair young woman you are."

Ariana sighed, knowing Eleanor spoke the truth. Her father never missed an opportunity to remind her of as much.

Eleanor moved toward her herb cabinet and began filling a little sack. "Your only hope is to capture the attention of a foreigner to our land. My vision tells me such a man arrives this very day. Even more fortuitous—he does not plan to stay for any length of time. Such an advantageous situation is unlikely to arise again soon."

"Aye." Ariana's belly churned with an equal mix of nerves and anticipation. The thought of escaping her oppressive household held great appeal, but the danger of finding herself tied to a man more acrimonious than her father distressed her. "But I will not even try to catch his eye if he looks to be cruel or harsh in his nature."

Well-worn hands patted Ariana's smooth ones. "You will do what is best, I am certain."

Nodding, Ariana pulled open the door before turning back to the wisewoman. "What if I cannot make

myself attractive to him? What if this whispered curse
of the Glamorgan woman is truly at work tonight and
the man sees right through me? And even if I can intrigue this stranger, Father will not let me marry."

Thomas Glamorgan's hateful disposition demanded everyone around him suffer fully for the
weight of his family's curse. Ariana knew he would
never consent to burdening some unsuspecting
stranger with the millstone of his bewitched daughter.
No, he would far rather suffer and wail about his fate
than try to change it.

The old woman handed her the small cheesecloth
sack she'd prepared and smiled with the knowing of
Eve. "I've taught you how to use these herbs before, my
child. They can help you in your quest. And if it is
meant to be, you will know. All obstacles will fall away
if fate wishes to see you wed."

A tremor of fear skittered down Ariana's spine, followed quickly by a strong dose of resolve.

"Thank you." She kissed her friend's cheek.

Gathering her cloak more tightly about her, Ariana
stepped out into the misty afternoon, a morose ballad
of star-crossed lovers on her lips.

Peering into the deep green forest before her, she
willed her eyes to see through the thicket of oak trees
to Glamorgan to discern this mysterious knight for
herself, but her ability with the sight could not be
forced. As fickle as Welsh weather, her limited gift
allowed her to see things only at the most inconvenient times.

She would simply have to see the man for herself.

Stuffing Eleanor's linen pouch full of herbs into her

troublesome loose sleeve, Ariana hurried toward the keep and wondered if this would be the night she would meet the warrior of her dreams.

Chapter One

∼∽∾∿

"I don't know if there is a woman to meet your needs about Glamorgan, Sir Barret. If you would be willing to extend your stay in Wales, perhaps, we could find someone suitable in the outlying areas."

Thomas Glamorgan's words from the great hall caught Ariana's attention as she hastened through the keep toward her bedchamber. Too intrigued to consider the impropriety of her actions, she paused just outside the entrance. If she did not listen to her father's conversation herself, she would certainly never hear news of it otherwise.

"A fortnight?" A deep masculine voice rumbled through the hall and tripped over Ariana's senses. "I will be in Wales less than a sennight 'ere I sail for France on a mission for the king. I assure you, my lord, I have the ear of King Henry and if you can be of help to me, he will no doubt remember the kindness. But I cannot wait for days to find a wife. I have been granted a Welsh keep, but only if I can find a Welsh wife to go along with it."

Her fingers froze in the midst of fiddling with her amethyst bracelet. The voice in the great hall could only belong to one man—the foreigner Eleanor foresaw.

And he was looking for a bride.

Sweet Arianrhod, the situation seemed too good to be true. Hadn't she promised herself she would not indulge in hopeful flights of fancy anymore? Hadn't she tucked away her fairy-tale dreams of marriage and family?

Yet she couldn't suppress the happy tune that danced about her head any more than she could still her racing heart as she strained to hear their conversation.

"But Barret, surely you jest." Her father spluttered in indignant surprise. No doubt the notion of undertaking such a task in a rushed manner galled her father. The Lord of Glamorgan was a man of cherished routines, as predictable and full of gloom as his daughter was eccentric and full of life.

Still, Ariana knew her father to be a man who both feared and respected politics. He would be swayed to help the man if only for a small assurance his borderland keep would be at peace in any disputes between the Welsh and their more powerful English neighbors.

"Glamorgan boasts no highborn ladies traipsing about on a daily basis," Thomas managed between incensed coughs. "It will take time to invite the most eligible girls for your inspection. You would not want some serving wench for a wife when you seek a mistress for Llandervey."

"I do not seek an heiress, merely a reasonable, biddable woman with many childbearing years ahead of her." The stranger's tone rang clipped and sharp, as if annoyed.

Had he honestly just said he sought a *biddable* woman? Dear heaven, but that wasn't a good sign. No one had ever accused her of being compliant.

Still, the richness of his voice itself piqued Ariana's curiosity enough to draw her glance around the door-frame. She yearned for a quick glimpse of the man who might be the key to breaking the curse—or simply dis-pelling the myth of a ridiculous family legend.

Easing around the archway, her mouth promptly went dry at the sight that greeted her eyes.

Utterly imposing, her father's uninvited guest com-manded attention. Stalking the great hall, impatience and frustration evident in every line of his large, mus-cular form, the stranger dwarfed her father by two hand spans. Ariana guessed his shoulders to be twice the width of her own, while his waist and hips narrowed under the swirl of his midnight-blue hauberk.

He looked entirely too ominous in his unrelieved dark garb and road-dusty chain mail, especially standing beside her father whose hunched posture and ill-fitting attire announced to the world his bro-ken spirit.

"Barret" as her father called him, did not look like a man who would appreciate being tricked into mar-riage. Yet, as intimidating as the man appeared, Ariana couldn't break her gaze as she stared at him.

Sable brown hair fell across the shoulder of the for-eigner's dark hauberk, nearly blending in with the black wool of his tunic, which looked surprisingly clean for a knight. Warriors of her acquaintance were all so concerned with fighting and weaponry they appeared to have little time for bathing.

Too bad she could not make out his features from her hidden observation spot.

"What of your own girls, Glamorgan?" The stranger pressed. "Have you no daughters ready for marriage?"

Ariana's heart faltered in her chest for one hopeful moment, though she knew her father would never allow her to wed an unsuspecting stranger. Consumed with his own bitterness, Thomas Glamorgan seemed to enjoy seeing everyone else around him suffer.

"None of interest to you," her father snapped, recovering himself.

Surprised at the depth of her disappointment, Ariana squeezed the bag of Eleanor's charmed herbs still hidden beneath her sleeve. Nothing gave her courage like the reminder of Thomas Glamorgan's insistence that his daughter remain as cursed and unhappy as he. If she did not take fate into her own hands, how would she ever escape her oppressive family seat? Worse, how would her brother's daughters elude the same barren existence?

"Very well." The knight's jaw clenched in obvious affront. "My one concern is to return to France and complete a mission for my king. Garner any women you think might be remotely pleasing and I will view them this eve."

Ariana felt as shocked as her father sounded.

"You cannot mean that," the Lord of Glamorgan returned. "A man of your stature and prestige could command a wealthy heiress. You can surely wait a few days if it means a hefty gold dowry?"

"No." The knight raised his hand to forestall further discussion. "I have my reasons."

Wishing the man would have related those reasons, Ariana wondered what could make him so careless about choosing his spouse. Did she truly want to wed a man who seemed so unfeeling?

Then again, suitors were not exactly lining up at Glamorgan's gates. She could scarcely afford to be choosy about her husband.

Suddenly aware the stranger would see her on his way out if she did not escape the corridor, she attempted to pass the hall and gain the privacy of her rooms when her father's voice halted her.

"Ariana! Come in, my dear, and greet our guest."

Her heart hammered in her chest, as much from being caught skulking about the door as from nervousness at meeting the knight. Flustered hands straightened her surcoat as she cleared her throat and strode forward. Heat rose in her cheeks.

Hope sparkled through her when the stranger turned green eyes upon her. For one shining moment, it seemed as if the veil of the curse had lifted. His gaze penetrated her with the intense scrutiny of a man seeking a mate, and in that moment, she connected with him on some unspoken, fundamental level.

And then it vanished.

His brow furrowed, and she knew he felt the bond fade, too. He looked at her then as all men looked at her, with vague, unseeing eyes.

The curse still loomed, but by God, this man had seen through it for one incredible instant.

Thomas Glamorgan scarcely bothered to look at her,

however. "Roarke Barret, this is my only daughter, Ariana. You'd be most welcome to take her for your bride if she weren't—"

"No." The knight interrupted him just in time to prevent her father from revealing her affliction. He peered at her for a long moment before shaking his head. "You have made it clear you do not want to give up your daughter. I will see the other women tonight."

With those words, the English knight brushed past her with such abrupt quickness she barely noted anything else about him besides a vague impression of heavy brows and a stony set to his jaw. Mostly, she recalled fascinating emerald eyes.

The stab of disappointment caught her off guard. Except for her father's perpetual misery and bitter resentment toward her, the curse had never bothered her before this year. She never envied her friends the lustful looks men bestowed upon them. But as her twentieth summer loomed, her deathbed promise to her mother began to prey upon her mind. And in truth, her feelings began to change on the matter, too. She did not want to die a spinster like all of her aunts had for the last hundred years. She wanted a family of her own, with children and the freedom to pursue her music whenever she wished.

And a handsome man to notice her.

It was a strange and new feeling, this disappointment. And it suddenly hurt very much to be passed over as if she were worth less notice than the keep's hounds.

"He did not see you, of course." Her father's voice interrupted her thoughts as he stared at her through the cloudy white film encroaching over his failing eyes. He looked down his hooked nose at her, a difficult feat considering his shorter stature and stooped shoulders. Yet Thomas Glamorgan could lift his chin just enough to glare at his daughter in such a way that made her well aware of her unworthiness. "The curse prevents any man but me from seeing you as you really are."

Determined not to raise his suspicions by allowing him to know how much the knight's rebuff stung, Ariana straightened. She wasn't cursed, by God. The Glamorgan legend was a myth perpetuated by rumor and gossip.

She hadn't just dreamed that moment of elemental connection with Roarke Barret. The knight *had* admired her for a moment. Perhaps it had been a sign that he was the man destined to dispel the long-standing fable surrounding the women of her line.

She mustered a smile for her father, unwilling to anger him and risk not being allowed to participate in the evening meal. She had plans to cross paths with Roarke Barret again. "I am hardly invisible."

Although she often wondered why she never warranted a second glance from any man. She had often seen the most humble village women chased with lustful enthusiasm by suitors. Yet, despite what she considered a mildly attractive exterior, no man ever looked at her with anything more than a fleeting glance. Before her mother died, Lady Glamorgan declared the curse utter nonsense, insisting men would travel far and wide to beg for the hand of her beautiful daughter.

But her mother's prediction had yet to come true. Indeed, men were more apt to look right through her.

She awaited her father's answer while he called for

messengers to be dispatched to every nearby nobleman regarding the English knight's visit. Preparations would be made to find the man a bride, and from her father's expression, Ariana had no doubt that he would not allow that woman to be her.

His mouth hardened into the thin line that constituted his version of a smile. "My sister once compared it to being as attractive as a lovely tapestry upon the castle wall. A man might observe beauty in her, but not the kind that was in any way tempting."

Did her father take malicious glee in hurting her? Sometimes it seemed that way, but Ariana maintained a smooth mask of indifference, assuring herself that Welsh men were merely too superstitious about Glamorgan women to look her way. Curses were not taken lightly in a country shrouded in mists and legends.

"Fortunately she found fulfillment in the convent." Her father began a familiar diatribe. "'Tis a shame you have not yet joined her."

After dutifully listening to his lecture on her short-comings and an adamant declaration that he would not suffer her under his roof much longer, Ariana departed the hall.

For once, she hoped her father was correct. She did not want to abide in the dark gloom of Glamorgan Keep any more. If only the stranger could be persuaded to take her to be his wife, she could leave her wretched household forever.

Surely once *one* Glamorgan woman married, all talk of a curse hanging over the females of their line would quickly fade. Her nieces would one day wed and have babes of their own.

Ariana prayed this stranger was The One. The man who would be her destiny.

The knight of her dreams.

Roarke Barret stomped along yet another darkened interior corridor of Glamorgan Keep in search of the kitchens, wondering if the miserly lord had deliberately misled him about the whereabouts of the food rations. The stoop-shouldered Welshman and his gloomy household had cast a pall over a previously fruitful day. In the ten years since Roarke had left his birthplace on the Barret lands in England, he'd met men more cruel and wicked, but none more wretched.

The fact that he had entrusted the sour-faced knave to find him a bride didn't exactly fill him with confidence, but he was running out of time to accomplish the matter and Glamorgan's keep had been the last substantial holding on his way to the coast. Roarke had foolishly delayed his nuptials so long that he had little choice now but to rely on Thomas Glamorgan. Still, heaven only knew what manner of women would be paraded before him this night.

Not that he expected to discover wedded bliss with his new wife. Far from it. He had stopped believing in dreams—especially the love and marriage kind—on a rainy day ten years ago when his mother's perfidy had come to light. The same day his world had crumbled beneath him and revealed him as a bastard instead of a true Barret.

And although he'd searched for a true place to call home ever since, he'd discovered only a power-hungry lord for a true father and other half brothers who lacked the sense of honor that had always been second nature to his mother's other son, Lucian.

A man five times the man Roarke had ever been.

Now he tread the endless corridors of Glamorgan, certain he was at last on his way to securing his own lands and his own place in the world. Squinting into the shadowy passages, he tried to decide if he should forsake the rations until he returned to the keep later that night for supper, when he heard a light footstep on the stone walkway.

The footfall was accompanied by a fanciful love song trilled out in soft, sweet notes.

For a moment, he envisioned that delicate feminine voice accompanied by his lute. A musical harmony that would feed the soul more than any hunk of day-old bread he might find in the kitchen.

But then the voice halted along with the feet, bringing him back to cold reality and the need to distance himself from whimsical thoughts.

He discerned the slender female form in the corridor a few feet away, the memory of her song making a greater impression upon him than any visual image of the young woman.

"My lord." She couldn't hide the surprise in her voice. "I did not expect to meet anyone else in the living quarters."

He recognized the voice of Glamorgan's mysterious daughter he'd met earlier and regretted not being able to see her more clearly. Her raven-dark hair and striking amber eyes had snared him for a moment, making him wish he could choose a wife on the basis of attraction.

A foolish notion.

No doubt, he was better off being blind to Ariana Glamorgan's enticement in this dim hallway.

"Perhaps I misunderstood your father's directions to the kitchens," he began, realizing his voice took on a gruffer note than necessary. "I seek rations for my trip but am unable to find the stairwell your father described."

She surprised him by laughing. A rich, musical sound that caught him off guard. "Perhaps my father misled you on purpose, my lord. He is reputed to have acquired much wealth through unrepentant stinginess. The kitchens are on the other side of the great hall, and I would be glad to show you the way myself."

The desire to walk alongside this enigmatic woman churned through him with palpable force. All the more reason to deny himself the pleasure. A beautiful woman held too much power over a man. Even his own mother's beauty had made her a target for another man's lust.

Nay. He would not allow himself to be tempted by such a woman, no matter how alluring her siren's song. Not now, and not tonight when it came time to choose a bride.

"I will not detain you any longer." He inclined his head just low enough to catch a whiff of her rose-scented hair. Another tactical error. Straightening, he brushed past her, seeking freedom from the dark intimacy of the shadowed corridor. Freedom from his own hungry thoughts. "Thank you, my lady."

And although he managed to escape their conversation, Roarke knew her haunting song would echo in his head long afterward.

Chapter Two

Reaching the safety of her chamber, Ariana eased out of her cloak and tossed the woolen garment across the neat, creamy-colored linens of her bed. Despite the cool autumn weather, her whole body felt alive with heat in the wake of her chance encounter with Roarke Barret. The first man who seemed to see beyond the fog of the Glamorgan legend, the man who could be the key to her destiny.

Excitement tripped through her despite his refusal to let her accompany him to the kitchen. Now more than ever she needed to find a way to make herself eligible for marriage, to present herself as an option tonight at the supper where he would choose his bride.

She twirled about the bright chamber hung with colorful tapestries and the few other decorative pieces she'd managed to smuggle from her dead mother's belongings before her father, in a fit of morose heartache, had everything else burned. She hugged herself to calm her thudding heart when a soft tap sounded at the adjoining door.

A voice whispered through the heavy wooden barrier. "It's Ceara. May I come in?"

Ariana hurried to unlatch the door and admit her cousin. "You know you are always welcome."

Ceara Llywen hurried into the chamber as if demons were in pursuit. Long cinnamon-colored hair floated more regally behind her. Though still awkward and shy at sixteen years old, she was quite beautiful and happily unaffected by the family curse thanks to her relation on Ariana's mother's side. Ceara's amber eyes, so like her own, were wide with dismay. "Is it true a stranger has come to seek a bride?"

"Aye, but you've no need to be frightened of him."

Ceara moved about the room, fingering small objects as she flitted from one spot to another. Now she ran her fingers over the intricately carved mahogany that framed a looking glass. "Is he not a nobleman?"

"Aye. Or soon will be. The king just granted him a Welsh keep, it seems." Ariana responded distractedly, trying to decide if she wanted to delve into the bag of Eleanor's charmed herbs in an effort to work a little magic tonight.

Not that Ariana credited the bag of dried plant leaves with much more power than a good-luck charm. But what if the herbs really could help make her visible to the stranger?

Ceara cleared her throat. Replaced the looking glass. "What if your father seeks to wed *me* to the man?"

The question, so full of trepidation and fear, captured Ariana's attention.

"And you would not want to marry him, Ceara, honestly?" Ariana set down the mysterious bag of herbs and settled beside her cousin, unwilling to allow her own desires to infringe upon Ceara's tender heart.

"Nay!" Ceara's violent head shake sent cinnamon strands dancing over her shoulders. "I do not wish to wed any man. I hope with all my heart I might take the veil once your father realizes how adamant I am in my course."

Though Ceara was not cursed by Glamorgan legend because she was Ariana's maternal cousin, she longed for the fate Ariana had fought the last four years. Sadly, Ariana wondered if her father might not force Ceara to wed against her will just to spread the legacy of Glamorgan unhappiness.

"Even if I did marry," Ceara continued, "I would never, ever, wed such a man as the giant who rode here this afternoon atop that great black beast."

Eleanor's prediction floated back to Ariana.

The knight we have dreamed of enters the realm before nightfall.

"You saw him when he rode in?"

Ceara nodded. "I have never seen a horse or man so huge. He is a man of war and English besides. They thrive on battle."

Ceara's parents had been killed two years earlier in an uprising along the Welsh-English border. She'd lived at Glamorgan ever since, a ward of the most notoriously miserable household in Wales.

Ceara did not want to wed. Ariana did. Thomas Glamorgan wouldn't let Ariana marry an unsuspecting foreigner, but would gladly allow Ceara to marry a man she feared.

A far-fetched scheme began to take root in Ariana's mind.

"If you do not wish to be considered as a bride for

the stranger, Ceara, I have a wonderful plan that will benefit both of us." Ariana smiled to encourage her cousin. "But it will require you to stay in your rooms tonight. You will have to allow me to bring you supper."

Would it ever work? Would she dare a ploy so underhanded to escape Glamorgan?

Ceara nodded eagerly. "It is my fondest wish to avoid the great hall this eve."

Taking a deep breath, Ariana strengthened her resolve. "I want to pretend that I am you."

"What?"

"You know I have been visiting the wisewoman to help me find a way to overcome the rampant unhappiness associated with my family, do you not?"

"I knew you went secretly to her cottage, but I did not realize what for. Do you think she can really help you?"

Briefly, Ariana explained Eleanor's vision and the little bag of herbs she'd received from the wisewoman. Toying with the amethysts on her bracelet, she blurted out her plan. "I want to take a chance and test the power of those charmed leaves tonight, Ceara. If there is any way to ensure the stranger sees beyond the fog of the so-called curse, I am ready to give it a try. If he chooses to wed with me, all talk of a curse will cease and my nieces will be free of this madness."

Wide-eyed, Ceara listened, then shook her head. "I think you have to accomplish more than getting him to marry you," she whispered.

"What—*Ceara*," Ariana chided her cousin with dawning realization. The Glamorgan woman always suspected it would take physical union with a man for the curse to be broken, though they had no way of knowing for sure. "Once we are married it should only follow that he would claim his marital rights."

Ceara laughed, appearing more at ease now that the burden of dinner was lifted from her shoulders. "I hope you are correct, cousin. I would hate to see you wed this intimidating foreigner for naught."

Silence fell for a long moment before Ceara continued, "Why would you pretend to be me? You want this man to see you for who you really are, but you would pretend to be someone else? I do not understand."

"You know Father would never allow anyone to marry me who did not know about the legend surrounding our family. But if Father thinks it is *you* the stranger wants, he will gladly speed things along just to be spiteful."

Ceara's eyes widened. "You really think you can fool Uncle Thomas?"

"Yes, although I will do my best to keep my distance from him, lest he discover the trick." Ariana stood, impatient to begin the necessary preparations. She still needed to collect a few of the herbs she needed to bring her luck tonight. "But if we are to succeed we must hurry. Are you willing to try?"

All obstacles will fall away if Fate wishes to see you wed....

"But *I* won't actually be marrying anyone?"

"Of course not!" Ariana laughed, her spirit soaring along with the song in her heart. She pulled Ceara over to the small looking glass that hung near her wardrobe. "But you *would* have to part with something very special." Absently, she twisted one of Ceara's long red locks between her fingers, so different from her own raven tresses.

Explaining her scheme to her cousin as she gathered her cloak for one final herb-gathering venture, Ariana felt the first real stirring of hope—an emotion she had feared long squashed by her father. But just now, as the afternoon shadows lengthened and the evening loomed full of possibility, Ariana dared to believe in her dreams.

Under a smattering of warm spring sunlight, Roarke dived into the bracing waters of a Welsh stream, hoping to wash away his fiery attraction to the lord of Glamorgan's daughter along with the dirt from the road.

His long strokes knifed through the murky water, focusing him on his one goal—obtain a Welsh wife to secure his Welsh lands. The English king's command had been explicit and Roarke planned to fulfill it in the morn. At long last, he would accomplish his most closely held ambition.

Despite his noble parentage, Roarke's bastardy had cast a shadow across his name and rendered him all but penniless. Although he'd been raised as a legitimate son of the Barret house, he'd later discovered his mother had forsaken her wedding vows during the Crusades when she thought her husband dead. She'd kept the secret her whole life, but shortly after she died the truth had been revealed, much to his devastation.

Since then, he had tracked down his real father—a man he would never be proud to claim as kin—and relentlessly pursued his own lands. It had taken constant attendance to King Henry to earn a place at his side and finally a respected place as one of his closest knights, but at long last, his lands were within his grasp.

Of course, true to his luck he had been given a keep among the notoriously rebellious Welsh. The keep would be difficult to hold, but worse yet, his claim was contingent upon marriage to a Welsh wife.

Another man might have taken his time to find just the right woman to wed. Not Roarke. When last he'd chosen the ideal woman to marry—a vibrant childhood friend who had been sold into the convent by her parents—his half brother Lucian had wooed her away. Likewise, Lucian's father had loved their mother to distraction and it hadn't prevented her from straying the moment she thought he was dead. Roarke had come to think he'd be better off choosing a practical woman of a more grounded, sensible nature.

His new wife would be respected as part of his household, but she would never be a part of his heart.

Scrubbing his hair clean in the glistening waters of the stream, Roarke tried to forget a voice inside him had decried his own dictum concerning a wife when he had gazed into Ariana Glamorgan's eyes. For one awkward moment, he felt as if a lightning bolt had struck him; his senses overloaded by a wisp of a Welsh girl. But as they'd spoken in the corridor afterward, he'd realized she was too fanciful, too dreamy-eyed to be the kind of woman he needed.

The sharp snap of a twig on the south side of the stream brought his ruminations to a halt. Ceasing his strokes, Roarke tread water, waiting for another noise to follow.

He was being watched.

Not a superstitious man by nature, he knew the eyes that followed him were no ghostly trick of the haunting Welsh landscape. If ten years of service to King Henry had taught him anything, it was the sixth sense of knowing when he was being observed. The further he advanced in the king's good graces, the more often predatory eyes followed him.

"Show yourself," he ordered, irked when a bird chirped heedlessly above him. He swam to the shore, hoping to draw out the watcher. Before he reached the bank, a feminine voice called down to him.

"I did not mean to interrupt your swim, my lord." Ariana Glamorgan stepped from the thicket, a fistful of herbs in one hand, her lightweight cloak clenched to her bodice with the other. Dark hair tumbled around her shoulders while her lips curled into a saucy grin. "But since you commanded I present myself, I thought I had better come forward."

Shoving aside thoughts of the watcher who had been following him of late, Roarke wondered if he imagined the teasing note in her tone. No daughter of the dour Lord Glamorgan could possibly be indulging in open flirtation. Yet there she stood, peering down into the water at him with curious eyes. "You are gathering herbs so late in the season, Lady Ariana?"

"Aye." She sifted through the small green stalks she carried and tore away some excess stems in favor of the waxy leaves. "Herbal knowledge is a Glamorgan tradition. Perhaps you are familiar with the women of my clan?"

"I know naught of Welsh custom or nobility." Although he wouldn't mind getting to know this brazen creature with eyes that seemed to peer into the water for some hint of his nakedness. He could not recall meeting a more engaging female than this dark-haired temptress who appeared everywhere he wandered today, but Ariana's curious gaze and teasing smile were hardly the qualities he sought in a wife. And he would never make an overture toward the daughter of his host without her father's consent. No matter what stray stirrings he felt for this woman, he would not act upon them. "But I do not wish to detain you in your search."

"Very good." Nodding slowly, she seemed unusually satisfied at his response. "And I do not wish to detain you, either. Surely you have important plans afoot if you are to meet your bride this eve."

True enough. Though he found he didn't look forward to sitting in the great hall tonight half as much as he wished to keep Ariana nearby for a few more moments.

"I trust you will be joining us at dinner?" He surprised himself by asking the question since he could not act on his attraction to the woman anyhow.

"Perhaps." She shifted on her feet as if suddenly nervous. Wary. Lifting her gaze to peer into the sky quickly shifting to twilight, she reached one slender arm to point heavenward. "There is the first star of the night, my lord. Let us wish upon it that you may find the maid of your dreams for a bride."

Damn.

She could not have found a faster way to cool the fire in his blood than with her fanciful wishes.

"I assure you I am no dreamer." The chill of the water seeped into his skin, calling their conversation to an end and drawing Roarke to the task at hand this eve. "Perhaps I should allow you to do the wishing for us both."

As if sensing the darkening of his mood, the lady took a step back, her hand falling to her side once again. "Although I am quite accustomed to casting extra wishes on behalf of those around me, I would not steal that right from a stranger. May you find that which you seek, Lord Barret."

She disappeared into the forest as quickly as she had arrived, noiseless and invisible in the growing dark. Roarke knew a moment's pang at having scared her off with his surliness, but there had been no point in idle chatter with a woman he would never see again after tonight.

Hauling himself out of the water now that the maiden had left, Roarke scaled the slippery moss-covered rocks in time to spy his friend and fellow knight Collin Baldwin tromp down the bank opposite where Ariana Glamorgan had recently stood. Friends from Roarke's days at Barret Keep, he and Collin had traveled together ever since—Roarke seeking to expand his fortunes, Collin seeking any joy that life had to offer.

"I thought you were growing fins down here, Barret." Collin scrubbed a hand over a scruffy beard he'd been growing since they entered Wales and threw Roarke a length of linen. "Are you aware Glamorgan's dinner awaits?"

"Aye." Unwilling to speak of his interlude with the lady Ariana, Roarke blotted at the rivulets on his chest before taking up his tunic. "And though you are simply eager for your next meal, I am seeking a wife. Such pursuits are not easily forgotten."

"Should be a pleasure fondly remembered if you did it the right way. Do you even speak the Welsh tongue?" Collin had been scouting Glamorgan lands for signs they were being followed. Now, he whickered to Roarke's horse while he waited for Roarke to dress. "If you wed a low-born wife, as you seem intent upon, she will not know English or French."

"And what, pray tell, will we need to speak to one another about?" Roarke wondered aloud, mentally plaguing his friend for raising the subject again. "The last I knew, the begetting of heirs did not require a great deal of talk."

Searching his saddlebag for fresh clothing, his fingers brushed the small lute his mother had given him. Although she bade him play the stringed instrument for peace of mind, Roarke associated it with his mother and her dreamy-eyed weakness. The lute rarely left the bottom of his traveling bag, but he could not help his occasional need to prevail upon it, taking solace in the haunting sounds of the strings.

"Ah, you may have to talk a little, my friend." Collin raised a blond brow, his big body lounging against a tree. "You would not be so cruel as to force a woman the way Fulke Kendall did your mother."

Roarke tensed. Only Collin could push him this far. And only Collin had interpreted Lady Barret's faithlessness as merely an act of aggression on Lord Kendall's part. "Since when does a man have to force his own wife? I plan to wed the woman who will bear my sons. 'Tis more than my father did."

"Speaking of your sire, what news have you from Southvale? Surely you must have inquired after Lord Kendall's health while you were in London."

"Reports of my father come to me without my asking, as you well know," Roarke muttered, seating himself on the mossy bank to lace well-worn leather boots.

Collin skipped rocks across the creek while he waited. "Has he heard of your new lands? Do you think he will try to make peace with you so he might add Llandervey to the Kendall holdings?"

"I will not allow hard-earned lands or wealth to be sucked into the noble house of Kendall." He tugged his bootlaces harder, the leather lightly biting into his hands. "Fulke can maintain his wealth of holdings and I will be happy to keep my own." Strapping on his sword and smaller knife, he strode toward Glamorgan Keep, alert to any small movements in the forest.

In case the watcher returned? Or did he hope to catch another glimpse of Ariana?

Collin hastened to catch up as the bell tolled the hour for vespers. "Think you Glamorgan has found a suitable wife by now?"

"If by suitable, you mean Welsh, then I am certain he has."

"It is not too late, Roarke. You could still convince the king to change his mind about a Welsh bride."

Roarke paused in the clearing just outside the keep gates to face his friend. "It is much too late. I care not who I take for a wife."

Torches flickered brightly through the narrow windows of the keep. Two horse-drawn conveyances deposited guests, mostly laughing females, at the front doors of Glamorgan.

"But if you had longer you might find happiness—"

"Happiness is not a component of most noble marriages." Roarke ground his teeth, trying not to remember his half brother Lucian had found utter fulfillment with his bride. "Frivolous emotion will not bedevil my household." Pivoting on his heel, he stalked toward the gates, ready to meet whatever woman Fate sent his way.

The kitchen staff was given orders to serve the meal late in the day so that as many women as possible could be gathered for Roarke Barret to view. By the time the delayed dinner hour arrived, Ariana's transformation was complete.

She peered back at her reflection, her raven locks artfully hidden underneath the long cinnamon tresses Ceara contributed from her own crowning glory. Her father would never suspect their deception.

"You look beautiful, Ariana. Far better than I did with that hair." Ceara stared at her cousin's face in the polished-silver looking glass. They each possessed the same red hair now, but Ceara's barely reached her shoulders, her locks dispensed with so Ariana might carry out her plan to break the curse.

She bit her lip, sorry to have taken something that most women held so dear. "I feel awful about your hair, cousin. My father will flay me alive when he learns what I have done."

Ceara smiled wistfully, twisting one of Ariana's new red strands around her finger. "Maybe now he will understand how serious I am about taking the veil. I have no need of such adornments."

Ariana only hoped her cousin's gift would not be in vain. What if she could not make herself attractive to Roarke Barret tonight? Heaven knew, she had failed miserably in her attempt to draw him into conversation by the creek.

"You, on the other hand, need this small donation very much." With a girlish impulsiveness she rarely demonstrated, Ceara hugged her cousin. "I consider it a worthwhile cause to help you leave this place. Do you think this stranger is really the one meant for you?"

"He seeks a bride as desperately as I seek a husband." Ariana hummed a tune, as she picked through the herbs she'd collected earlier and hoped she did not overestimate herself. She had no experience with interpreting male interest, thanks to her lifelong reputation as a cursed Glamorgan woman. But she would like to think she'd seen a flicker of interest—heat, even—in the knight's eyes.

"But he is so big." Ceara shuddered. "So dangerous looking. What will he do when he learns how you have deceived him?"

But Ariana had not thought that far ahead. Since seeing the knight and experiencing the strange tingle of excitement when she looked at him, she could only think about escaping Glamorgan and freeing her nieces from the family legend that seemed to have taken on a life of its own. "I'm not sure. I only know I must act quickly, or rue the day I did not take a chance when it came along. A man who cares so little about marriage as to choose his bride over the course of dinner may be very happy to have me in spite of my small ruse."

Ceara winced. "Men are usually quite insistent that their wives are not deceptive, cousin."

"Then maybe he will allow me to leave once he knows our marriage is false." She shrugged as she lit extra tapers about the chamber.

"Saints be praised, cousin. You know nothing of men! A man would never allow his wife to simply *leave* him. He could kill you for your treachery."

Heaven help her, Ceara was beginning to sound as morose as Ariana's father. Could no one in this household ever look at the bright side of things?

"I must try. This nonsense about Glamorgan women has plagued my family for far too many years." Ariana waved away her concern as she poured the herbs from Eleanor's pouch into a mortar to grind them. "But my father may be difficult when he discovers my deception. You must say I cut your hair as you slept, and that you knew nothing of my plan."

"I will emphasize the fact that the long-suffered curse might be broken with you, and he will be placated." Ceara sniffed the powder as Ariana worked. "That smells awful."

"Yet with any luck, my concoction will render me attractive."

Ceara crossed herself. "Dear Lord."

"'Tis no different than sowing the fields with herbs to induce good crops, or baking a coin into the Yule cake for a prosperous future. After a hundred years of spinsterhood, I think the Glamorgan women are entitled to a few desperate measures."

Determination renewed, Ariana headed for the chamber hearth and set the small pot upon the stones. She gave her cousin a gentle nudge toward the door and hoped she was doing the right thing. The stranger needed a Welsh bride as much as she needed to leave Glamorgan. Why shouldn't she be the woman to fulfill his need?

"You'd best bring some of your things from your chamber so you are prepared to lock yourself away in here for the night. Remember, you cannot go below stairs until at least tomorrow afternoon. I heard one of the maids say the knight wishes to leave with his new bride by midmorn."

Ceara hesitated, concern filling her amber eyes. "What shall we say when your father wonders why you are not attending my wedding?"

All obstacles will fall away....

Ariana would make sure of it. "I will have a maid tell him that I am consumed with sadness about the curse, and that attending the wedding of another, when I am destined for spinsterhood, is difficult for me."

Ceara snorted. "You? Ariana Glamorgan is the most doggedly cheerful woman in Wales! Do you think he'll believe it?"

"He'll probably be thrilled to hear I am appropriately depressed for once. Just keep to my rooms tomorrow until I am far away from Glamorgan."

"Godspeed, Ariana. And don't forget to disguise your voice just a little. Your pitch is higher than mine." Ceara gave her friend one last hug. "I will pray for you."

Ariana hurried Ceara out the door and turned back toward the chamber hearth, filled with resolve. Hope.

She sat before the low flame, costumed in imitation of Ceara and ready for the evening meal except for one thing.

The good-luck charm.

Her lips trembled as she prayed for help, asking for her endeavor to be blessed. Then, pouring the ground herbs into the palm of her hand, she closed her eyes and concentrated.

And tossed the powdery concoction into the fire.

Flames burst from the hearth stunning Ariana with a sudden roaring blaze. A strange sense of power rose within her, almost as if a storm gathered inside her, gaining momentum as it whirled through her being.

The tide of emotions churning through her leapt right along with the flames, culminating in a shimmering sensation of light all around her body, wrapping her in golden warmth from head to toe. And Ariana knew, without a doubt, the charm had worked. The amazing sense of strength still gripped her, but the shimmering sensations faded with the hearth blaze, settling into a dull glow that made her want to smile.

She picked up her polished looking glass and examined her face. There was no visible change, of course. But then, Glamorgan women had always been able to see themselves as they truly appeared. Only men overlooked a Glamorgan female, and it was whispered that no man could see the beauty within a Glamorgan woman.

Until now.

Her feet fairly danced in anticipation to venture below stairs. Straightening the mass of red hair atop her head, she felt a fleeting regret she could not meet the knight as herself. Why did she have to pretend to be Ceara the one time she might truly attract a man?

Refusing to be deterred, she launched into a sprightly ditty she often heard sung in the village and departed the chamber to woo her knight.

Chapter Three

Roarke was not the first guest to arrive at the evening meal. The Glamorgan great hall already hummed with chatter and music. Women of any minor rank or background milled about. Daughters of two area nobles wore colorful velvets and scarlets, decorated as richly as the limited notice of his arrival would have allowed.

Not that it mattered, Roarke thought as he assessed the room from the entryway. He did not seek an heiress or even a great beauty. In his experience, beauty lured too much attention from other men while a wealthy woman might seek to assert her power while her husband was away at war.

His mother had done both—whether she'd meant to or not—and he'd paid for her mistakes. Anne Barret might not have meant to be unfaithful to her husband, but she had fallen for Fulke Kendall rather quickly upon hearing of her husband's death. Roarke had tried to tell himself that perhaps his mother had already been close to her husband's fellow knight, but the thought failed to lessen the sting of his bastard heritage.

He had amassed his own wealth these last ten years. All he wanted from his marriage were heirs and the assurance from King Henry that Llandervey would belong to his family for as long as his line remained. Roarke sought a practical, simple woman for mistress of his new keep.

A hush rolled across the hall like a gentle wave as Roarke entered. The women sized him up instantly, each taking her own visual inventory as he crossed the hall to his seat at the head table beside his host.

Blessed saints, forgive me for this debacle, he muttered, horrified to think he requested this room full of women to choose from as if he were an Eastern sultan presiding over a harem.

The Lord of Glamorgan greeted him with the same dreary disposition he demonstrated earlier that afternoon, his stooped shoulders even more pronounced in the tailored cut of his evening attire.

"All of these women are aware I am English?" Roarke inquired as he took his place on the dais. He vaguely questioned where the man's daughter lurked, curious to see if she would have the same peculiar effect upon him as she'd had twice before. "I would not have a disillusioned father refuse me his daughter in the morning."

"Aye. They are all aware you are no Welshman." Thomas seemed to strain in an attempt to smile. "But none of these girls bring much to a marriage, so their fathers would consider you a good match despite that fact."

Nodding, Roarke wondered what unhappiness could make a man so perpetually miserable. "Is this the lot of them then?"

"Nay." Glamorgan swept the room with his eyes, as if seeking someone in particular. "My late wife's niece has not yet arrived, but I have high hopes you might turn your fancy to her. Ceara is a lovely little thing and smart enough to run a large household. She would make you a fine wife."

Detecting a hesitant note lingering in his host's voice, Roarke interrupted. "But?"

Glamorgan's shrug looked a little too casual. "She is rather shy and suffers from the notion she belongs in a convent. I've put her off about the matter, and perhaps you could convince her of the appeal of marriage."

Roarke thought she sounded ideal for his needs even though he knew from his long ago betrothal that convent life didn't assure a man his bride would be untouched.

Still, Roarke was about to mention that Ceara sounded very suitable, but he had lost his host's attention. Thomas Glamorgan halted in midsentence to see the sudden cause of a dramatic stillness in the room.

The near-sighted lord didn't seem to be able to discern the sight that had rendered the rest of the hall silent, but Roarke saw all too well.

A woman had entered the dining area.

A remarkable woman. Surely nobility by her proud bearing and graceful step. She was tall for a female, though Roarke doubted she would reach past his shoulder. Exquisitely dressed in a fine silk cotehardie and surcoat, both a vivid shade of green, she sailed into the room like a mermaid riding an ocean wave. Delicate features were set in an angular face with high cheekbones, tawny colored eyes and squared jaw. Hair the color of a summer sunset was carefully twisted about her head in an intricate knot, and Roarke was surprised that for a moment he found himself wondering if it would be soft to his touch. Then again, that might have been simply because she bore a striking resemblance to Lady Ariana.

"Your niece?" he inquired as the woman came close enough for the Lord of Glamorgan to distinguish. Roarke felt annoyed with himself for his careful perusal. The noise in the room increased again now that the newcomer had almost reached her seat at the high table.

Although Glamorgan affirmed his guess, Roarke would never have suspected the striking woman before him was shy, let alone intent on the nunnery. She looked supremely at ease, smiling at the assembled guests with genuine warmth. In fact, the woman was positively radiant. Her whole being seemed to glow with an inner light. She was not beautiful in the traditional sense, but she was immensely attractive.

And, consequently, all wrong for him.

"Roarke Barret, may I present my niece, Ceara Llywen?" Thomas Glamorgan squinted with failing eyes at the young woman as she curtsied before them.

"It is my pleasure, lady." Roarke ignored the urge to kiss the slender fingers she extended to him. What was it about the women of this household that drew him? He squeezed her hand briefly as he inclined his head above it, and pulled out the bench so she might be seated.

A soft floral scent emanated from her with subtle persistence. The same rose scent he had detected on Lady Ariana earlier today. And, strangely, he caught the strains of a popular love ballad as he helped her into her seat.

Ceara Llywen was humming.

"Ariana does not feel well," she imparted to her uncle as she sat down between them, her voice pitched a bit lower than her cousin's. "She asked me to take her place."

"Quite understandable," the man murmured, nodding his approval. "You look oddly suited to preside over the great hall this eve, Ceara. Have you cast aside your convent longing at the first sight of an English knight?"

Roarke almost choked on his wine. The poor niece flushed pink at her uncle's mean-spirited comment. Had Roarke not feared embarrassing her further, he would have defended her.

Instead of answering, she chose that moment to ring the bell and signal the meal to be served. A most uncomfortable meal, at that. It was impossible to look around the room without ten different women trying fervently to catch his eye, their ploys running the gamut from darting glances that ended in dramatic fluttering of long eyelashes, to the more bold adjusting of low necklines.

The thought of choosing a wife in this fashion held little appeal, yet it must be done. He vaguely wondered why he did not propose to one of the kitchen maids upon his arrival today and spare everyone their trouble.

His mood darkening as he downed several cups of

ale, he brooded why he should have to choose a wife in such a hurry anyway. Unfortunately, his lack of birthright forced him to dance attendance on a fickle king and marry at another man's whim.

"I beg your pardon?" Glamorgan's niece turned intense amber eyes upon him.

"What?" Roarke tried to gather his thoughts as he stared into those tawny depths and could not recall having said anything.

Her smile was not the weapon of an accomplished flirt, bearing none of the saucy boldness of her cousin. Rather, Ceara Llywen looked as abashed as a maid stumbling through her first conversation with a knight. "I am sorry. It sounded like you said 'It is damned unfair.' Were you perhaps referring to the meal?"

Ariana had waited through most of supper to find an opportunity to speak to the stranger about something more significant than the weather. For a brief moment when she walked into the room, she had thought he found her pleasing, but now she was not so sure. His mood seemed to become more forlorn as the evening wore on, leading her to believe he was displeased with the selection of women her father had found for him.

She grew more unhappy by the moment, as well. Ceara's hair itched her scalp dreadfully, and she longed to return to her room and dispense with the masquerade. She had no idea how to proceed with the brooding knight who did not believe in wishing on stars.

Even worse, she no longer felt that shimmery sensation she had when she first employed Eleanor's charm, and began to wonder if she possessed any power to attract the English knight anymore.

The thought frightened her to the core.

The moment she walked into the room and felt the eye of every male upon her was one of the biggest thrills of her life. A common enough occurrence for other women, yet Ariana never felt that ineffable sensation of being stared at in a decidedly male fashion.

But it was the eyes of the stranger she most coveted. She craved the warmth of that green gaze more than attention from a roomful of men. Despite Roarke Barret's dangerous proportions and formidable scowl, he'd clearly been taken aback by her father's cutting attempt to embarrass her earlier. Did that mean he might harbor a bit more kindness in his soul?

Or was she simply dreaming again, allowing her fanciful nature to see things that weren't there at all?

"Nay, lady. The food was the best I've eaten in weeks. Excuse my rude words," Roarke finally responded. His thigh barely grazed the fabric of her gown beneath the table, yet Ariana felt the warmth of his closeness through the delicate silks of her surcoat and tunic.

She shivered at the sensation, unaccustomed to contact with any man. "My father—that is, my *uncle*—often uses inappropriate language at supper. You will feel quite at home at a Cymric table. I am afraid our manners are not as polished as our English neighbors." Ariana hoped she covered her slip of the tongue regarding her father. It would not be easy to impersonate her cousin for long.

"Where is your father, Lady Ceara?" Roarke asked, latching onto her reference. "He does not join us at the meal?"

"He is dead, my lord, along with my mother. I have lived at Glamorgan Keep these past three years under the kind hospitality of my uncle, yet I am inclined to sometimes speak of my father as if he were still here. You must excuse me." Heart pounding at the lie, Ariana prayed for forgiveness as the knight inclined his head in repentance.

"I am sorry—"

"Thank you, my lord." Ariana halted his apology, hating the need to prevaricate and eager to change the topic. "If I may sir, I would be happy to point out some of the more refined ladies present. I am sure you are quite overwhelmed at the prospect of finding a bride in the course of the night. That is…unless you have already made your selection?"

At first, she was relieved to see the knight shake his head "no," then wondered if she should feel disappointed.

If he were to choose her, would he not have already done so by now?

"Despite the lack of exalted nobility among the women my uncle has gathered, many of them are capable of managing a household. Did you notice the young lady in the light blue dress? That's Mary."

Ariana gestured to a delicate woman a few years younger than she and hoped the knight would not find her appealing. She felt a little guilty pitting herself against the girls she grew up with, but they did not suffer the weight of family legend the way she did. Roarke Barret was her only chance.

The knight dutifully looked over the lady, but shook his head again. "Too young."

"Helen is a lovely girl," Ariana began, pointing out one of Glamorgan's prettiest maids. "She is more mature and very—"

"Haughty." Roarke finished her sentence, though not in the way she intended. Ariana had to admit the man possessed a sharp eye. Most men were fooled by Helen's beauty.

"How about the woman two trestles over in the comely red wool? She is—"

"Dull. She does not know how to enjoy herself and begrudges anyone else their happiness."

"My lord!" Ariana admonished, as shocked at his correct assessment as she was at his bold manner. "She is an accomplished young lady."

"I am sure she is, Lady Ceara, but she is also an unhappy person. She will not do." Roarke lifted his glass toward his man-at-arms on the opposite end of the room.

The blond giant seemed to take great pleasure from feeding one of the ladies a choice morsel with his fingers. Apparently the man was not as choosy as his tooperceptive lord.

Perhaps she should have been happy that Roarke Barret was not finding anyone else to suit his taste for a bride, but Ariana found herself annoyed at his smug attitude.

"You may have overestimated the women of Glamorgan, sir, if you thought you would be able to find a perfect bride here in the course of one evening."

The knight leaned close, his dark head inclined intimately toward her own. An unfamiliar sense of heightened awareness shot through Ariana at his proximity. Such intense regard by a man struck her as strange and new.

"I have no choice, my lady. I must wed tomorrow morning in order to secure a land grant." A shadow darkened his eyes for a moment, then was gone so quickly Ariana wondered if she imagined it.

"I do not mean to overstep my bounds, sir, but it seems you are rushing an important decision in your life. Could your nuptials not wait until your return from France?" Feeling rather breathless under Roarke's close scrutiny, she was relieved when a fresh platter of sugared fruit paused before their table.

"Allow me, Lady Ceara." Roarke chose a plum and an apple before waving away the server, then offered her the plum from his own fingers.

Ariana's cheeks heated as the fruit grazed her mouth. Her heartbeat jumped as he wiped the juice from her lips with his thumb, his callused touch surprisingly gentle.

"Delicious," he remarked, as surely as if he himself had taken a bite.

"It is good," she agreed, which elicited laughter from Roarke.

"It is not the plum I speak of, Ceara." His words were clear and distinct, yet the peculiar glint in his eye gave Ariana the sudden impression Roarke Barret imbibed too generously this evening.

"Pardon me, lady, if I speak too forwardly," he took her hand into his own, interrupting her thoughts. Ariana knew he must feel the leap of her pulse in her palm as he gently squeezed it. "But lack of time dictates I be quick about this business of marriage. Your uncle tells me you are eager to enter a convent. May I ask why?"

"A convent?" The warmth from his hand momentarily dulled her wits as she struggled to grasp his meaning. She made a concerted effort to pay attention to his words instead of the curious effect male attention seemed to have upon her.

"Your uncle suggested you were shy and convent-bound, but I see no trace of unusual shyness or rigorous piety in your manner."

Sweet Arianrhod. Her father must have spoken to Roarke about Ceara. Ariana mentally shook herself to ward off the strange feeling Roarke's hand upon hers was inspiring. Luckily, he released it at that moment.

"A convent is appealing to a young woman with no prospects. I do not wish to burden my uncle."

The knight frowned, as if this answer did not please him. Ariana puzzled over what response he might hope to hear from her. Did he seek a shy and pious bride?

"But he will have to dower a convent as heavily as any young groom for you, perhaps even more heavily."

"It is not the dowry that is a problem, it is more a lack of possible husbands. I would not ask my uncle to use any favors to procure a groom for me as he still has to find a husband for his own daughter."

Was she making any sense? She felt as if he knew she was lying, as though her burning face gave away all her secrets. He paused thoughtfully, as if he still had not heard the answers he sought.

Attempting to change the subject she blurted, "Did you meet Ariana?"

She could not believe she said the words. Some inner demon must have forced them out of her mouth. But she was curious to know his earlier impression of her, be-

fore she resorted to a small charm. Had he felt the same
pull of some invisible bond between them when they'd
met in the hall and along the bank of the creek?

His brow furrowed as if trying to remember. "You
and she rather look alike."

She nearly choked on a sip of wine. Replacing her
cup on the table, she coughed as delicately as possible
all the while hoping Lord Barret would not see through
her scheme.

Few men had ever been able to conjure up details
about Ariana Glamorgan's appearance, yet this man
had distinguished a very particular resemblance. All
without the benefit of any charmed herbs or the elaborate disguise she'd resorted to this evening.

Hope blossomed like a spring bud, urging Ariana to
wed the mysterious foreigner with the penetrating green
gaze. This was the man who could dispel the suffocating Glamorgan legend.

"I am surprised she is not already wed," Roarke continued, oblivious to Ariana's churning thoughts. "Is she
inclined toward the convent, as well?"

"*She* is too vibrant a spirit for such a dull existence,"
she replied, feeling oddly defensive of herself and her
choice not to enter the convent as a good Glamorgan
woman was supposed to.

Strangely enough, her annoyed answer seemed to
please Roarke and he nodded his satisfaction. Did he
find a vibrant spirit so reprehensible?

"I will not mince words, my lady, so excuse me if I
am too abrupt. Would *you* consider marriage to an English knight?"

Chapter Four

Ariana absorbed the words for an endless moment. She felt as if she were poised above a deep ravine, moments away from making a huge leap that would determine the course of her life. She took a deep breath.

And jumped.

"I would consider it."

Roarke's laugh was humorless. "Perhaps I did a poor job of phrasing the question, Lady Ceara. I plan to seek your uncle's permission to wed with you. I am not without care for your thoughts on the matter. If he consents, do I have your approval?"

The glittering intensity of his eyes frightened her for a moment, and Ariana saw into his soul. Whether it was her fickle gift of the sight or feminine intuition, she could not be sure, but she knew with unwavering certainty the English knight resented having to ask her the question. Her fears increased tenfold.

Before she could form her response, his voice turned hard and cold. "You do not love another, do you?"

"Nay! I know nothing of love."

"Good. May I speak openly with you, Ceara?"

Ariana could see no trace of the gentleness she'd perceived in him earlier. She nodded, unable to deny him anything.

"I believe it is important we be forthright with one another, my lady. Having known the wretched heritage of bastardy myself, I hold honesty and honor to be the mainstays of marriage."

A pain clenched in her belly as he spoke. The consequences of her charade pricked her conscience. But she couldn't turn back. She would restore honor to her family through this marriage. Would save the real Ceara from having to wed a mercenary knight she feared. "I understand."

"I offer you marriage in order to secure the lands offered to me by my king; lands I have worked for my whole life. I am a bastard, Lady Ceara. Alone in the world as you have been since your parents died. I am dependent upon my king for title and land, and for that reason I had to consent to a Welsh wife. Although there is no love between us, I expect there to be strict fidelity and truthfulness."

Her leap across the ravine was turning into a free fall. There was naught to hold on to as she sank headlong into the abyss of his green gaze.

"I do not wish to wed under false circumstances, Ceara, so I tell you this now."

He looked at her expectantly, his eyes slowly growing more gentle until he tipped her chin with his fingertip. "I tell you this in the interest of being fair to you. If you choose to become my wife, your position will be respected. Though I cannot commit my heart to the union, I vow you will have my protection and I assure you a place of honor."

Ariana struggled under the weight of his words, as if now there were a stone tied to her foot, too.

"You are very honest," she managed, her voice sounding husky and emotional even to her own ears.

Dear Gwydion, but Eleanor said obstacles would fall away if he were the right one. Right now, the obstacles mounted by the moment.

Yet...

Something about the man's intensity appealed to her. She believed him when he said he would protect her. There was a certain inner strength and determination about Roarke Barret that Ariana admired. This was a man who would never dream of backing down from a fight. He was no Thomas Glamorgan to cave under the weight of unhappiness.

"It is still a genuine proposal, my lady. You would have a keep of your own to tend, and children." He grinned broadly—much to her embarrassment. "'Tis more than you can say for your convent."

And it was far better than living under the weight of family legend and fruitless dreams. She wanted to know the love of children, even if she did not know the love of a man. Besides, he needed her. After a lifetime of near invisible servitude to her unappreciative father, Ariana knew well how to give of herself. She could make this man happy. Bring light and laughter to her household in a way she'd never been able to at Glamorgan. Not only that, but she would also be helping Roarke to fulfill his own destiny.

Surely fate would handle the rest.

"Aye." She smiled back at him, her face still warm with embarrassment, but her mind resolved. "It is preferable to the convent, my lord. If my uncle consents, I will be your wife."

Finding her footing, she sensed a long climb in front of her. But she felt more keenly alive than she had since she was a young girl. Her world was suddenly bursting with possibilities.

"Excuse me, Ceara," Thomas Glamorgan haltingly interrupted them. "But it grows late and the guests grow restless. I think 'tis past time we call an end to the meal." He looked questioningly to Roarke. "That is, if it is acceptable to our guest of honor?"

At Roarke's nod, Thomas signaled for the entertainment to commence. A neighbor to the Glamorgans brought out a small reed instrument and joined his daughter in a lilting duet homage to their Welsh homelands while the servants finished clearing the tables and picking up the trenchers for the village's poor.

"Have any of our girls caught your fancy then, sir?" Lord Glamorgan inquired.

Ariana only half listened to Roarke's exchange with her father, her nerves jittery and her resolve faltering. Roarke's speech about honesty had her questioning her motives, doubting her cause and overall sick to her stomach. How could she go through with her ploy, knowing Roarke only expected truthfulness from her?

Worse, how could she get married to a man who practically admitted he would never love her?

Her mind wandered as her father announced that Ceara Llywen would marry Roarke Barret in the morning. She kept envisioning someone among the crowd pointing her out as a fake. But apparently she really *could* pass for Ceara. They possessed similar features and identical amber eyes, though few people noticed their resemblance because of the stark contrast of their hair. Once Ariana put Ceara's red locks over her own and dotted a few freckles across her nose with the help of a few ashes from the fireplace, they looked like twins.

Except for their figures. Even at sixteen, Ceara had surpassed her cousin in curves. The extra padding Ariana used around her bosom and hips was uncomfortable, but the difference was quite noticeable without it. She would shed a little padding each day after she left Glamorgan until she was back down to her usual size.

With any luck, her husband would never notice.

By now, cups were raised from all sides in toasts to the new couple. Even Lord Glamorgan offered his blessing.

"You seem distracted, my lady," Roarke remarked. "Do you feel well?"

His question reminded her the charm might very well be wearing off. Either that; or perhaps her sense of daring merely faded now that her fate as Roarke Barret's wife had been decided. Something about the English knight unsettled her on a fundamental level. Rendered her breathless and a bit weak-kneed.

"Would it seem terribly rude if I were to withdraw from the celebration, my lord?"

"Not considering the haste of our wedding tomorrow. I wish to leave by the time the bell tolls for tierce at midmorning."

"As you wish," she agreed before backing out of the hall into the keep's entryway where the front doors were thrown open to the night.

She only took a few steps before he followed her. "Aren't you forgetting something, *mor-forwyn?*"

It was not his sudden use of Welsh that caught her off guard so much as what he called her.

Temptress. Siren.

"You are familiar with our tongue, my lord?" Her mouth went dry, as much because of the glittering intensity of his gaze as the warmth behind his endearment.

"I learned my first word tonight."

"You are aware of what you just called me then?" She could not guess where he had run across such a term.

"Temptress." The slow smile that crossed his lips called forth a peculiar weakening in her knees. He closed the distance between them until he was a hand span before her. Unwilling to move away, she tilted her chin to look up at him.

"And I heard the word in reference to you, lady. I overheard a bold cupbearer remark you went from nun to *mor-forwyn* in the course of one day. I admit I was curious to know exactly what he meant regarding my future bride, so I had him explain himself. I trust he did not give me false information?"

Judging from Roarke's intimidating height and far too intense manner, Ariana guessed he had scared the unfortunate lad out of his wits.

"No, my lord. But I hardly think 'tis a flattering name, whether it comes from a member of the kitchen staff or a future husband."

"Perhaps not. But for now, it is all I know of your language and I rather like the sound of it." His grin was utterly disarming, perhaps because it seemed a rare occurrence for the serious foreigner. Ariana could not help the answering smile that twitched at her lips.

"I expect one more thing before you retire, lady," he reminded her as she began once again to take her leave.

Ariana half turned, thinking he was going to mention another detail about their trip, like "bring warm garments," or some other practical concern.

She was not prepared for his sudden nearness. Nor did she have time to consider the heavy arm that swiftly encircled her before it pulled her toward him.

"I wish to seal our agreement properly."

Green eyes searched hers for a long moment, seeking her response. His words warmed her lips, sending a surge of sensation racing through her limbs and tripping along every nerve. Her blood seemed to dance in her veins, as spellbound as she was by the promise of his touch.

His mouth descended to hers slowly, increasing the dizzying swell of unfamiliar sensations in her body so that she had to hold on to him for support. He kissed her fully on the mouth, his lips tasting faintly of cinnamon and ale. The rough skin around his mouth surprised her when it prickled her, though she guessed all men who shaved their beards must feel as such. The scents of freshly bathed skin and an autumn afternoon mingled, as if he had just stepped from Glamorgan creek.

She would have put her arms about him to draw him even closer had he not pulled back at that moment.

Their gazes locked for one long moment, each taking measure of the other.

Caught up in the pure pleasure of the moment, Ariana wished he would kiss her again, create more of the shimmering magic that danced and skipped through her.

Then she saw the shadow that crossed his face, dimming the emerald eyes to mossy green, turning the softness of his just-kissed lips into a hard, straight line.

"Good night, Lady Ceara."

Setting her away abruptly, as if her kiss had been distasteful somehow, Roarke left her to wonder if he regretted his choice of brides.

Regretted having kissed her.

Regretted his need to marry.

She assumed he rejoined the merriment in the great hall, though her eyes did not follow him as he left. The night air grew suddenly chill in his absence.

"Nos da." Whispering the Welsh words to the vacated darkness, she sought her chamber with a kiss and a song on her lips, the refrain of a haunting melody echoing the fears she felt inside.

The morning mist hung shroudlike over the keep, enveloping it in gray stillness. Typical weather for a September morning, but it made for a depressing wedding day.

The heavy mantle of fog weighed as much as the guilt that burdened Ariana's shoulders. She had remained awake almost the whole night, working with Ceara to alter a wedding gown and two other tunics and kirtles to accommodate the more curvaceous figure she adopted in her guise as Ceara. As the night wore on, she felt less triumphant about her successful encounter with Roarke Barret and more remorse about using him so shamelessly to gain her own ends. How could she make sacred vows in front of witnesses under false pretenses?

Worse yet, how could she enter a consecrated holy church knowing in her heart that she misrepresented herself to Roarke?

And yet...

How else was she to restore her family honor and fulfill her mother's dying wish? The Glamorgan legend had plagued her family for a century, affecting generations of women who did nothing to deserve such a cruel and lonely existence. Although many of them took solace in the convent, the greater number did not have such a calling and remained a burden to their families, growing more unhappy with each passing year.

One aunt, two generations back, was rumored to have killed herself because of the misfortune of her birth, though the family asserted she fell from a slick window ledge while gazing out over a cloudy moor. Ariana's mother had struggled her whole life to bring joy to this sorrow-filled household, to coax her husband from the dark depression of the curse that cloaked his keep more thoroughly than any Welsh mist.

Now, it was Ariana's turn to heal that darkness.

The bell tolled for prime, reminding her she had two hours until her wedding. Three hours until she rode off with a man she'd known for less than a day. The man who was to be her destiny.

If he did not discover her secret before then.

"Ariana!" Ceara snatched a length of linen from Ariana's hand and stuffed it into a traveling bag. "You must finish packing so you can get dressed! We will never finish if you keep brooding. Are you having second thoughts about this wedding?"

Ariana laughed, feeling nervous and edgy. "*Second* thoughts? I have not had time to have *first* thoughts about it yet." She laid a few other personal items into her bag, wondering if she had packed everything she needed.

"Is it so wrong to fight this fate, Ceara?" Fear constricted her throat. Had she been so wrong to deceive last night? "Is it too much to want a family, a home with a husband and children?"

"Nay." Ceara neatly arranged the garments in the bag before packing any more. "I do not think you will be forsaken for trying to rectify a grave injustice that has gone on for too many years."

Emotion knotted Ariana's belly. "You are so good to me, Ceara."

Her cousin smiled as she went about her work, single-handedly packing everything Ariana needed on her journey. "You must remember your aim is worthy." Ceara put down the shifts she was holding and went to her cousin. "But as much as I want you to succeed in this, if you do not wish to go through with it, there is still time to admit our deception."

Tears burned Ariana's eyes. "Nay! That is not what I want! But he is bound to find out sooner or later and when he does, what will happen?"

"He is full of pride and has fought for what is his. Just look at how coldly he goes about the business of choosing a bride. He doesn't even know your father, yet he is perfectly willing to accept whomever Uncle Thomas puts in front of him. He will be equally cold about dispensing with a wife who does not serve him well."

"Perhaps he seems aloof because he is in a hurry," Ariana remarked, trying to reign in her scattered emotions.

Ceara shook her head sadly. "This *is* a far cry from the 'grand adventure' you spoke of last night." Amber eyes that mirrored her own fixed Ariana in their unblinking gaze. Ceara looked older and wiser than her sixteen years, and Ariana was tempted to heed her advice. "You can end this before it is too late."

There was still time to call it off. She would be safe from Roarke here, and protected.

And alone for the rest of her life.

"I cannot. I must go through with it now, and we both know it." She would simply look at this as another way to use her healing skills. Only now she'd be healing her family. Her heritage. "Eleanor said if it is right, all obstacles will fall away."

"Obstacles have surrounded you at every turn already, cousin! And doesn't the curse stipulate that the man must love you?"

"Not exactly." Ariana pulled the woolen shawl more tightly about her shoulders as she paced the cold stone floor. "There are no real instructions for how to break the curse, only speculation by Glamorgan women. But gaining the genuine love of a man might not be necessary. It might be broken merely if he—that is, if we—" She made a helpless gesture with her hands.

"Are intimate?"

"Yes." Ariana tossed a last handful of things into her bag. "I am going through with it. If anything, our conversation has only made me sure that I am doing the right thing. Would you ask the maid to bring in the bath now? I want to start getting ready."

Ceara stepped into the hall to do her cousin's bidding and soon ushered two servants into the room with a tub. When they were gone, she helped Ariana settle into the warm water.

"So is this charm of Eleanor's still affecting you now?" she asked, throwing rose petals into the water before she took up the soap.

"No. Indeed, I don't know that there is any real power to Eleanor's herbal potion."

Ceara frowned. "I thought this was something very powerful, something Eleanor had been working on for years?"

"Aye. So she told me." Ariana splashed water over her face and shoulders. "But she would also do anything to help me marry. Including trick me into thinking I could face the English knight even when I stood trembling in slippers."

"By the rood, Ariana. You think she merely *pretended* to have concocted some powerful potion?" Ceara scrubbed more forcefully.

"Ow!" Ariana finished her hair herself. "I don't know, but I cannot fathom how she would have come by the recipe for something so fanciful as a brew to make a woman more appealing. She is a healer, not a sorceress, after all."

"Praise God."

"Aye. Except that now I will have nothing to inspire

false confidence. I think I will attend the wedding heavily veiled. Which is just as well because my hair will still be wet at this rate." She rinsed the thick black mass quickly and stepped from the tub, drying the tresses vigorously with several linens until it was just damp.

They worked in silence, nervous and tense about the day ahead of them. Ariana combed her waist-length hair, plaiting the strands to be pinned atop her head.

Ceara handed her a newly worked hairpiece over her shoulder. "I sewed my old hair to a strip of cloth this morn, so you will have an easier time fixing it in its place each day."

The hair was tightly bound together in small sections, then sewn to a strip of cinnamon-colored linen, not much darker than the hair itself. The cloth would allow Ariana to secure the hair easily to her head without all of the elaborate pinning and tying they did last night before dinner.

"Thank you, cousin," Ariana whispered, tears springing quickly to her eyes. "I feel so awful about taking your hair."

Ceara ran her fingers through the short strands that fell between her chin and shoulders. "Think no more of it. It is not as if I were bald as Uncle Thomas. I think when I join the convent I will keep it this length. It would be much cooler under a habit. And if I change my mind, it will grow back."

While Ariana fretted, Ceara smothered a giggle. "Besides, if I decide I really would rather wed, I shall wait 'til I am an old maid like you before I choose a husband, and by then it will be long again."

Ariana laughed, too, though her heart felt heavy with

guilt and worry. Her scheme had the power to hurt Ceara and Roarke....

But it would save her brother's little girls. If she were successful, they would benefit, which made her guilt a little easier to bear.

Distracted with such concerns, the morning raced by until she was dressed and ready to go below stairs. Then she recalled Eleanor's charm. Quite probably a bogus brew designed to help Ariana feel more brave. Should she bother mixing the herbs today?

It certainly couldn't hurt. Especially when the thought of facing Roarke Barret while memories of his kiss teased her senses. She needed all the courage she could muster. Slowly and purposefully, Ariana added all the right ingredients. She whispered a healer's chant, mixed the herbs and then threw the mixture into the flames.

Nothing.

No shimmery sensation.

No blaze of fire.

Her father called to her, though of course it was Ceara's name he called, not her own. They were waiting for her so they could begin the procession to the chapel.

But she tried one more time. Using all of her concentration to block out the various knocks that came to Ceara's door, and the shouts for Ariana to please talk to Ceara so she will come down, Ariana went through the ritual one more time, focusing on her goal the way Eleanor taught her to. She put all of her strength and all of her hopes into the herbal concoction as she crushed the herbs beneath her pestle and once again threw the mixture into the flames.

For nothing.

The charm would not work today. Had probably never worked outside of Ariana's wishful imagination. She had no choice now but to face Roarke Barret with only the help of a few false freckles and a cinnamon-colored hairpiece on her own wedding day.

Chapter Five

Saints protect me.

Whispering one last prayer that she was doing the right thing, Ariana pulled her heavy veils over hair and face and hoped Roarke did not seek to lift them. She might not look any different today then she had the night before, but she felt less sure of herself without the help of Eleanor's mysterious charm.

Quietly, she stepped through the door that adjoined her room to Ceara's and then out into the passageway from Ceara's room. She ran into her father, whose face was mottled pink with annoyance.

"I am ready, Uncle," she said sweetly, her voice low and modulated the way Ceara's was. It mattered not how she spoke to Roarke, but to fool her father she had to be especially careful.

Thomas Glamorgan opened his mouth as if to chide her, then smoothed one hand across his bare head, as if taming unruly locks that were no longer there. "You look lovely, niece," he said, his voice straining with the effort to be pleasant.

Ariana wished she did not have to deceive him today. For all of his flaws, she loved her father, and it grieved her to leave him without saying a real goodbye. No matter how difficult he made her life, or how much he blamed her for the unhappiness he suffered, her father was not solely to blame for the pall that hung over the keep. Misery, like the curse, had a way of clinging to Glamorgan.

As they proceeded to meet the well-wishers, her mood brightened. With a holiday declared until after the wedding cup was drunk, the villein made merry into the night and then slept well past prime. Now they welcomed the cause of their celebrations with shouts and autumn wildflowers, which were strewn along with brightly colored fall leaves in Ariana's path. Shades of red, yellow and orange carpeted her every step while the chapel bell announced her arrival.

Her worries returned as she climbed the church steps and spied Roarke, who appeared more forbidding than the fierce gargoyles that silently waited for the ceremony to begin.

He was not outfitted in wedding attire. He could have been dressed for a day of riding or a day of battle except for the gold medallion he wore about his neck, hanging from a slender flaxen rope that was so fine and sleek it looked as if it were woven with a woman's hair.

Aside from that peculiar decoration, the English knight showed no outward sign it was his wedding day. His lack of finery caused Ariana to wonder if he would bother waiting for the toast to be raised before he mounted his horse to leave Glamorgan Keep far behind him.

Even dressed as he was, he would have been quite handsome, Ariana thought, were it not for the scowl that furrowed his brow.

Was it because she was late?

Or because he resented having to wed her at all?

Wondering where the man who had tenderly kissed her last night had disappeared, she was not eager to take the steps that would close the space between them. But the ancient, stooped village priest who would officiate beckoned and her wedding day commenced.

Her groom barely acknowledged her, but the women who attended the ceremony seemed to admire her. She could see their assessing glances as they noted the rich fabric of the exquisite gown, one of many her father had ordered for her over the years. During the long night of preparations for the ceremony, she and Ceara altered it to accommodate a fuller figure, so the fit was just right. A deep crimson velvet, the material alone had cost a fortune. The bodice boasted rich embroidery and a few small jewels along the neckline.

The veils were hardly unbecoming, either, though they completely hid the bride from the world's view. Red-and-black silk covered the back of her head and neck in a wimple. Over top of it, two layers of heavy white Flanders lace fell from a thin silver circlet to cover her face and fall midway down her back. The intricate fabric was artfully arranged to allow the less decorated portions of the lace to cover her eyes so she might see through the veils.

When she reached Roarke, he turned formally toward the priest and awaited his words.

He was going through with it.

Ariana breathed her relief. Doubts had plagued her all morning that the English knight would change his mind and choose another bride. And it was not just because the charm failed. The fact he ended their kiss so abruptly the night before made her think he found her lacking.

Now the sacred words were being read that would officially bind them together as man and wife, a surge of guilt spread through her. She vowed she would be a good wife to Roarke to make up for the way she had tricked him into wedding her. Heaven knew the man didn't seem to care much about whom he married.

Her hand shook slightly as Roarke slid a heavy band of thick silver upon her ring finger. Devoid of any decoration, the ring was not particularly becoming around her finger, but the weighty silver comforted Ariana as it slid onto her hand. Although Roarke Barret came to her with no love in his heart, his commitment to her was strong and true. A man of honor, he would not take his vows to his Welsh wife lightly.

As she looked forward to the wedding night that would free her from the Glamorgan legend, she could almost feel the stranglehold of her family heritage begin to loosen its grip.

Sneaking surreptitious glances in his bride's direction, Roarke wondered if the temptress he'd kissed last night lurked anywhere beneath the pile of veils he was now marrying. He could scarcely see his future wife, but he trusted Ceara awaited him beneath her elaborate garb.

Truth be told, perhaps it was just as well that she remained hidden from his eyes. He had scarcely kissed her last night and yet thoughts of her had plagued his dreams. Invaded his waking thoughts. And since his father had treated his mother with nothing but coarse lust and then scorn, Roarke strove to maintain absolute self-mastery where his own baser urges were concerned after discovering his true parentage. He was no better than his father if he could not control himself.

For that matter, Roarke did not appreciate his own fickleness where women were concerned lately. He had been attracted to Ariana Glamorgan by day and Ceara Llywen by night. All the more reason he needed to settle his future as a sedately married man.

Now, as he glanced sidelong at Ceara while the priest spoke the words that bound them, he saw no hint of the amber-eyed siren he'd met last night.

It was peculiar.

First the strange meetings with enticing Ariana Glamorgan, and now his odd reaction to her cousin Ceara. What the hell was the matter with him? Even before discovering the truth about his parentage, Roarke had never been indiscriminate with women. In that way, at least, he was certain he did not take after his father.

He would be wed any moment and on his way to Llandervey, which was all that really mattered. It would be just as well if his wife remained veiled and inaccessible to him today anyhow. That way he would not have to worry about the unsettling way her kiss called forth a level of ardor he'd never known himself to possess.

Until tonight, of course.

After promising dutifully to love and cherish her,

Roarke felt a moment of guilt, knowing he would be unable to fulfill any vows regarding love.

"Do you, Ceara Llywen, take Roarke Barret?"

Roarke barely heard her muffled acknowledgment through the shroud of fabric she wore, but she agreed.

She, too, made further vows the church required, but Roarke did not pay much attention again until he heard the pronouncement that they were truly man and wife.

It was done.

Llandervey belonged to him now. The strategic keep on the western sea had caught at his imagination from the first time he'd heard mention of it. Now that he was properly wedded to the right woman, he could not wait to seize it for his own.

He would have left at that moment, impatient as he was to see Llandervey. But the people of Glamorgan clamored for him to stay and drink a wedding cup with Ceara, and Roarke could not refuse.

Llandervey could wait a little longer.

It pained him to have to delay over the wedding cup, that much was abundantly clear. Ariana saw the longing in Roarke's eyes as he looked at where the sun sat on the horizon, before he agreed to participate in the celebration.

He did not even kiss her after the ceremony. Though not required by the Church, the act was a tradition. One Roarke would rather not observe with her, apparently. Her nuptials had been quick and terse, but the brevity of the ritual did not disturb her half so much as speaking vows to her husband while using another woman's name. Would their marriage even be recognized once she revealed her true identity to Roarke?

Her fears were chased away by the appearance of her father after the vows.

"Let me be the first to congratulate you, Ceara," he said, fiddling with her veils to give her a kiss.

Thomas Glamorgan looked taken aback for a moment when he lifted the heavy material and met her eyes. Ariana knew a moment's panic, thinking her ruse was discovered, but then her father seemed to dismiss the feeling and proceeded to kiss her on both cheeks.

"Good luck, Ceara, my dear." The words seemed to pain him, but Ariana thought it unusually kind for her father to make an effort to be pleasant. She kissed him back, praying he would one day forgive her deception.

She accepted the arm that Roarke held out to her dutifully, and was not surprised that he did not look at her, even though her face was now uncovered. It was the same lack of acknowledgment she had known all her life.

The villein danced and made merry all the way back to the keep, singing ballads of love and romance and reveling in the simple pleasure of a beautiful autumn day now that the morning fog had lifted. Ariana hummed along with them, the fear in her heart lifting when she indulged in music.

The skies had cleared since Ariana first awakened, a rarity for this early in the day. The fading grass was still damp with morning mist and the sun shone brilliantly, as if trying to remind the world of his glory before the waning time of year took over and darkness became more prevalent than daylight.

Roarke leaned close as they walked. "I am sorry to say we will not be able to spend much time with your uncle, my lady, before we depart for Llandervey. 'Tis almost tierce now." He spoke without looking at her.

"Of course. It is my own fault, my lord. I apologize for arriving later than I would have liked at the chapel this morn. It took longer to pack than I suspected."

They strode in silence amidst the well-wishers and merrymakers who joined them on the way back to Glamorgan. There were several trestles erected outside laden with breads and pastries of all kinds, as well as fruits and meat pies. It was light fare for a wedding breakfast, but the people of Glamorgan could not spare many hours to celebrate at harvest time.

Wine had been limited to two rounds by the cupbearers, so the newlyweds' farewell party was a sedate one. Ariana knew it was time to leave when the gangly, scruffy bearded knight who rode with Roarke approached them. Ariana had met him briefly last night. Collin…she could not recall his last name.

"I do not wish to tear you away from your good family, my lady," he began, his incredibly blue eyes unseeing as he looked at her. "But if you wish to be settled comfortably into your new home by night fall, we had best prepare to leave."

"Yes, of course," she replied distractedly, her gaze wandering vaguely over the wedding guests. She spied Roarke talking to her father's steward and approached him.

"My lord? Should we be leaving?"

Her husband did not even turn in her direction to answer. He looked skyward to judge the time of day and nodded. "I shall find your uncle so you might say your goodbyes."

Soon she was giving her father a teary-eyed kiss on the cheek, being swept atop her mount and waving farewell to the people of Glamorgan.

Although she would not miss the morose household that sought to strangle her spirit, Ariana could not help a pang of regret at not being able to say a genuine good-bye as herself.

Everyone she knew and loved was left behind, maybe forever, so she could be joined to a stranger who would scorn her when he learned the truth of who she was.

"Your bride is a beautiful woman, Roarke." Collin remarked as they neared Llandervey in their trek.

Roarke shifted uneasily against his horse, unwilling to discuss Ceara when he needed to remain alert. Watchful. The journey had been easy thus far, and by Roarke's calculations the keep would be in sight momentarily. But he'd never fully shaken his sense of being watched over the last fortnight. Even now, he kept his traveling party close together, his bride within arm's reach, in case they were being followed.

Llandervey would be a most welcome sight, and not just because he was eager to see if Ceara's kiss tasted as sweet as he remembered.

"She is fair enough," Roarke agreed, his thoughts far away as he remembered how ten years ago his half brother Lucian Barret had traveled many leagues with another woman intended to be Roarke's bride. Lucian had traversed distant lands and difficult terrain with a killer on his heels. Only now did Roarke fully appreciate all that Lucian had sacrificed for him.

But then, Roarke's Barret kin had taught him far more about the meaning of honor and nobility then his Kendall father ever had. One day, Roarke aspired to be the kind of man Lucian had become. He would never succeed, however, if he lost focus on the trip when someone shadowed their every move.

"Fair?" Collin turned to peer down the line of the small traveling party, presumably to find Ceara. "You have not looked at her then, I'll warrant."

Roarke's hand settled over his sword as they neared a small outcropping of trees near the road. "Perhaps I have other concerns beyond my bride's beauty. Have you seen no signs of our watcher?"

"Nary a trace. It is your wedding day, Barret. Be of good cheer." He lowered his voice meaningfully. "Besides, you are certain to frighten your lady. Have you not seen how nervous she appears?"

Damn.

He'd never considered her worries for a moment, unaccustomed to thinking of a woman's needs. With one last glance at the thatch of trees, Roarke turned to study his wife in the middle of their small retinue of his men. She looked even slighter atop the large mount she rode. Her travel garments emphasized her slender waist and generous curves, while her wimple had loosened around her hair, allowing the cinnamon strands of her hair to cloak her shoulders.

But her eyes skittered along the horizon, nervously seeking a glimpse of the terrain ahead even though her view had to be impeded by his men all around her. He thought to call her forward to ride by his side now that the keep must be near.

Collin's low whistle distracted him as they reached the crest of a small hill.

Roarke stopped suddenly, his halt bringing the rest of the line to an abrupt standstill. At the top of the rise they could see Llandervey, lone and magnificent against the vibrant backdrop of a churning sea. The sun setting behind the massive stone structure imbued it with an unearthly glow, as if it were a dream come to life for Roarke.

Which, in fact, it was.

Huge rounded towers fortified the barbican at all four corners of the outer walls while the keep itself replicated the four rounded towers on a smaller scale. A small village sat close by the outer walls, where families toiled to bring in the last sheaves of wheat before the sun sank from the sky. If properly manned, Llandervey was an enemy's nightmare, there being little to do in a siege except starve out the lord and his followers.

"Now *that* is beautiful." Roarke had possessed a keep once. Briefly. But it had never really belonged to him, entrusted to his keeping by his half brother Lucian. He'd coveted his brother's possession so thoroughly it had been painful to give the property back, making him realize he could never be content until he'd earned lands of his own.

Collin whistled appreciatively. "You have been well rewarded, Barret. How will you man the walls?"

"We will have to train some Welshmen, I guess. My wife brings me a respectable dowry, enough to train more men-at-arms. Between those men and the five seasoned knights Henry promised me, it will be enough."

"Your keep is remarkable, my lord." Ceara joined them so silently Roarke never heard her approach. She looked out over the valley dreamily, obviously recognizing the worth of Llandervey. "I trust you are well pleased?"

"Aye."

"It is obvious you are well loved by your king to be given such a prize."

A better husband might have taken more care to show his wife their new property, to welcome her to her new home with words of tender encouragement, but Roarke had long ago forgotten such manners. Life as a mercenary knight had proved a coarse existence, stark enough to make his gentler upbringing a distant memory.

If she noticed his rudeness, Ceara did not comment. Seeming genuinely impressed by the huge keep, she watched the sunset with a beatific smile on her face.

"You look well pleased, my lady," Collin noted when they stood idle several minutes.

"I have dreamed of seeing the sun slip into the western sea, but never thought I would actually witness it. It is a miracle to behold."

Roarke's own thoughts echoed her words, but he said nothing before he nudged his horse into motion. There was much work to do in the short time that remained before he sailed for France. There was staff to be assembled and directed, a steward to be instructed and fortifications to be inspected.

The task in the forefront of his mind, however, was the same one that prevented him from making conversation with his new wife and preoccupied him all day. He would consummate his marriage to Ceara.

Normally, the notion of bedding a woman would be a welcome diversion. But the woman in question inspired an ardor in him that he had not expected and did not welcome. Memories of her kiss had haunted him all day, making him fear he'd chosen the wrong woman to wed after all. Wedded life held little appeal if he had to continually battle his own lust.

Spending the night in her bed promised to be an exquisite test to his self-control.

Ariana blinked back tears by the time she reached the large, private solar attached to her new bedchamber. Roarke had not so much as looked at her once all day.

As a new husband, could he not at least make an effort to look in her direction? To make conversation?

The crowning insult had come when he made no mention of their wedding night before he left her alone in her private chambers. He'd made it very clear, however, that his rooms were on the third floor, just above hers.

Meaning he would not sleep beside her.

How could she consider herself married if he would not look at her, let alone sleep in the same chamber?

Tired and out of sorts, Ariana slumped heavily into the chair beside the door and sighed. The ride to Llandervey had been interminable, and made worse by the fact that she did not sleep a wink the previous night for all the wedding preparations. Now, exhausted and miserable, Ariana gave into the luxury of weeping over the whole state of affairs.

Deprived of Eleanor and Ceara.

Resented by her husband.

Accustomed to being of good cheer even at the worst of times, Ariana did not usually indulge in weeping. But if she could not appeal to Roarke to consummate their marriage before he left for France, she would not have another chance to dispel the old Glamorgan myths until he returned in the spring. She *must* succeed tonight.

Feeling considerably better after crying, she forced herself to begin the task of unpacking. The problem of her wedding night would have to wait until she was organized.

Furnished elaborately with several chests, two tables, two benches and a lovely wooden chair, her huge solar was well appointed. Fine, detailed tapestries that looked freshly beaten hung proudly on three of the walls.

The bedchamber looked no less grand. Heavy curtains surrounded the monstrous bed, though they were currently tied back with golden rope. A sniff told Ariana the linens were freshly aired, and she wondered who had known to prepare the rooms ahead of time.

Her rooms opened onto the gallery, where she could overlook the great hall. A convenient location, though it would no doubt be noisy many evenings. Opposite the doors to the gallery were several narrow windows, five of which were graced with intricately worked stained glass of every imaginable color depicting several scenes from Arthurian legend. The wizard Myrddin Emrys, or "Merlin" to the English, appeared more often than Arthur himself, suggesting the craftsman had been Welsh, as history had it that Merlin hailed from Cymru.

And the Welsh loved their wizards. Myrddin might be their most famous wizard, but he was certainly not the only one. Welsh history abounded with magic and sorcery, mystery and legend.

Ariana marveled over the thick glass, running her finger over the heavy panes as she followed the rise and fall of Arthur and the doomed fate of the wizard at the hands of Nimue.

The sorceress.

What wisdom did Nimue acquire that she so thoroughly captivated Myrddin's attention? If only Ariana had that kind of appeal....

A knock at the door pulled Ariana from her brooding thoughts. She opened it to discover a girl, not even as old as Ceara, carrying a heavy flagon of wine and two ornate silver cups.

"*Noswaith dda,* my lady." Smiling and rosy cheeked, the girl greeted her warmly in Welsh as she bustled through the doorway and settled her burden on a tray atop a small chest. "I am Emlyn, your maid. We have been awaiting your arrival."

Ariana smiled to hear her native tongue. "The rooms are very welcoming, Emlyn. You have obviously been working hard. How did you know of our arrival?"

"The English king camps close by, my lady, as he prepares to depart for France. He sent word that the new lord and lady would be arriving. Begging your pardon for being so bold, my lady, but we are all so glad you are one of us!"

"Meaning a Welshwoman?"

"Aye! None of us wanted to continue to serve after the English took the keep, but the English king swayed us by promising us we would have a lady of our own in the keep. Will you be wanting a bath tonight, my lady?"

"Yes, please." Ariana wondered if there were others among the household who would not be so welcoming as young Emlyn.

"His lordship asked me to tell you he will come to you after his talk with the steward."

All thoughts of possible resentment at Llandervey disappeared at the thought of Roarke joining her tonight. "Lord Barret told you that?"

"Aye, my lady." Emlyn blushed as she trotted off to find a tub. Ariana could not believe her ears.

Roarke planned to come here?

That meant she would have a chance to consummate the marriage tonight. If the wisdom of the last five generations of Glamorgan women was to be believed, the so-called curse could be broken if she was intimate with a man. Ariana could save her nieces from spinsterhood and reclaim her own future as a mother. A wife.

And by God, if she could do that, she would gladly spend a lifetime making amends to Roarke for pretending to be someone she was not.

Chapter Six

An hour later, Ariana was clean and freshly scented, her false red hair brushed to shimmering perfection beneath a simple bed cap. She wore a magnificent lavender silk shift made for her in France as she paced her chamber and told herself to stay calm. Roarke was a mere man, after all. The fact that he was also a warrior of great prowess and just happened to hold her fate in his hands hardly mattered.

A curt knock at the door froze Ariana in her slippers. It could only be him.

"Come in." Her heart beat so hard she could feel the pounding in her ears.

"Good evening, Lady Ceara." Roarke stood silhouetted in the door, filling the frame with wide shoulders. His face lurked in shadow, but his voice sounded deliberately kind. "Have you rested since our journey?"

"No, my lord." Her voice was breathless, barely above a whisper. Her fear made her anxious. She wished she could run and hide, fearing he might find fault with her and cast her off despite their vows. "I have been busy unpacking and settling in. Are you? Rested, that is?"

Entering the chamber without haste, he closed the door behind him. The room was cast in shadow, the only light shed by the small, dancing flame of the hearth. As he neared Ariana's spot at the fireside, she could discern his features more clearly.

Remote and expressionless, his green eyes revealed little of the warmth she caught in them the previous night. The dark slashes of brows above them were forbidding in their inward slant. Still, his lips appeared soft and inviting, just the way she remembered them from his kiss.

"I have been occupied with the business of securing the lands and discussing the defenses with the token men-at-arms the king left here. The keep has been scantily guarded since falling into English hands, but apparently the design of the place is so intimidating, no rebellions have been waged against it." His body's proximity to hers inspired a shiver over her skin.

"I am taking great care to secure the whole residence, so you might rest easily whilst I am in France. I must leave at first light."

Although she had been prepared for the news, Ariana was surprised at the depth of disappointment she experienced. "First light, my lord? How will you possibly have everything ready so quickly?"

"All will be in readiness, I assure you. Although it will be completely up to you to manage the household. I trust you are capable of the task?"

"Of course, my lord, but I have so many questions

about what is expected of me while you are away, and—"

"Take them to the steward. His name is Philip Thornhill, a very capable sort." Roarke looked into the flames as he spoke, his voice soft and low but curt, indicating the discussion was closed.

Ariana tried another tact. "Would you care for some wine?" She stood, reaching for the exotic flagon Emlyn had brought earlier.

"Nay. I will not sleep much this night and have a long journey ahead tomorrow." He stepped closer to her, closing the space between them, though he still did not look directly at her. "I wish to retire with you for a brief period, Ceara, that we might know each other as man and wife before I leave. It is important to me that our union be legal in the eyes of the church."

Heart fluttering awkwardly while her breath stopped short, Ariana could not believe her good luck. Maybe Roarke wasn't as impervious to her as she'd feared. Still, his words now cast her into the most awkward moment of her life.

What came next?

She licked her lips as her mouth went dry. "As you wish, my lord."

He turned his gaze toward her then, finally. And his eyes were full of warmth. Nay, *heat*. She shivered as his bold, green gaze swept over her.

"Come with me, wife."

Lacing thick, rough fingers through hers, Roarke led her from the solar and into the darkened sleeping chamber. A small fire burned in the grate, casting golden shadows across her husband's broad shoulders as she followed him. His touch was warm and solid against her cool skin, bringing with it vivid memories of last night's kiss.

She'd had no time to contemplate this moment until now. Her mother's life claimed by a fever when Ariana was only nine, she'd received no instruction for how to behave on a wedding night. And with the rest of Cymru thinking she was cursed to spinsterhood, no one else had taken it upon themselves to explain such matters to her.

More's the pity, she thought. If ever she could have used an advantage with such knowledge, it was now.

When he finished untying the heavy blue bed curtains, Roarke turned to her. Had he been so tall last night when they kissed? Funny, she didn't recall the way he loomed above her, her head scarcely reaching his chin. He'd changed since their journey, his hauberk traded for a simple tunic and woolen braies.

Curiosity called her to touch him, to discover for herself what those strong male muscles would feel like against her skin. But she didn't dare. Would never be so bold.

Roarke forced himself to withstand his wife's perusal, hoping if given time, her anxiety would lessen. He could almost feel her nervous fear humming all around him like a palpable thing, her whole body taut with unease around him.

"Do not be afraid." He kept his voice low as he spoke to her, but she startled at the sound anyway. He reached out to touch her, willing his hand to gentleness despite his hunger for her touch. Her taste.

"I am unsure how to proceed," she confessed, her

gaze dancing around the chamber. Alighting on anything but him as he smoothed his thumb across her exposed shoulder.

He half wondered if it would be kinder to simply take her quickly. It seemed to him that waiting for something she feared must only drag out her sense of alarm. Then again, he might just be searching for ways to justify what he really wanted to do. His hands twitched with the need to circle her hips. To draw up the hem of her night rail by slow degrees. To test the soft skin of her thighs.

"Perhaps if we started with a kiss," he whispered, drawing her close. His eyes focused on his target, following the nervous flick of her tongue around the rim of her soft mouth. "You were not opposed to my lips upon yours yesterday, were you?"

"Nay." Her eyes drifted closed until his mouth slanted over hers.

She tasted as fragrant as she smelled, like sweet nectar or fresh honey. He cupped her chin in his hand, tilting her face so that he might have better access to the warmth of her mouth. His heart hammered in his chest with the need for more, and yet he could sense the wisdom of holding back, as well. He'd never been with a woman who had inspired him to take such time and care, but Ceara seemed a prize worth savoring.

His hands settled on her waist, absorbing the feel of her soft curves through the fabric of her thin gown. And yet, her curves were not quite as he remembered them....

Before he could ponder the matter, however, she broke their kiss. Her cheeks flamed with high color evident even in the shadowed bedchamber.

"Forgive me, my lord, I am merely…" She seemed to cast about for the right words, her discomfiture obvious.

Who knew consummating a marriage would be so difficult? Still, Roarke was not without care for her maidenly fears. She'd been bound for the convent, after all. For that matter, she was an orphan raised under the care of a cantankerous relation. Perhaps no one had ever discussed matters of the marriage bed with her.

"On second thought, perhaps a glass of wine would be best, my lady." His errands around the keep could wait a few hours. And Collin had already gone out to ride the perimeter in search of their watcher. Roarke had only one night with Ceara and he didn't intend to hurry it. "I do not mean to rush you through your wedding night when such a thing should be a momentous occasion for a young woman. Will you pour?"

Perhaps grateful to escape the tension between them, Ariana hurried off to the small sideboard to retrieve the wine while he settled himself into the bed linens. He enjoyed watching her move about the chamber, her slender form obvious underneath her night rail thanks to the help of the firelight.

Lifting the leather-encased flagon with two hands, she hefted the wine above the first cup. The ornate silver pitcher was an unusual serving piece, perhaps one of her family's treasures that she'd unpacked. After filling cups for both of them, she retraced her steps to the bed and climbed in beside Roarke.

"Here you are my lord, to your success in France." She raised her drink to his in cheerful toast. "May you return home soon."

Touching his cup to hers, he drank to the sentiment even though he knew she would be disappointed in that regard. A knight never returned home quickly. Especially one intent on making a name for himself with his king.

She would discover as much for herself some day. And while he hoped she did not grow to resent him, it did not change the fact that he needed a wife to secure his legacy, to provide heirs for the lands he would amass.

Her voice called him from his thoughts. "Does the wine not possess a strange flavor, my lord?"

He drank another sip. Drained the cup. "I taste nothing amiss. But then I am not fond of Welsh wines."

It had been on the tip of his tongue to tell her that he preferred English ales, but a wave of fatigue overcame him. His senses felt suddenly thick, as if Ceara had moved far away from him.

"Ceara?" He thought he called out to her, but if she heard him, she did not acknowledge him.

Instead, she seemed to be making herself comfortable on the soft feather mattress beside him. His mind refusing to make sense of anything, Roarke wondered vaguely if there could have been something in the wine.

The last thing he recalled before darkness prevailed was his hand curving around his wife's hip, drawing her close to him in sleep.

Roarke knew something was very wrong the instant he awakened, but strangely enough he could not think of it. He always awoke clearheaded and alert. A light sleeper all of his life, he usually awoke several times a night, always knowing instantly the approximate hour and exactly where he was.

Right now he could not recall either.

He looked around him as if in a fog, straining to see more clearly. His first distinct realization was that he was covered with a woman's hair. Red hair. He pushed the long cinnamon-colored strands off him, savoring the softness of each before he found their source and carefully studied the woman he bound himself to yesterday.

Her skin was clear and smooth and unmarked by the ravages of childhood fevers or other illnesses. Her figure was slender except for the generous curves of breasts and hips. Although, as his gaze strayed over her body she seemed smaller somehow today. More delicate.

She was a beautiful woman, his wife. He'd been so worried about taking her too roughly last night. She'd been a virgin after all. And then when she'd kissed him, touched him so tentatively, it was all he could do not to shred her thin shift from her curves and lose himself in her. It had been his right, yet he'd wanted to take his time. Help to ease her fears.

He'd asked Ceara to pour them both wine, and then…

Blinking at the soft trickle of sunlight filtering into the high window of Ceara's room, Roarke's mind suddenly cleared.

It was first light.

He was supposed to be on his way to meet King Henry, as they would sail for France today.

Roarke vaulted out of bed, all thoughts of Ceara fled as he tore from her chamber and up the stairs to his own rooms. Berating himself every step of the way, he shouted out orders to half the household as he hastened to don travel garments and chain mail.

"Philip!" he shouted for the third time, nearly colliding with the sleepy steward as the man in question arrived at the entryway. By now, several other household servants arrived to help pack.

"Here, my lord."

"You are to answer to my wife, Philip, and no other. She speaks for me in my absence. No one else gets in the keep while I am away, unless it is King Henry himself, should he arrive here before me. I will return within a half year, and I expect things to be in good order. The men-at-arms are in charge of themselves, neither you nor my lady wife need to concern yourselves with their doings. Do I make myself clear?"

"Perfectly. All will run smoothly, my lord, I assure you."

"Collin Baldwin?"

"Loading the horses, my lord."

Had Philip seemed less capable, Roarke might have asked the king for another day, but he trusted his English steward to oversee the keep and Collin was already prepared to leave.

His one concern was his marriage. He did not think he consummated the union last night, and now Ceara could easily get an annulment. But he'd hardly confess such a concern to Henry, damn it. And he didn't believe in lying to the king in order to give himself more time.

Roarke swore profusely as he stomped down the stairs and paused outside her door.

What to do? Should he mention his concern to her?

If he did not, she might wonder if he even wanted her for a wife and be open to harmful counsel by her Welsh countrymen should she keep correspondence with anyone.

Disgusted with himself for not taking care of this matter last night, he decided to speak with her and entered her chamber without knocking.

She stood at the window, watching the preparations in the courtyard below until his entry startled her.

"My lord." She straightened, holding her chin high despite the nervousness in her expressive golden gaze. "I hoped you might say goodbye. We need to discuss the matter of last night's wine."

"I am late," he began abruptly, sounding harsher than he had intended. "About our wedding night…" He did not even know what to say. There was a chance they consummated the marriage and he just did not recall. Last night was somewhat of a blur.

She stepped closer, lifting the exotic flagon she'd used last night to pour their wine. "I believe our wine was poisoned." Proffering the vessel for his inspection, she wiped the spout and showed him a grainy residue. "Not with anything lethal, merely an herb to invoke drowsiness."

"Poison?" His mind churned with thoughts of all he needed to prepare for his trip, but that lone word caught his ear. He sniffed the contents of the silver pitcher before replacing it on a nearby chest.

"I thought the drink tasted strange, but the brew affected me so quickly I was not able to connect what happened until I awoke this morning." She tugged at her kirtle, her hands fluttering restlessly over the silk. "I do not think you are safe to go abroad today, my lord. What if someone wishes you harm?"

"I would be more concerned if someone should wish *you* harm, but I will inform the steward to look into the matter." He couldn't credit anyone wishing to poison their wine. And although he knew he'd made some enemies among the English king's other knights, he did not envision any nobleman concocting tainted herbs. "Perhaps we merely drank a brew gone bad."

"But what if—"

"We can speak of it more when I return." He hated to leave on such an awkward note, but he had no time to tarry. "I apologize for leaving you so shortly after the wedding, but I have promised my king."

Perhaps sensing his resolve in the matter, she nodded shortly. "I understood that when I agreed to be your wife, my lord. You need not concern yourself with me. I wish you Godspeed and a safe journey." She stepped quickly toward him and kissed his cheek.

There was much more that he wanted to say to his fair Welsh wife before his departure. *Don't stage a rebellion while I am gone,* for one. But that seemed rather harsh in light of her gentle manner and sweet gesture.

"Thank you. I will return in the spring, Ceara. I hope you are well adjusted to life here by then. I trust you are content to be an Englishman's wife and understand the implications of that?"

Her brow knit for a moment, as if she had given little thought to the question.

"I am pleased you are a foreigner to Cymru, my lord. It gives us both a fresh start of sorts."

Her answer was not what he'd expected. But he was late. And her answer at least struck him as honest.

Unwilling to settle for a kiss on the cheek—especially after last night's debacle with the wine—Roarke hauled her close. He savored the soft feel of her against him. Slanting his mouth over hers, he claimed her mouth for his own, inhaling her warm lavender fragrance as he coaxed apart her lips.

He kissed her until she sighed. Then kissed her until she moaned softly beneath him. But only when she wrapped both arms around him and clung to him did he consider he'd kissed her well enough.

By God, he did not want to leave her.

Hunger churning through him as he pulled away, he set her aside with more than a little regret.

"Farewell then, Ceara, until we meet again."

Ariana's heart fell as she watched Roarke leave her solar. Why had he refused to listen to her suspicions? As a healer, she knew how to be on guard for possible poisons in the future. But what of Roarke? If the vile herb had been intended for her husband and not her, he needed to be very careful of the food and drink he consumed.

Glaring at the tainted wine and its unusual vessel, she vowed to speak to Emlyn about the matter shortly. Hadn't the maid said there were members of the household who did not relish the notion of an English lord? At least, if that was the case, the trouble would remain here at home and Roarke would be safe abroad.

Assuming his sword arm was as strong as it looked. The man could not have been more imposing if he'd been carved out of marble.

And he struck her as quite clever. Though her experience of knights was slim, she conversed with enough of those who passed through Glamorgan Keep to know Roarke was much smarter than the average warrior. She noticed he read the wedding certificate before he signed it in a very fine hand. She heard him speak with her father at length about the political climate on the continent. And during their marriage feast, she even caught him comparing notes with one of the villein about Welsh and English planting seasons.

So he had the wits to keep himself alive in battle.

Yet Ariana could not shake the deep sense of foreboding that settled over her as she peered out her narrow slit of a window to watch him ride out of the courtyard and to the south with Collin. As if he rode into certain death.

She crossed herself quickly at the thought and closed her eyes to say another prayer for his safe return, but the moment her lids fell a startling picture formed in her mind. A knife at Roarke's back. A dark shadow lurking behind him.

Her eyes flew open against the horrible sight, her breathing fast and shallow in the vision's wake.

The sight.

"No!" she cried hoarsely, one palm curling protectively around her forehead, as if to keep out the pictures in her mind.

Although Ariana could not call forth her power with the sight at will, whenever it came to her, it had always been accurate.

Roarke was in grave danger from an unknown enemy, the kind he was not prepared to fight. Ariana knew it as surely as the sun rose in the east. She was not having a mere attack of nerves at being left alone in Llandervey. She knew, without a doubt, that she had just peered into the potential future.

Unless she intervened.

"Where is Eleanor when I need her?" she wondered aloud, leaving the slender window to pace the floor of her simple chamber. But she could no longer call upon her old teacher and confidante. Time to trust her heart and instincts to do what was right.

Roarke needed her. He did not know the danger that awaited him.

Not that Ariana knew precisely where danger lay, either, but her vision would come true unless she was there to stop it or to at least warn Roarke what fate might have in store for him.

But how to tell Roarke? If he had not been inclined to listen to her fears about the tainted wine, he might not be impressed with her claims of having the sight.

Still, she had to at least let him know. Although he might not believe her as he had no experience with her visions, she could at least warn him and stay close to make sure the vision did not take place.

If anything were to happen to Roarke Barret, Ariana would surely be cursed for the rest of her life with one great lie over her head. Her nieces would still be destined to live out the same barren existence all Glamorgan women had for five generations, and Ariana would never fulfill her mother's dying wish.

Moreover, she owed him. She'd promised herself she would be a good wife to this man and now she'd been presented with an opportunity to fulfill that vow.

Besides, she could not bear the thought of harm coming to Roarke. In the short time she had known him, she had already formed an attachment to the green-eyed stranger who'd held her so tenderly and kissed her so thoroughly.

Their fates were bound somehow, and she would not allow anything or anyone to harm her husband until they had a chance to find out why.

Late the next night, cramped in the airless hold of a small seafaring vessel, Ariana half regretted her determination.

Stretching a knot from her neck in her confined space, she squinted between the slats of the crate in which she'd hidden herself and wondered what Ceara would think of her cousin's latest adventure. Would she think Ariana foolhardy? Addlepated? Hasty-witted? Aye. Aye. And aye.

Merciful heavens, but she had gone too far this time to follow her husband across the channel to France with his king and all his knights nearby. But then, she'd been too afraid to approach Roarke among his intimidating company once she'd finally caught up with him on an English hillside while they loaded their boats to set sail.

She had departed Llandervey less than an hour after her husband. She'd asked a distracted Philip Thornhill where her husband planned to meet the king and the steward gave her excellent directions without realizing it. When she'd rode up on the party preparing to sail after endless hours on horseback, she'd made a fast decision to hide. To wait for the right moment to speak to him alone instead of blurting out her warning to him in full view of his lofty assembly. Besides, her every instinct insisted he would have brushed aside her concerns and departed anyway. At least if she followed him, she could make sure her vision did not come true.

And perhaps she would be granted her wedding night after all.

Although that had not been on her mind at the time she'd left Roarke's keep, she could not deny that she'd thought about it—often—over the course of her long journey. She'd been nervous two nights ago. And then enticed. Curious.

How unfair that the tumult of feelings and worries had not been eased by a night spent becoming her husband's wife in every way. Other brides only had to worry for a day about their wedding night. Ariana would be tormented every day until she could accomplish the deed.

Still, her means to that end were not comfortable. She could scarcely bend her big toe without bumping the sides of her crate, and she wondered if she hadn't made a huge mistake. She'd left the keep with no thought as to how long she would be gone or what she might need for a journey. She'd grabbed two changes of clothing, soap and a hairbrush. Then on impulse, she took a slender silver blade encased in smooth leather and fastened it to her garter.

Now she was a stowaway in Henry's boat as the knights made their crossing to France. They had been at sea for what seemed like hours when the scramble of feet on deck roused Ariana from her endless roil of fears. She felt dizzy and short of breath anyway, but the hustle of the crew above deck gave her hope she would be able to come out of hiding soon.

How she would be able to escape the crate undetected remained a mystery. Discovery by anyone but Roarke would be extremely dangerous.

Although discovery by Roarke would be hazardous, too, she began to realize. No matter how she made her presence known to him, he would be furious to learn that she had come to France. She knew very little of her husband's character, but of that much she was certain. Heaven knew, he would never understand her reasoning.

Her need to follow him sounded ridiculous even to her own ears. She followed him because of a vision— because she possessed the sight.

He might not even believe her, let alone understand.

The small ship she rode in was pulled roughly to the shore, bumping over rocks and sharp sticks she could almost feel through the bottom of the wooden boat. She latched her crate for unloading.

But the unloading never came. The men deserted the boats and many of the supplies seemed to have been carried ashore, but other crates and weapons remained behind, as if the boats were going to be docked there for a while.

Finally, she climbed out of her hiding spot and carefully opened the door to the hold for a look out over the deck of the boat. Night had fallen. Fires were being lit all over the camp, tents were already erected, and a pen for the horses was hastily constructed.

She spotted Roarke easily. A head taller than most of the men, he stood out in a crowd.

Quietly lowering the door to the hold, Ariana began searching the contents of the remaining boxes, hoping to find something to aid her in her escape.

She found what she needed on her fourth try. Men's attire.

Removing her dress was awkward in the small hold. She could not even stand upright, let alone reach around the back to unhook all of the clasps. But she eased out of it at last and stuffed the garment into her bag.

The clothes she chose were too large, requiring considerable rolling and tucking before she managed to fit into a heavy pair of braies that she gartered tightly to her legs with leather straps. She then donned a worn white tunic and black hauberk held fast with several rounds of leather strap to stay fitted to her body.

The full hood on the hauberk disguised her hair and features as well as the oversize clothes hid her figure. From a distance, no one would pay her any attention.

Thankfully, the boat had been pulled ashore, so Ariana did not have to swim to reach land. She slipped soundlessly from the hold, feeling bold and daring in the close-fitting male garb.

The men relaxed about the campfires. Now that the tents were set up and their immediate gear was unloaded, they ate and drank in good humor. Whores appeared out of nowhere, drawn to men with coin more quickly than clouds gathered in a sunny Welsh sky.

Ariana studied their tactics with interest. Of course many of the men were receptive to the women's wares immediately, but other men needed cajoling to part with their coins for the company of a woman.

That particular scenario was of vital interest to her.

She noted the women touched the men in a brazen fashion. Standing behind a seated man, one of the women placed her hands on the man's shoulders and leaned over him to press womanly flesh against her potential customer's cheek. Apparently, it was an effective move, because the man pulled her quickly into a nearby tent.

Ariana watched the women's antics avidly for a few more moments until she spied Roarke striding toward the fire closest to her. All interest in the women died when it occurred to her that one of them might be sleeping with her husband tonight.

Before he was seated, not one, but two women appeared at his side to tempt him. Draping themselves about him shamelessly, Ariana could see the pouts and fluttering eyelashes they used to entice him.

Roarke did not take them up on their offers, nor did he dismiss them out of hand. He smiled winningly at them, enraging Ariana and filling her with envy.

Ariana grew more incensed by the minute. One of the women pawed her husband, kissed him profusely on several occasions, and tried to seat herself across his legs. By the time Roarke parted company with his admirers, Ariana was torn between scratching Roarke's eyes out and swimming back home to annul her marriage.

As her eyes followed Roarke to his tent, Ariana unwittingly moved toward him, stepping slightly beyond the protective shadow of the forest. Into the light.

Her anger had made her careless.

Chapter Seven

❦

"And who might you be, lad?" a slurred male voice shouted across the rocky terrain near the water, freezing her in place. "Have you no duties to attend that you be sneaking about?"

Heart slamming wildly, Ariana stepped cautiously back toward the trees, praying the man's words were not directed toward her. She vowed to curb her every impetuous instinct in the future if only she had not been spotted.

A big shadow rose like a growing mountain from a seat at a nearby fire, then stomped nosily toward the wooded area. Toward *her*.

"You will have to answer to me if you think you can ignore a question from a knight." A monstrous hand fell upon her shoulder as she sought to run away. Yanking backward on her cloak, the man wrenched her to the cold earth.

She struggled to regain her footing, knowing she could outrun her lumbering captor if only she could free herself. She'd outrun her father's men more than once on her secret outings into the forest to visit Eleanor. If only she could…

Her hood tore off in his hand, exposing her hair. Her face.

"A woman." His voice held a note of awe before dark menace crept back into his words. "Hellfire, that's just what I needed."

The fear skittering down her spine turned to ice-cold panic.

"You do not understand, sir. I am a noblewoman." It was worth a try. Her mind worked vainly to formulate some line of reasoning that would force him to free her.

And he was a knight after all. A successful one at that, judging by his clean, shaven face and his newly polished chain mail.

"Then you've fallen on hard times, if your garments are any indication." His smile told her he did not believe her for a moment. Lowering himself to the ground, his knee bit into her thigh.

Dear God, he thought her a whore. And to be fair, what other woman would be traipsing about the English camp in the middle of the night?

"You do not understand." She edged her hand toward the knife she'd secured to her garter, moving slowly so as not to attract his attention. "I am—"

"She's my wife." Another voice roared in her ears. A welcome voice despite the fury that rolled through the words. "And you'd better get the hell off of her right now, Edgar."

* * *

A few minutes later, Roarke stalked back to his tent, towing his new bride along with him. He hoped he could restrain the potent anger and gut-wrenching fear that still roiled inside him. It had taken every shred of self-control he possessed not to knock Edgar Hughes's teeth down his throat when he'd found the man on top of Ceara. Thank the fates he'd been bathing nearby when he'd heard her scream. But right now, his temper simmered so that he wasn't sure how much will he had left to converse civilly with Ceara.

"Thank you, my lord." Her soft-spoken gratitude drifted over him as he hauled her back to his tent, away from the curious stares of a handful of other men who had witnessed his exchange with Hughes.

"Do not thank me." He thrust her into the darkened tent on the far perimeter of the camp, a strategically located spot that allowed him to keep an eye on his fellow knights in case of treachery. His friendship with Henry had its rewards and its dangers.

Following her inside, he extinguished a candle he'd lit earlier. Now the soft lines of her face and the reflection of her wide eyes were cast in shadowed half light from the filtered rays of the moon. Long red waves tumbled haphazardly down her back.

Perhaps he'd frightened her because she stared back at him in silence. Hellfire, of course he'd frightened her. But it couldn't compare to the scare she'd given him.

"What are you doing in France?" He forced himself to speak softly despite the waves of anger rushing over him, wondering how she could have ever booked passage across the channel so quickly. "Answer me."

"You'll think me foolish, my lord." She bit her lip. Hesitated. "I followed you because I am certain you are in grave danger."

"I will be engaged in battle several times in the next six months. It is the nature of a knight, if you will recall."

"Not that sort of danger, my lord." She cleared her throat, as if to rid her voice of the tremor that unsettled her words. "I had a vision as you were riding out of the keep grounds that you would be betrayed by one of your own people. I came to make sure that does not happen to you."

"You had a *vision?*" No amount of self-control could have kept the disdain from his voice. By God, what was the matter with her?

"Aye. I know it sounds far-fetched, but—"

"Far-fetched does not describe the half of it." His voice rose just a bit above a whisper. "It sounds ludicrous, Ceara, as I'm sure you are well aware."

He pressed her shoulders down so she might sit on the bedroll, hoping to put her more at ease. He even forced himself to sit beside her on the dark woolen blankets. "Do not make me ask you again. What the hell are you doing here?"

"I have the sight, Roarke. I actually saw someone stab you in my mind's eye. It was horrible and I—"

"The sight?" He had heard the Welsh were superstitious folk, but this was too much. "And you expect me to believe such fanciful nonsense?"

He saw her stiffen. Straighten. But by all that was holy he would not feel sorry for her after she'd nearly been defiled in his own encampment. He took a deep breath. Started again.

"What made you come here? Are you working with the Welsh to form a group of resisters to English rule? Perhaps you have French sympathies and wish to warn friends of our presence?" His voice grew louder with each scenario he painted. "Or are you simply a mentally unwell woman, and that is why your miserable old uncle was so eager to be rid of you?"

He almost shouted. A sure sign his temper was spiraling out of control. Grinding his teeth, he lowered his voice when he posed his next question.

"Who attends you on this trip, my lady?" He brushed past her to peer outside the tent before turning back to Ceara.

"Where is your man-at-arms? Who guards your person?"

"I am alone."

"You crossed the sea *alone?* You traveled to France *alone?*"

"Think you I could not make my way here by myself?"

"I know damn well you could not steer a boat on the sea yourself—" He paused abruptly, slapping his forehead in sudden realization before massaging his temples with one large palm. "You stowed away on one of the ships. I thought your uncle was giving me a convent-bound girl, not some adventure-seeking witless fool! Have you no sense?"

"I considered your well-being to be worth the risk, my lord. But I knew if I were to warn you of the coming treachery I must face the potential dangers."

"Worth the risk? You thought defending a veteran warrior against an imagined plot of treachery was worth the risks of debauchery, rape and who knows what else?" Roarke seized her arms, pulling her to him as if he could will his message into her by force.

Her eyes flashed in the darkness, but her lips remained sealed.

"Do you know what a man like Edgar Hughes would have done to you?" God, he could not bear the thought. Could not crush the image in his mind of her slender form underneath another's man's thighs.

"I have seen many English crimes perpetrated against innocent Welsh women and children, Roarke. I am aware of the dangers. And I tell you again, I weighed the risk and still wanted to warn you." She leaned closer to him, arching her back so that her face hovered inches from his own. "I knew you would not believe me. But I know that what I saw in my vision will happen unless I am here to avert it. And I do not want you to die."

"Good God, you really believe you are here to save me." Roarke slid his hands down her arms before turning away from her. Had anyone ever attempted to save him before? The notion humbled him. Quieted him. His anger deflated by slow degrees even as he knew he must make her understand her own foolishness.

"Ceara, even if I could forgive you for what you have done, my king would not allow me to overlook your actions. I have no choice but to censure you in some way." What to do with a woman who put herself in such danger? The whole English encampment would be buzzing with talk of his bride's antics tomorrow. He would have to explain her actions to Henry. Would be bound to address the matter.

Ariana's heart lodged in her throat at the thought of censure. His criticism shouldn't sting so much considering she'd been on the receiving end of her father's barbs her whole life, especially since her mother's death. But somehow, Roarke's disappointment in her stung even more.

She tensed, but refused to let Roarke see her fear.

"You understand that you should have stayed at Llandervey where I left you. If I allow this transgression to go unchecked, it would be much noted by my fellow knights, and certainly my king." Roarke swore under his breath. "But you are my wife, and I will not allow anyone to harm you. Perhaps it would be best if you were confined to a local convent until I am finished in France."

"You mean to sentence me to a nunnery?" To be shut away from all hope of love and laughter and life ranked as her worst nightmare. It was the way all Glamorgan women died. "I will not go."

"Your escort rides out at dawn, wife, and you will most certainly be with him."

He rose as if to leave the tent.

Anger swept through her at his presumptuousness. He had scarcely listened to anything she'd told him tonight. Ceara had warned her that other men would not be so easy to manage as her father, but she did not truly believe it until now. Scrambling to her feet, she used all her strength to take him by the arm and make him face her.

"Has it occurred to you, *husband*," she stressed the word as unpleasantly as she could, "that I am not even legally bound to you? I am not obligated to honor your request."

She blocked his path, daring him with her glare to do battle with her. She would not be dismissed and ignored. At the moment, he looked too surprised to argue.

"Did you think me so naive as to not realize that our marriage is not even legal yet?" She felt the heat rising in her cheeks, but ignored it. "Did you think I was such an innocent as to be tricked into thinking I should sit about your keep for half a year or who knows how long when I am not even truly wed to you? If you were to die in this campaign, my lord, whose protection could I possibly seek? Our union means nothing on paper alone, and my reputation would be in too much dispute to secure another husband, considering I would be left with nothing."

"I will not die." The solid strength and sheer male power of him under her fingertips seemed testament to that fact, but she knew he could not make such an impossible claim.

"You think to dare God with your invincibility, my lord?" Why would he not even take into consideration her claim? Resentment sizzled. Boiled. "And from what I can see, you are only too glad to be away from your convent-bound bride on this campaign. Although you could not muster the strength to fulfill your marital contract with me, you seemed to have plenty of vigor and warm smiles to bestow upon a common whore tonight!"

She did not realize she was shouting until the stark contrast of Roarke's utter silence greeted her concluding words.

Ariana could tell he was shocked by the slight inclination of his brows and his lack of speech. But more than that, he was furious.

Good. Better than having him feeling nothing.

After a long moment, he stalked closer in the shadowed tent. She forced herself not to shrink back although the urge to back away was strong.

"You waste your words and your anger. Neither sways me. I wed you with good intentions, Ceara, and you know well that I mean to honor you. You have no reason to fear for your position in spite of the state of our marriage." His voice was controlled, but the tension rippling through his muscles told her that her words were hitting their mark.

"Why should I trust you about our marriage when you made it so painfully clear that you wed me only because the king commanded it?"

"A good wife respects her husband's word."

"When I am *truly* your wife, I will respect your word." It galled her to have to look up at him while she spoke, but he was so near, she could not do otherwise. Through the hair's breadth that separated them, Ariana felt the heat of his body, the beat of his heart.

Or was it her own?

She found herself wanting the curse broken even more than before. A strange urge to know this man, to be close to him, took her by surprise.

Her unsteady emotions confusing her, Ariana tried to step away from him, but his arms were about her instantly, making escape impossible.

"When you are imprisoned in a convent and under lock and key, it will not matter that you do not respect my word. Mayhap your time among the Christian sisters will teach you to be less rebellious."

She opened her mouth to argue, but Roarke halted

her words by covering her mouth with his own. Her mind fought him even as her body relaxed against him, welcoming his embrace.

Roarke possessed her with his kiss, claiming her mouth and stealing her will.

Desire swept through her, as fierce and strong as the fury that filled her moments before. Somewhere in the back of her mind, she wondered what moved him to kiss her when she was so unappealing without the use of magic, but she was too unnerved by the sensations swirling through her to wonder about it for long. His strength surrounded her, holding her up while her legs seemed to dissolve beneath her.

Warmth spread through her as his hands moved from the small of her back to trace the curve of her arms and shoulders, slowing their path at the column of her neck, and resting on either side of her face.

Slowly, he pulled away from her, cradling her face in his hands.

"Sit down, Ceara. You must be exhausted from your journey."

Barely recovered from his kiss, she did as he asked.

Roarke smiled at her as he pulled her down beside him. She was surprised to see genuine warmth in his eyes. And he'd kissed of his own free will. She'd needed no fanciful charm to bring about such a feat.

"I was very frightened, my lord."

"I wonder."

His gaze wandered slowly over her face, taking in every feature in the filtered rays of moonlight as if memorizing her. She marveled at the feel of him look-ing at her. And this was far more then the second glance she'd sometimes craved from other men. His perusal was slow. Steady. Thorough.

Ariana felt giddy with her small triumph. A joyous tune sprang to her lips, though she managed to contain it to a happy hum.

"I am sorry about our wedding night, Ceara. 'Tis not the way I wanted things to go, you can be sure. But I cannot change what happened, and I am not sure it is right to give in to your demands just because you followed me here. To do so would give a wife far too much power."

The glow of her small triumph vanished along with her glad song.

Words of protest bubbled up to her lips and Ariana wished fervently to spew them out. *Of all the arrogant, high-handed, illogical, ridiculous...*

"You must leave tomorrow, for it is too dangerous for you here. I am sorry if you do not look forward to the convent, but were it not for me, you would be bound for the nunnery for a lifetime. I cannot believe it is as harsh a punishment for you as you say."

It took all of her willpower to resist the urge to scream in frustration. Why had her father shared that bit of news about Ceara with Roarke? It would have been difficult enough to contend with the false hair, padded figure and painted freckles, but now she also had to pretend to be a different manner of woman all together. She was so much different from sensible, pious, sweet Ceara.

"If it were for a few nights, it would not be a punishment, but six months would be a difficult adjustment for me, especially now that I am a married woman. It seems to me if I am safely ensconced in a convent, you will have even less qualms about devoting yourself to gaining an annulment."

"I do not know how you came about such a notion, my lady, but I have no plans to annul our marriage. I need you very much."

Ariana studied the intent green eyes for telltale hints that he spoke falsely, but she could see no such signs.

"Very well then. If I can convince you of the significance of my vision, then perhaps I will go."

Roarke laughed.

"You find it amusing that I will do as you wish?"

"I find it amusing you think you have a choice."

"You were not laughing when I arrived here tonight, husband, and I will wager you did not think I had a choice but to stay at Llandervey yesterday morning."

The flexing of his jaw muscle and renewed glitter of his eyes told her he did not find her remark entertaining. "I trust you learned something from this episode?"

"If a vision warns me that I need to protect you in the future, I shall be more discreet in doing so."

He looked ready to strangle her with his bare hands, but he took a calming breath, obviously preparing a diatribe for her benefit.

Following his previous example, she silenced his outrage with a kiss.

It was not an all-consuming sort of kiss like the one he bestowed upon her, but it effectively surprised him out of his tirade. Ariana pressed her lips gently to his and, for good measure, stroked the side of his face ever so lightly with her fingertips.

"Where shall I sleep, my lord?" She vowed she

would not let this night pass without some attempt to woo him into her bed. Surely she could charm her own husband more effectively then any of those camp followers she'd seen earlier.

Roarke did not answer right away as he deliberated the question. Ariana could not recall ever seeing the man hesitate before.

"You will sleep by my side."

Chapter Eight

Roarke regretted the words as soon as they left his lips. It was ludicrous for him to sleep next to her and not consummate their marriage. He'd regretted leaving her this morning and now here she was. In his tent. Within arm's reach.

And dear God, but she seemed to be undressing.

"I brought a few items of clothing with me, but I left the parcel near the beach." She unfastened the cord that tied a man's tunic to her waist, her movements graceful and feminine.

"I'll get them." He turned away from her abruptly, thinking the night air would clear his head. Although no amount of bracing cool air would rid him of the image of Ceara sliding out of her clothes.

Watching him depart the tent, Ariana clutched the loose tunic to her body, hoping her instincts for attracting her husband were working. She would feel more certain of herself if he had opted to remain within the tent. With her. But the few minutes that he was gone gave her time to think. Plan.

Somehow she needed to convince him to consummate their marriage tonight, and not send her to a convent tomorrow. It seemed like too much to maneuver, even for her. She'd done more than her share of helping fate along the past few days. Right now, she needed a sign that she was doing the right thing in her quest to stay by his side. She had no wish to transform into a shrewish wife within her first fortnight as a bride. She only wanted to save Roarke. Create the warm, thriving household she had dreamed of as a child.

"Here you are." Roarke's voice startled her at the flap of the tent. He tossed her dark traveling bag at her feet, a gust of cold night air swirling into the tent behind him as he entered.

She had thought about undressing in front of him in the hope of enticing him, but no matter how badly she wanted her marriage to become a reality, she could not find that sort of bold courage. His eyes glittered hotly in the darkness, searing her skin as he gazed upon her.

"If you would excuse me for a moment, my lord?" She sidled closer to the exit, called by the cool, crisp air outside. "I need some privacy to ready myself for sleep."

Roarke beat her to the tent flap. "I will go. You can change in here."

"But I need to…be outside." Her face warmed as she hoped he'd infer her meaning.

His jaw flexed. Tightened. Turning to the flap, he peered out into the night and the thick cover of forest behind his tent at the far edge of the camp.

"You have but two minutes before I come out after you." Holding the canvas aside for her, he allowed her to leave.

Ariana crept away as quietly as she could, not wishing to disturb any of the other knights now that the camp appeared quiet. Still. Clutching her bundle of clothes, she hid among the trees to dress and hastened to ready herself for sleep. Not wishing to traipse through the trees nearly naked, she left her undergarments and a small amount of padding under her night rail. By the time she approached Roarke's tent again, he had lit a candle within.

A courtesy to her so she might make herself more comfortable? Or perhaps he merely had tasks of his own to accomplish before sleep. Whatever his intent, she could see the outline of her warrior husband clearly, his fine male form making her breath catch.

Soundlessly, she neared the edge of the forest when she heard a rustling sound nearby. Roarke? Nay. She could still see him within his tent. Holding herself still another moment, she wondered if it might be a night animal of some sort.

Until she spied a man circling the rear perimeter of Roarke's tents stealthily, as though searching for a back entrance.

Immediately alert, she crept closer to the man as he stole toward Roarke's lodging. It could be his friend Collin, and she did not wish to cause Roarke any more distress by sending up a premature cry of alarm. He was irritated enough with her already. Instead she watched the figure, garbed in dark colors and bearing no visible standard, as he positioned himself against the back of Roarke's tent.

Once in position, the man reached slowly across his midsection toward his belt for his knife.

Ariana gulped back the gasp that rose in her throat, fearful she would give herself away by the sound. She blinked once to be sure she did not imagine what she saw, for it appeared to be one of Roarke's fellow English knights who held the weapon.

But as the dull gleam of silver flashed subtly in the moonlight, she knew her eyes did not deceive her.

Roarke's shadow within the tent darkened as it neared the canvas. His massive form lowered itself into a sitting position on the ground, as if he were preparing to oil his chain mail or polish his sword before sleeping. Ariana's eyes followed his every move as carefully as the watcher seemed to.

When the watcher raised his dagger again, panic swept through her in a cold wave. She wasted no time in running headlong toward the man with the knife.

"Roarke!"

Her cry was blood curdling enough to frighten the would-be murderer. His feet fairly flew away from the tents.

"Stop him!" she cried, pointing out the disappearing shadow to Roarke and the handful of other men who appeared from their tents at her scream.

"Roarke!" she shouted, able to breathe again once she saw him alive and unharmed. "A killer lurked behind your tent, my lord."

Why was no one running where she'd pointed?

"I'll go," a young knight spoke up from the small crowd. "But I did not see signs of anyone."

No one else seemed concerned that a murder was

nearly committed just moments ago. Roarke in particular stared hard at her, looking none too pleased she had just saved his life.

Uncomfortable, she squeezed the bundle of her discarded clothes more tightly to her.

Roarke separated himself from the rest of the group to close the distance between them. He tossed his cloak around her shoulders none too gently.

"My lord, a man approached your tent, with a knife," she stressed the words forcefully, but he did not seem the least bit interested in what she had to say. Her own heart still pounded angrily in her chest, the rush of fear fresh in her blood.

"This is my wife," he announced suddenly, turning to the rest of the assembled camp. "She will be leaving as soon as she possibly can."

His green eyes flashed an unmistakable warning as he looked about him, sending a distinct message to the other knights to disperse. Slowly, the men departed, laughing and jesting amongst themselves.

"My lord, you do not understand, a man would have killed you—" she began before another man approached them.

"You will not dismiss me, Barret. I demand an explanation at once."

The dark haired, plump man who interrupted her could only be one person. Even without the robes that accompanied his station, King Henry III was immediately recognizable as royalty.

Ariana curtsied low before him, her white gown grazing the hard packed earth.

"Rise, fair lady, and explain your presence to me."

His tone intimidated, but the king's expression did not. A smile lurked at the corners of his lips as he bade her tell her tale.

"Certainly, Your Highness." Knowing she would be foolish to mention her vision to her husband's sovereign, she peered into the forest one last time, hoping the young knight who had chased Roarke's attacker would return the traitor in hand. "I followed my husband to France today after a frightening incident in which I believed he was meant to be poisoned—"

"This is truly your wife, Barret?"

"Aye, my lord." Roarke hardly looked pleased to admit as much.

"You did her injustice with your description. She is ravishing." He returned his gaze to Ariana. "Pray continue, lady."

She felt herself blush to her toes. Surely she was not as cursed as her father would have her believe if even the English king could dole out such compliments. "I meant to warn him of possible treachery at work and then tonight I discovered a man approaching his tent with a knife. I thought I must have misconstrued the situation, but as Roarke neared the wall of the tent, the man raised his weapon to strike."

"And thus the scream?" The king looked amused.

"Yes, Your Highness."

"And what of the night's earlier intrigue, Lady Ceara? I have heard you encountered one of my other knights and I would have been most displeased if your husband had not arrived to save you."

"My husband has informed me that I used very poor judgment in trying to protect him."

The king looked skeptically between husband and wife. "I detect a great deal more to this story, Barret, but I suppose that is your business. She may accompany us to Rennes tomorrow, but then you must make arrangements for her return. I need your Welsh wife in Wales, keeping peace with her people."

"There is a convent not far from here, my lord," Roarke interjected.

"Any woman so eager for more nights with her husband is certainly not meant for the convent." The king smiled wickedly at Ariana. "And who knows when we will pass this way again. I want her back in Wales as soon as possible, not locked in a French convent where she does neither of us any good. She rides to Rennes."

He kissed Ariana's rather longer than was necessary. "I bid you *nos da,* my lady."

She thought she would swoon—not from the kiss, but from utter joy at the opportunity to remain with Roarke a bit longer. "*Nos da,* Your Highness. And thank you."

Ariana could not believe her good fortune. She would go with Roarke tomorrow and stay by his side for as long as it took to make travel arrangements. That would surely present opportunities for them to know one another better and break the curse.

The thrill remained until she looked at Roarke.

His scowl sent a shiver of foreboding straight to her toes.

"To the tent. Now."

Roarke took his wife by the arm to be sure she did not cause any more trouble. He was not yet recovered from the shock of discovering his quiet, unassuming young bride had followed him to France. Now this.

He pulled her into the tent, securing the opening behind them.

"Never in my wildest dreams did I envision having a wife to be this inconvenient," he began without prelude.

"Someone is trying to kill you, my lord, and I suspect it is one of your king's own men."

"A very good reason for why you don't belong here."

He recalled the watcher who had followed him from England to Wales and cursed Henry's insistence she stay with him.

"Do you have enemies, my lord?"

"I did not work my way up from nothing without making enemies, wife. But that does not make your notion of someone trying to kill me any less ridiculous." His worst enemies were members of his own family, but he did not consider them threats to his life. Roarke's father had a legitimate son, Miles, who was two years older than Roarke. The next legitimate son, Niall, was younger than Roarke, but would inherit before Roarke could.

Not that he wanted to.

"If my tale were not true, why would I purposely draw so much attention to myself tonight?"

Why indeed? Even Roarke had to admit it seemed a rash act for her to take without some provocation.

Whirling away from her, he lifted the tent flap and strode into the night air. If there was any hint of someone's presence behind his tent, he meant to find it.

He returned in no time, the proof he sought in his hands.

"It seems I owe you an apology, my lady." He turned the short dagger over in his palm, still amazed his wife told the truth. "And my thanks, as well. Were it not for you, I might very well be dead on the blade of a spineless backstabber."

Clenching and releasing the handle of the weapon several times in quick succession, he flipped the knife deftly from blade to handle to blade again. Hellfire, what a mess.

Who wanted him dead? More importantly, who was vile enough to try to kill him by such foul and underhanded means?

"You say you thought it was an Englishman. Why?"

"He had the proud bearing of a knight, first of all. He carried himself with the strength and grace of a warrior, even though he was skulking about. And he seemed to have come to the outskirts of the camp from within. If it were a French knight, I would have expected him to be walking toward your tent from the shelter of the forest, as I was. And I saw no sign of a horse."

"It makes no sense." Yet he was surprised at her logic. She was exceedingly sharp for a sheltered young woman.

"You said yourself you have enemies."

"Aye. But none that I thought would try to kill me." He searched the depths of her amber eyes, wondering if he should confide what else he knew. He did not wish to put his wife in danger, but she seemed determined to throw herself in the midst of things. Perhaps if he was honest with her, she would realize she played a dangerous game by following him all over creation.

"I have been followed on and off for the last sennight. I see a shadow darting among the trees, I hear the rustle of feet nearby, yet whoever it is has made no attempt on my life. And he has had ample opportunity. Many better opportunities than tonight. But the watcher has made no move to kill me."

"Thank God for that." She had gone pale at his story, her tawny eyes moving uneasily over him.

Good.

Maybe she would learn to stay safely away from him.

"I may be in danger, my lady. And to have you near by gives an enemy another way to harm me. If he were to steal you away, it would put me at a great disadvantage."

"I do not want any harm to come to you, my lord."

Her words were spoken in earnest, Roarke could tell by the vehemence in her voice, the determined set of her chin. She was uncommonly beautiful.

And quite brave, now that he thought back on the events of the evening. Of course it was foolish to come to camp tonight. He would rest easier if she were safely settled in the convent.

But regardless of her real reasons for returning to him, she did not hesitate to come to his defense. And she did not merely scream from the safety of the forest; she had awakened the entire camp with her shrieks as she ran headlong into danger. Had the attacker not been scared off, she would have been standing face-to-face with a potential murderer. Surely he could abandon his foolish notion of punishing her by denying her their wedding night. Or was he only telling himself what he wanted to hear so he could possess her all the sooner?

"Nor would I allow any harm to come to you, Ceara."

He crossed the tent to stand before her, determined their union as man and wife should be made legitimate tonight.

Ceara Llywen was his wife by decree of his king. He could never love her, but it was his duty before God to respect her as his wife and give her his sons.

Tonight, he would claim her for his own. Despite the return of the heated attraction he felt for her, Roarke would control his passions. She tempted him far more than any other woman ever had, but Roarke would never allow his desires free reign.

All would be well.

A gentle shiver reverberated through her when his hands moved over her shoulders to clear them of the soft cinnamon tresses that rested there. Amber eyes watched him warily, widening at his caress with a mixture of fear and curiosity.

Or was it anticipation?

Certainly not. She was an innocent, bound for the convent were it not for his sudden appearance in her life. Ceara would have no idea what it meant to belong to a man.

Intrigued by the bare white skin at the neck of her gown, Roarke allowed his hands to follow his eyes to the base of her throat, where a slender purple vein jumped erratically beneath his gaze.

She was a peculiar woman, his Welsh wife. Surprising him at every turn, Ceara Llywen was not at all what he expected. Yet he could not say he was displeased.

Ceara had a perpetual habit of singing or humming, even at the most incongruous times. Whether she was happy or sad, irate or pensive, a tune of some sort emanated from her person. And while the odd trait continually surprised him, Roarke found he enjoyed Ceara's songs and celebration of life.

He thought briefly of the lute he had packed among his things. Roarke's father found his talent detestable because music was a jongleur's pursuit. But Ceara would see the beauty of the instrument, hear the call of the strings.

She had proven herself brave, intelligent and loyal. She possessed great courage to follow him to France, though the move had also been foolhardy. And she demonstrated obvious intelligence when she recognized the value of Llandervey, when many women would have been disappointed at its lack of aesthetic appeal.

The longer he allowed himself to look upon her, the faster the little vein leaped and the darker her eyes became.

"You saved my life this night, Ceara Llywen. 'Tis only fair I grant you that which you followed me to France for."

Chapter Nine

Anticipation curled through Ariana at his words. "I followed you to France to protect you, my lord. I sensed you were in danger."

Roarke's touch set her whole body to trembling, stirring her insides. In fact, the shiver that tripped through her veins in response to the warmth of his palm was even more heady than the shimmering sensation the magic ignited.

"That was not the *only* reason you mentioned for following me." A grin played at the corner of his mouth.

She concentrated, but could not imagine to what he referred. Her vision prompted her to follow him at all costs. She did not want Roarke's death on her hands if she could prevent it.

He pretended to be deep in thought, stroking his chin while he glanced off into space. "I remember you were concerned about my not 'mustering up the strength to fulfill our marital contract.'"

Heat flooded Ariana's face as the exact nature of her

excuse came to mind. She stepped away from him abruptly, ashamed of her brazen words, but Roarke did not let her go, increasing the strength of his grip around her upper arms.

"That was hardly a reason for following you across the sea to foreign lands, my lord. You give yourself far too much credit." She waited for him to respond, but he stared back at her in unblinking silence, an impudent smirk about his lips.

"Are you suggesting that my saving your life has earned me your dutiful stud service?" She shot the words back angrily, despite her embarrassment. He was overbearing and full of his own importance by half. Of course she couldn't afford to turn down his offer for the sake of her pride, no matter how arrogant his words.

The smile spread lazily across his face, rendering him more handsome and more irritating. "Aye."

Exerting all her force to extricate herself from him, Ariana struggled away but it was not until that wicked grin turned into a benevolent smile that he released her.

"You have changed your mind then?" She could still hear the teasing note in his voice, though he affected a wounded look.

"'Twould serve you right if I set your precious new holding on its ear in your absence," she tossed back, thoroughly annoyed. She saved his life. He could at least be gracious about it.

He caught at her hand, pulling her back to him. "That you will not do, my lady."

When she did not look at him, he wrapped his hand about her chin to tip it up toward him.

He was no longer smiling.

"I will send you back to Llandervey a well and truly wed woman, Ceara, and you will keep peace in my absence." His gaze held hers as surely as his palm cradled her face, staring so intently he seemed to will her to agree.

With the whole of his form, he coaxed the answer he wanted. The hard length of his thigh pressed against hers, warmth emanated from his body in the chill night air.

"I will, my lord." Her anger forgotten, Ariana saw more than just strong will in his eyes. She saw a man who took his possessions very, very seriously.

The grip on her loosened, but his gaze never wavered. His lips descended to hers slowly, gently, until at last his mouth settled upon hers with quiet force.

She hesitated only a moment. Then, as his kiss worked its potent magic, she sighed against him and thought no more about it. The lips that covered hers prevented all thinking.

She began feeling instead.

His scent and arms surrounded her. The warmth of his body burned through her gown, heating her skin as thoroughly as his kiss heated her insides.

Ariana swayed and fell into him, her body molding to Roarke's muscle-hardened form. She did not understand the guttural groan that emanated from within him, but suddenly his hands were everywhere on her. Roaming with abandon down her spine and up her arms, easing over her throat to the hollow between her breasts.

She awoke from her splendorous daze as she recalled the false padding she wore in her guise as Ceara. "No!"

Roarke looked puzzled, his own eyes glazed with passion as she imagined hers must be.

The confounded padding! She shed some of it today, but not all. She could not ruin the moment by allowing him to discover the elements of her deception filling out her gown.

Roarke smiled suddenly. "You are shy, wife. 'Tis only natural." He leaned over the candle that still burned in the tent and extinguished it with his fingers, leaving the tent lit only by the full moon.

"Come to me, Ceara."

"I am used to a lady's maid, my lord. I do not know—"

"I am perfectly capable of undressing you." She heard the restrained laughter in his voice.

"Please…I feel so…ill-prepared." Her heart raced. She was so close to getting what she wanted. So close to breaking the curse after all this time.

"It would please you to ready yourself for bed?" Roarke asked, a hint of regret in his voice.

"Yes."

"Very well. I shall leave you for a few moments. But I will be right outside. 'Twould not be safe for me to go any farther."

Relief flooded through her as he departed, giving her the time she needed to remove Ceara's curves from her slender body.

She flew to her travel bag, shedding the white linens stitched together for makeshift padding. Untying the fashionable barbette that covered her hair, she knocked her hairpiece askew in her haste and had to quickly re-adjust it as she tied a white nightcap in place. Ariana had barely settled back onto the blankets when the tent flap opened.

She prayed he would not notice the difference in her figure. The shift was loose enough that he should not see it with his eyes, but Ariana fretted he might feel the lack with his hands.

Yet she swore his eyes settled unerringly on her hips and breasts, despite the full coverage of her loose night rail.

"You are lost in that garment, wife. Like a child playing dress-up in her mother's clothes." His voice hinted he was amused.

"'Tis my only shift, my lord." She cast her eyes to the floor, feeling awkward and inadequate. "I had to travel lightly."

"Ah. That explains it then." He seated himself on the bedroll, which was no more than two woolen blankets upon a thin pile of dried grasses, and proceeded to remove his boots. And the belt that carried his sword. And his hauberk.

Leaving him clad in tunic and braies.

Ariana watched him avidly, fascinated by the play of muscle along his thighs, his arms, his calves. Even in the moonlight, their taut movements were clearly defined beneath the close fitting garments that remained on his body.

"Come here, *mor-forwyn*." He caught her staring at him, but her interest seemed to please him. He smiled warmly at her, the soft curve of his lips as inviting as those vividly green eyes.

Hesitantly, she stepped forward, suddenly shy. This was the moment she'd waited for—the act that might break the curse for all time—but she could not deny her fear.

She had little notion of what went on between a man and wife except for a few things Eleanor had confided. Ariana had dismissed much of the Bohemian wisewoman's tale as too lurid to be true. Yet the story came back to her now, and frightened her just a little.

Roarke Barret was a strong and powerful man. And he was huge.

She could not have gone to him had she not seen the gentle assurance of his gaze. The invitation in his eyes propelled her forward despite her fear.

Strong, sword-roughened hands greeted her slender ones, drawing her down to her knees between his legs. "Do not be afraid, Ceara."

Cringing inwardly at his use of her cousin's name, she longed to tell him the truth of her identity. Her deception struck her as especially dishonest were she to maintain that she was Ceara even in the marriage bed.

Sliding his arms about her, he gathered her close. His thumb traced the outline of her jaw.

"Roarke?" She must tell him. Not about the ridiculous family legend that had surely never been true, but about her pretending to be Ceara. Perhaps she could convince him Ceara really wanted to go to the convent, though Thomas insisted she wed. Surely she could embellish the tale enough to make it believable.

And she desperately wanted to hear him call her by her real name this night.

"Mmm-hmm?" His hands trailed down her body in a smooth sweep, lingering on her waist and pulling her hips forward against his own.

"Roarke, I must explain something." Ariana closed

her eyes against the wave of heat that rippled through her body at his touch.

"Nay. You need not." His fingers dug into the softness of her hips, pressing her tightly to him so that she felt every bit of his strength.

"Please, I really do." She pushed against his chest, her good intentions weakening in the face of his slow seduction.

"Nay, wife. You have no need to explain yourself to me. You are more beautiful to me as God made you."

His words puzzled her, even as his lips found the warm pulse of her throat and brushed against her skin there.

"But—"

"'Tis true." He ran his hands meaningfully over her breasts, pausing to feel the tightened tips with callused palms. "Who thought you needed to catch my eye with the help of a false form? Your uncle? Your cousin?"

He knew about the padding. Realization of his meaning shocked her. And embarrassed her to the core.

Sweet Gwydion, could the man be any more observant?

"No, my lord, I—"

"Shh." His hands continued their exploration of her body, caressing her breasts and belly with aching thoroughness.

"You are just right." He kissed her lips, quieting the mumbled protests that sprang to them.

"Unspeakably lovely." His tongue darted out to part her lips in bold invitation.

"Perfect." The word was barely a breath against her mouth before he tipped her head back to drink more deeply from her.

His words were a balm to her soul. Never, even in her dreams, did she imagine a man would say such things to *her*—the cursed daughter of Glamorgan. She allowed her eyes to drift closed, giving in to the gentle force of Roarke for just a few more moments before she told him the truth of her identity. She would tell him. Had to tell him.

But dear heaven, his touch aroused a swell of delicious heat inside her, making her body ache for more.

His skin warmed her as surely as a fire against the cold chill of the sea air surrounding them. She reveled in his hard warmth, running her fingers tentatively over him.

The noise Roarke made in the back of his throat warned her she woke a sleeping beast. Fascinated by the texture of him through the linen cloth, adventurous hands untied the laces to feel his skin directly against her palm.

No sooner did she touch him then she was beneath him, her back pressed into the crackling rough warmth of woolen blankets over dried grass and hard packed earth. The weight of Roarke's body pressed upon her belly and hips, though he raised himself slightly above her on his arms.

"*Mor-forwyn*...siren." He looked at her, green eyes narrowed with hunger. "Your pull is strong this night."

Then all else was forgotten as he kissed her again, his mouth teaching hers in wanton movements with his tongue, calling forth from her an answering passion she had not known existed inside her. His lips sent ripples of pleasure throughout her, curling around every nerve and settling finally in an aching knot in her belly.

The kiss so encompassed her, she did not realize her shift worked its way up her thigh until his hand was suddenly upon her bare hip. The blatant intimacy of his touch startled her.

She would have spoken, whether in joy or protest she knew not, but Roarke's mouth was so quickly upon her flesh again; this time working its magic on her neck and the base of her throat, that she could not speak. Her head fell back in utter abandon as his tongue snaked its way to the curve of her breast.

"So sweet."

His words echoed her thoughts, his touch feeling less foreign as he spanned her waist and belly, igniting a blaze deep inside her. His fingers traced circles along her hip and thigh to land at the juncture of her legs.

By now she trembled in wonder and anticipation. She clutched his neck, her fingers flexing against his skin as he sifted through the silky curls of her womanhood. Found the source of the fire that burned within her.

She cried out at the invasion of his fingers, but his lips quickly captured the sound. Hungrily she kissed him, clinging to him to ensure he didn't let go of her now. She needed his kiss. His touch. All of him.

Taut as a bow, his body was rigid in its discipline as he touched her. Ariana was grateful for his consideration, but she wondered at the unleashed power behind his touch. She absorbed the tension emanating from him every time she lay her hands on his chest.

That strength fascinated her. Thrilled her.

"You are mine." He stilled for a moment above her, his eyes penetrating hers with their fierceness.

She felt the unfamiliar presence between her thighs. His presence.

"Roarke—"

He was poised to take her, shifting subtly to gain better access to her body as he pulled her closer.

And pulled her hairpiece off in a sweep of cinnamon strands across the blankets.

"What in the name of all that is holy?"

His question was more a roar than an actual utterance. He held Ceara's hair in his hands as if it were the most horrifying sight he ever beheld.

Sweet Arianrhod.

She tugged her night rail over her legs, fearful of the fury in his eyes. Her own ebony tresses fell partly to her shoulders, still awkwardly pinned in places.

"'Tis my cousin's hair, my lord. I tried to tell you before…." She plucked nervously at the pins in her hair, self-conscious of her new appearance. Her heart still pounded from the thrill of their intimacy, and now it thundered even harder with fear. Regret.

"Your cousin's?" His roar shook the delicate strands of hair as he spoke. "And who the hell are you, woman?"

"Ariana Glamorgan. I—"

"Glamorgan? Kin to Thomas?" He shook his head in angry frustration, green eyes narrowed in hard disapproval. "What have you done with my wife?"

"I *am* your wife, my lord."

His cold stare searched deliberately over her, searching for imperfections. Spying the freckles that dotted her nose, he wiped his thumb roughly across them, smearing them.

"I am wed to Ceara Llywen, lady. Not any Glamorgan. Where is Ceara?" He extricated himself from her, haphazardly replacing his tunic and braies.

"You wed me, my lord, using Ceara's name." She freed her hair from its pins, grateful for the additional coverage it provided her body. The coldness of his appraisal quickly doused all the delicious heat she'd felt so recently. She scrambled to tug her gown around her body, tucking even her toes under the white linen as she drew her knees up to her chin.

"Liar! If you have harmed my wife, I will kill you and your traitorous father both. Where is she?"

She'd made a horrible, horrible mistake to mislead this man. "Please, Roarke, you must believe me. You have never actually met Ceara Llywen. It was me from the first night at Glamorgan Keep. I disguised myself as my cousin Ceara from the very beginning to deceive even my own father. Ceara never wanted to wed. She allowed me to cut her hair so I might fool Father. He had nothing to do with my deception, I swear it."

Tension filled the tent, as suffocating and dark as any Welsh rain cloud.

Please, let him believe me.

"Why would you deceive your own father? Would he not give you to me of his own volition?"

At least he listened. She would tell him everything here and now. Bare her soul and pray obstacles started falling away soon.

"He thinks I am a lost cause at nineteen summers and so he did not offer me. He thinks Ceara is a prime candidate for a husband, no matter how strenuously she insists she would prefer the convent. Ceara did not want to attend the dinner you requested because of her call-ing, of course, but...well, I did." She thought it best to tell him the whole truth now before she lost everything. "I wanted a chance to wed with you, my lord."

"But to take it that far?" He tossed aside the hair-piece she'd worn since their wedding. "Your father ex-pected you to sup that night. You could have taken the meal with us all." He scrubbed his fingers through his hair in an aggravated gesture. "As Ariana Glamorgan, that is."

"Aye, but then you may have chosen Ceara over me because..." She forged ahead, sounding like a selfish, witless fool. "As a rule, men never notice me."

"I find that rather difficult to believe." He rubbed the remaining paint from her face which gave the impres-sion of freckles. "You are even more fair without your artifices and false hair. I was attracted to Ariana Glam-organ before I ever laid eyes on you in all this red hair."

Under other circumstances, Ariana would have rev-eled in his simple words, but Roarke looked strictly for-bidding. Green eyes assessed her, measured her, weighed her story.

"No man has ever suggested as much to me before." She took a deep breath. Prayed for courage. "It has long been whispered throughout Wales that the women of my line are cursed to spinsterhood. And indeed, no Glamorgan woman has married for some hundred years."

Silence greeted her admission. She became aware of the night wind whistling through the trees outside. The candle balanced on a flat rock near the bedroll flickered in answer.

Finally, some of the tension seemed to slide out of his shoulders. "The fact that you had to deceive Glamorgan to marry me tells me that even your own father believes you to be cursed?"

He didn't have to shout those words for them to sting more than anything else he'd said to her this night.

"Aye. The sorrowful legend of his house has brought his spirit low." Even now she sought for reasons to excuse his behavior, to make Roarke understand Thomas Glamorgan's dark moods. "He was not always so mournful. But after my mother passed he grew inconsolable. And the more I grew to resemble her, the more it grew difficult for him to see me and the more he wailed his fate."

Roarke snorted. "*His* fate? What of his only daughter's? Had he no care that you were left to your own devices to find a husband? With his position and wealth, I would think Glamorgan would have been overrun with suitors despite this family legend."

"The Welsh love their folklore, good and bad. And my heritage has long been a favored fireside tale." Her hand fell to the hairpiece he'd set aside, her fingers sifting through Ceara's beautiful red hair. "It is said one of my ancestors stole another woman's love. The spurned woman cursed my long-ago relation along with all future daughters of the Glamorgan line."

"But you don't believe this?" He tipped her chin to look at him, the expression in his eyes unreadable. Compelling.

She knew better than to accept such tales. Didn't she? "Do *you* believe it?"

"Never." His hand cupped her face. "And you are proof that particular bit of folklore is naught but a fairy tale. But I have one more question for you. If you are truly the same woman I married," he toyed with a lock of her dark hair, examining the color and texture before smoothing it behind her ear. "Tell me how I came to learn the meaning of *mor-forwyn*."

Smiling at the memory, she savored the feel of his touch. Marveled that he could be so gentle with her when she had deceived him. "By means of an unfortunate young member of the kitchen staff, my lord."

His touch lingered. Teased her with hope that maybe they could still recover a connection based on honesty. Trust.

Then Roarke's fingers fell away as he sighed heavily. "You realize our union is not legal."

"Maybe not in the strictest sense—"

"Not in any sense." He laid back on the bedroll beside her, but did not turn toward her. His gaze seemed fixed on the canvas roof above them. "Ariana, is it?"

"Aye." Her voice cracked a bit, though she attempted to hide the swell of fears by clearing her throat.

Slowly, he turned to her. "I have no choice but to return you to your father with all due haste, and I will take the bride your father intended for me—your cousin Ceara Llywen."

"No." He couldn't. Not after she'd succeeded in marrying. She'd come so far from her ominous heritage. "Don't you think we have a certain accord between us? After you married me, I made myself a vow I would be the best of wives in return."

Finally he turned toward her. But the look in his eyes was not understanding. Nor was it considering. Nay, he looked at her with what she could only interpret as…pity?

"I'm sorry, Ariana. You deserve so much more than—"

"No." Anger swept through her, red hot and fierce. "By God, you shall not pity me, Roarke Barret. Return me to my father if you must, but I assure you Ceara will refuse to wed."

"If she is the saintly woman both you and your father describe, Ceara will be dutiful to her uncle." Rising, Roarke tied his tunic and lashed his sword to his side as if to leave. "And now I must discuss the matter of correcting this mistake with my king."

Desperate for any words that might make him change his mind, Ariana rose to her feet, planting herself between him and the exit. "Ceara was only too happy to deceive my father so she didn't have to wed you last time. What's to say she will not go to great lengths to avoid marriage again?"

Slowly, he shook his head. "I am already married to Ceara Llywen in the eyes of man and God."

And, before she could consider how to respond, Roarke gently edged her aside and stalked from the tent.

Ariana did not move for long moments after his departure, still reeling from his declaration.

Did he really mean to return her to Glamorgan? That he would wed Ceara? Ceara would never forgive her. She had been intimidated by Roarke on sight and wanted nothing to do with him or any marriage.

Then there was the matter of the Glamorgan legend. If Roarke gave her back to her father, her Welsh countrymen would continue to whisper the women of her family were cursed. Her nieces would have no hope of marriage unless they were spirited far away from their homeland and away from the rumors. And Ariana would never fulfill her mother's dying wish.

She lay awake and cold on the bedroll for long hours into the night, hoping Roarke would return so she could reason with him. But as the moon sank low along with her spirits, she fell into a dark and dreamless sleep.

Alone.

Chapter Ten

Two moons later, Roarke still fumed that Henry would not excuse him long enough to take Ariana home. He muttered and cursed as he pulled himself out of a freezing cold creek in the French countryside to dress for the king's latest celebratory meal. He'd far rather be given leave for two days to see his wife—his false wife, he reminded himself—safely to Wales. But Henry had been adamant about Roarke being part of this ill-planned campaign that would never secure Normandy for the monarch who didn't have any idea how to hold on to his lands.

For the last eight weeks, the English troops had battled their way through the French countryside, winning two small holdings, imprisoning a few nobles for ransom, and moving as quickly as possible to Nantes.

The king hoped to take the keep at Nantes, but wanted his men honed and ready for the possibility of a long siege. Tonight's meal was a small reward before the biggest undertaking of all. Under normal circumstances, Roarke would have been glad for the interlude, but not this time.

Not with Ariana Glamorgan among the English victory party.

The king had installed "Lady Ceara" in the same room as Roarke in the keep because Henry did not know the truth of Ariana Glamorgan since Roarke had never admitted the whole sordid mess of his marriage. He'd gone to the king's tent the night Ariana confessed the truth to him, but the more he rehearsed the words in his mind, the more ludicrous the tale sounded even to his own ears. First, he didn't want to risk bringing the king's wrath down upon Ariana's head. She had suffered enough after a lifetime in her father's household, it seemed, and Roarke refused to see her ostracized by Henry's anger.

Second, if he admitted his plan to exchange one bride for another, it would mean he would have to declare his marriage unconsummated. A notion that chaffed his male pride like new chain mail on a squire's back.

How could he ever explain what had prevented him from taking her—the strange set of circumstances that continually swirled around his marriage?

False marriage, he silently amended, lacing his hauberk over his tunic in the crisp autumn air.

It would be dangerous to allow himself to think of Ariana Glamorgan as his wife. She'd threatened his peace of mind since the moment he'd accidentally torn off her hairpiece and uncovered her true identity. Heaven knew he'd wanted her that night, more than he'd ever wanted any woman. Sharing quarters with her ever since had been a perpetual sensual torment. But how could he consummate a loveless marriage with her when she'd been deprived of love all her life? He knew what it felt like to be spurned by your own father.

But no matter how much his true father's rejection had once pained him, Roarke had always recognized that at least his Barret father had loved him and accepted him as his son, even though he'd known full well his wife's faithlessness. Roarke had been raised by a good family, and somehow that helped lessen the sting of Fulke Kendall's contempt.

But Ariana deserved more. Better. She might think she could be happily wed to a man who would never be able to give her his heart, but Roarke refused to accept that for her. So she followed the English troops until he could return her to Wales, remaining in the background of the various skirmishes they encountered while he worried daily about her safety.

Roarke dressed hurriedly, his back turned to the cold afternoon breeze. He refused to use the chamber room in the keep because Ariana was there. He had no desire to see her since she tempted him to the very limits of his control. He only hoped she had the good sense to stay above stairs safely locked in the chamber while the English knights celebrated their triumphs.

The thought gave him a sudden chill of foreboding. Ariana do something safe? Sensible? It would be quite out of character.

He quickened his pace as he returned to the French keep.

A grand old structure, the keep dated back at least two hundred years, no doubt one of the biggest fortresses built in the eleventh century. Strong and stalwart centuries later, it had not weakened, only grown a bit out of date. The battlements were no longer high enough to escape the improved longbow recently perfected by the Welsh, and worse, the wall surrounding its village was still made of wood.

King Henry had quickly burned it down. Such a fence was useless for keeping out determined predators.

Roarke paused briefly at the great hall before continuing upstairs to warn Ariana to stay locked in their chamber.

And there she was.

Hovering about the entryway to the overcrowded hall, she glanced anxiously in either direction. Roarke made it to her side just in time to pull her back into the shadow of the portal.

"Roarke!"

He could feel her heart race for a moment before she pulled away from him.

"How dare you frighten me so! I am nervous as it is." Straightening her gown, she lifted her chin.

"What do you think you are doing?" He struggled to maintain his composure in spite of his warring desires to shake some sense into her or kiss her into passionate submission.

"The king ordered me to join him for dinner, but I am hesitant to enter a room full of knights drinking themselves into ill humor and celebrating vile acts of war."

"I will explain your absence to the king." He prodded her in the direction of the staircase leading to the sleeping quarters. "You will return to your chamber."

"Nay! I could not offend His Majesty." Patting her hair with a nervous gesture, she sounded truly mortified. "He has been so kind to me."

Ariana was lovelier with dark hair, Roarke decided. While red locks were becoming enough, raven tresses were uniquely suited to her. She dispensed with the false hair immediately after he discovered her identity. Because it was night both times the English knights saw her, her change of color went unnoticed. Collin knew the truth, of course, but his loyalty was to Roarke and he could be trusted with the secret of Ariana-Ceara.

Roarke noted Ariana was more slender now. Her cousin Ceara must be a more voluptuous woman, judging from the padding Ariana shed from her person. Some men might find the loss of bountiful womanliness a lack to be mourned, but Roarke admired her willow-like grace, and the quick efficiency with which she moved.

"He will understand, lady. You must leave here 'ere the night takes on an unpleasant tone."

In truth, it already had. Many of the English knights were drinking since the siege was won several hours ago, and by now the level of conversation in the hall was alternately bawdy, boastful and downright lewd. Roarke shoved her more forcefully toward the stairs.

"You will make certain he understands I did not disobey him purposely?" Her lashes fluttered without guile. For all of her rash and reckless behavior, Ariana behaved with as much shy awkwardness around him as a girl recently turned woman. For a moment, he allowed himself to recall her artless, but enticing kisses.

"Aye." He was in no mood to converse with her in

sight of the hall. From his position in the corridor, Roarke could see a young serving maid being debauched in full view of the company by Edgar Hughes. The maid's cries brought only laughter and shouts of encouragement from the diners.

Disgusted with his king for suggesting his wife partake in such a meal, Roarke scooped Ariana off her feet and carried her from the noise of the hall.

"Roarke!" She protested loudly, but did not struggle against him. As they passed a couple half-undressed on the stairs, Roarke hid her face against his hauberk and strode more quickly to their chamber.

By the time Ariana was safely locked in their room, he fought to control his anger—at her for being in France in the first place, at his king for demanding Roarke keep her here instead of leaving her in the convent, at himself for not locking her in her room earlier.

Depositing his burden on the bench before the hearth, he tipped her chin up, forcing her to give him her complete attention. "*Never* go to the hall unescorted. Never."

"If you were here with me, I would not have been forced to go by myself in the first place."

"No one forced you, Ariana." Her name slid easily from his lips. Immediately, he wished he had not used it. Use of her first name suggested an intimacy between them he fought wholeheartedly. "Your name is not Welsh," he observed, unaware he spoke the thought aloud.

"My mother chose the name, and she hailed from Bohemia since my father was forced to search far and wide for a wife."

"Bohemian?" Roarke peered closely at her face. "You have a bit of that coloring, perhaps."

"Honestly, my lord, it would make it much easier if you were to stay closer to me. I would have appreciated knowing you did not want me below stairs earlier today. 'Twould have saved me considerable trouble in readying myself for an audience with your king."

Her dress befitted a royal audience. Richly embroidered with silver-and-green threads, the heavy purple velvet fell in simple lines to flatter her slender curves. The white tunic that peeked out from under it teased invitingly as it dipped and reappeared around the slight swells of her breasts.

Although as lovely as her clothing appeared, nothing had matched the sight of her naked and hungry for his touch. A sight he wished was not imprinted in his head to torture him endlessly.

Unaccountably irritated that she went to such trouble to please another man, Roarke's voice turned harsh. "Well do not trouble yourself in the future. It would be easier for both of us if you avoid the king. I think the less he knows of you the better."

He had not intended to hurt her with the simple truth, but in the glow of firelight from the grate, he could tell by the stiff way she nodded that he'd upset her.

She made no reply for a long moment, one brow arched high in curious regard. "Then save yourself the difficulties, and stay wedded to me."

"*Stay* wedded? I am afraid that is impossible, when we are not wedded in the first place."

"That can be remedied easily enough." She rose from the bench to address him directly. Her hand rested softly upon his arm to plead her case. Roarke felt a curious response to that featherlight touch, a catch in his breathing that could only be attributed to her nearness.

"Nay." His argument lacked persuasion thanks to the hoarse rasp of his voice as he caught her scent.

"Have a priest wed us all over again, this time using my name." She squeezed his forearm, her touch burning right through the sleeve of his tunic. "You were ready to take any woman who came your way when you arrived at Glamorgan a scant few weeks ago. Why must you be so particular about your bride now?"

Because you are entirely too threatening to my control.

"And how would we explain to the church about my previous wife, Ceara Llywen?"

"I will account for my actions to the priest."

Unwilling to let himself be swayed by the desperation in Ariana's eyes, he turned away. "When he learns your father meant Ceara for me, the church will stand by your father's decision."

"The church will not allow you to give a ruined woman back to her father."

Her soft, silken words drew him to her with the strength of iron chains. "You are not ruined, Ariana, and we both know it."

Although in his thoughts, their marriage had been thoroughly—repeatedly—consummated.

"But what does that matter? By the time you return me to Glamorgan Keep, we will have been together several months."

"Not if I can help it." He savored the surprise in those amber eyes of hers. For once, he managed to shock her.

"What do you mean?"

"I asked King Henry to grant me leave to bring you home, and today, due to his extraordinary good spirits, he granted it. With my word I would return in all possible haste, of course. But he granted it. We leave in two days time."

His pleasure in surprising her vanished when the color drained from her face.

"You really mean to do it." Her words were breathless, her eyes wide. Hurt.

"Take a leave?" Damn it. He hadn't meant to cause her pain.

"Return me for Ceara."

If Roarke did not know Ariana was one of the most determined, resourceful women he had ever come in contact with, he would have sworn her hands shook. "Aye."

"But even if you return me with all possible haste, I still will have been living with you for eight weeks. No one will believe we have not lived as man and wife. You simply cannot return a wife!"

The nervous darting of bright amber eyes urged Roarke to be patient with her. She was genuinely distraught. Even though the treacherous wench deserved to be trapped by her own scheming plans, Roarke felt uncomfortable upsetting her.

Taking her hand, he led her back to the bench and sat down beside her. Of their own volition, his fingers remained around her chilled, quivering fingers.

"Any healer can attest to the truth that we have not consummated our marriage. There will be no doubt of our word."

He would not have thought it possible for her to turn a shade paler, yet that is precisely what she did. Her hand went rigid in his grasp.

"You cannot be serious." She shook her head in vehement denial, although he assured her it was easily done.

Lifting herself slowly from the bench, blotches of fiery red colored her pale cheeks in a sudden indication of her response to his words.

"You'll have to mention that fact to my father. I'm sure he would enjoy subjecting me to such humiliation for my defection." Each word was a bit more amplified than the next, although she never actually raised her voice. She trembled with rage, her heavy black hair swirling like an angry sea about her shoulders. "Is this how your knightly code of honor tells you to conduct yourself with a woman who saved your life? Repay her by casting her back, unwanted and of ill repute, to her family?"

Though her words pricked his conscience, he tamped down any regret by recalling her deceit from the moment he met her. "I owe you my thanks, lady, but I will not compromise my word to your father to take his niece. Nor will I repay your kindness to me with a marriage that can never give you what you need."

Although he didn't dare think about Ariana with any other man. His hands clenched. Fisted.

"Very well then. Return me for Ceara. Saddle yourself with a woman who fears you, a woman who detests your way of life. See if a woman bound for the convent is more pleasing to you." Ariana turned away from him in a swish of purple velvet skirts. "You are so coldly practical, you scarcely care who is at your side anyway."

Roarke watched her walk to the door and open it. Hellfire, she actually thought she could show him the way out. He thought to argue with her, but what would be the point? She was not his wife, and—in a few days hence—he would never reside under the same roof as Ariana Glamorgan again. He would allow her anger.

After he made one thing clear.

"I once vowed to maintain my honor at all costs, Ariana, since without honor, I am not worthy of any woman." He recalled the way he'd compromised his integrity long ago, the way he'd nearly stolen Lucian's Barret keep out from under him because he'd been too blinded by selfishness to understand Lucian's torment. "No matter what your cousin looks like, no matter what her disposition, I will have her for my wife because I gave my word to your father and because I made vows to her before God."

He departed her chamber before he gave in to the lure of her wide, tawny eyes. Later, he could not recall what made him pause outside the wooden barrier as she closed it. Instinct, perhaps.

But he did not miss her cry as he left, the pained noise of a wounded animal. Nor did he miss the muffled words that followed the anguished sound.

"You made those vows to *me,* Roarke Barret. To me."

The night was cold and lonely in the sprawling French keep, made lonelier still by the raucous shouts from the celebrating knights that continued into the morning hours.

Moonlight streamed through the casement where Ariana shoved aside the heavy black tapestry that covered it. It was unseasonably warm for the time of year, and though the night air chilled her, she heaped woolen blankets over herself so she might enjoy the crispness of the air and the gentle light of the moon. Ariana slept little, counting the huge stones in the wall next to her bed to keep her mind off Roarke.

He was sending her home.

When she naively planned her marriage to him, she never imagined this sort of outcome. She pictured him deserting her. She envisioned her husband angry enough to kill her. But any scenario she painted included her consummating her marriage and saving her nieces from spinsterhood first.

Over the last few weeks she had caught him staring at her sometimes. And perhaps because she had never before known the heated glance of any man, she was always aware of his eyes upon her. It filled Ariana with hope, making her dare to dream that maybe he was coming to care for her a little.

Until tonight.

Now she knew Roarke was serious about returning her to Wales and taking Ceara for his bride. For the past eight weeks, she'd hoped he'd merely said as much in anger. But his announcement they were leaving in two days threw cold water on that spark of hope.

A woman's shrill, drunken laughter caused her to wonder where Roarke went after he left their chamber. She recalled the night she'd first landed in France and spied him sitting with a young woman practically draped across his lap. Was he with another woman now?

His nightly routine of checking on her was the only time Ariana could count on seeing him during the day. Often he did not even speak to her, but the fact that he came every night, and took care of her even if he was furious with her, gave her a small measure of comfort. Roarke Barret was a man of honor.

Ariana lost her place after fifty-eight stones and went back to the beginning to start counting again.

What to do now? How could she make Roarke change his mind before they reached Wales?

She counted to ninety-four stones when she fell asleep in the fading moonlight, praying for a miracle.

Chapter Eleven

The miracle arrived in the form of a knock at the door.

Ariana barely heard it at first, so deep was her sleep. She became aware of it slowly, as its gentle rap persisted.

"Who is it?" she called, heart jumping.

"Roarke."

She hurried to don her tunic, chew a mint leaf, rinse her teeth and splash cold water on her face, scarcely daring to believe he wanted to see her.

The sun was barely risen. She could not have been asleep for more than a few hours. Her chamber was frigid now, reminding her she'd never pulled the tapestry back to cover the casement opening.

Teeth chattering, she opened the door to admit her visitor.

Shoving past her, his eyes swept the room as if in search of someone or something, pausing when he found his quarry in the direction of the bedpost.

Following his gaze, Ariana was surprised to see a

young merlin perched atop the post, looking majestic and out of place on his carved mahogany seat. Only then did she notice the heavy hawking glove on Roarke's hand.

"There you are, you witless pigeon." Roarke extended his hand to the bird, but the merlin rotated away from him.

Ariana stifled a giggle. "He does not appreciate your barbed words, my lord."

"He's a half-trained brancher, according to the falconer," Roarke confided, eyes still on the bird. "But I cannot imagine what they have been training the thing for if it does not have the sense to stay out of the keep."

"How did he ever get in?" Ariana could not take her eyes off the creature's soft brown-and-white feathers. He stood proud and erect, still as a watchful griffin over Ariana's bed. Turning around to see if Roarke was still there, the bird displayed marvelous blue eyes.

Roarke glared at Ariana. "It seems you do not have the sense to cover your windows, my lady. Apparently he saw an opening and thought he would have a look around. Worthless fowl."

"But how did he fit through that narrow space? His wings must be twice as wide as that casement."

"No doubt he hopped in from the sill. Though I wonder what a half-trained winged predator would want in the interior of a keep?" He whistled softly to no avail.

"Perhaps he would come to me," Ariana suggested, eager to try her luck.

For a moment, she thought Roarke would deny her request, but after a moment, he handed her the hawking glove. "You have hunted with falcons?"

"Glamorgan has a large mews. I love to help the falconer." Anything to avoid her father's somber company. "I do not often hunt, but I like to watch the birds and help train them to their calls."

As if anticipating this new development, the merlin rotated back to face them, following the shift of the glove with intent eyes. Ariana barely began her whistle when the bird flew to her hand and perched docilely upon her arm.

"Fickle beast." Roarke moved to put the hood back on the merlin's head.

"Nay," Ariana warned, familiar with how depressing unwanted confinement could be.

"You will never get him out of the keep without a hood."

"Perhaps, but let us talk for a few moments while he gets used to me. I do not wish to frighten him unnecessarily." She wondered if it pained Roarke to have to converse with her even a short time. Yet, his studious avoidance of her eyes told her he was no longer completely unaffected by her.

"What made you rise so early to go hawking, my lord? Most of the keep must still be abed." She stroked the feathers carefully, well aware the bird was potentially dangerous.

"Aye. And I cannot abide idle time. I regret the need to be in France at all, but it grows especially tiresome when we laze idly about between campaigns. I long to return to Llandervey, to survey the property more thoroughly, to get my accounts in order." His smile was wry as he seated himself beside her on the bed. "It is ironic that in order to secure the peaceful life I seek I have to lead the life of a warrior. But I will lose my value to the king as I grow older. I mean to enjoy what I have won."

"I hate to disappoint you, my lord, but your sword arm does not look ready for retirement." A large understatement. Ariana could not imagine a more perfectly formed knight. She imagined what it would be like to sidle closer to him. To rest her head upon his broad shoulder. "Mayhap you should not train yourself so hard."

Roarke made a disgruntled sound. "And forsake my ambition of being a landed nobleman to the faster sword of some bloodthirsty French blade? Never."

She laughed, happy to be engaged in conversation with her husband, knowing the miracle she prayed for last night manifested itself already. Perhaps she should learn to seek healing in smaller ways. The warmth of contentment stole over her, followed by the even warmer caress of Roarke's glance. As always, she felt it as much as she saw it. She dared not look back, afraid if she did he would cease his perusal of her, and for all the world, she wished it would never end.

"As it seems you and I are the only ones awake this morn, how about spending your last day in France hawking with me?" He looked as shocked to have uttered the invitation as Ariana felt to receive it.

His words wound themselves around her heart and squeezed. Whether he regretted his offer or not, Ariana was not about to let him withdraw it.

"I can think of nothing I would like better."

"I cannot imagine why you insisted on bringing that ill-bred brancher." Roarke frowned as they searched the skies for the blue-eyed merlin. The bird disappeared high above the trees long moments ago and was nowhere in sight.

Roarke's huge falcon stood perfectly still upon his arm. Ariana thought bird and man were well matched, both strong and full of self-control.

"He will be back." Ariana assured him. She sensed her bird preferred to hunt without an audience, but did not bother to share her insights with Roarke. He would only think her more foolish than he already did.

"Aye. You will no doubt find him back at the mews when we return to sup."

His words still hung in the air when the merlin reappeared, silently as he departed, with two fat songbirds in his talons. Ariana beamed her pride. She did not bother to stifle her grin as she arched a knowing brow at Roarke.

Despite Roarke's grumbles about the bird, Ariana had thoroughly enjoyed their morning together. She hoped to use the rest of their remaining time to get closer to him, mayhap convince him not to send her away.

The boy from the mews who accompanied them rushed forward with a sack for the plump game. By now, the bag bulged with the results of their morning of hawking.

"Very well then, he came back," Roarke acknowledged. "But what good is a hunting bird if he does not respond to the hunter's calls?"

He handed the falcon and his glove to the boy, signaling the hunt was at an end. Once the bird was hooded and jessed to the staked post used to carry more than one bird, the boy reached for the merlin.

"His greatest merit is not his ability to hunt." Ariana did her best to give the boy the bird, but it would not budge, remaining firmly attached to her glove.

"And what other possible merit could a bird of prey have?" Roarke scoffed as he leaned over to help her remove the whole glove.

"I am not certain yet, but—" She halted her thought when the merlin, obviously opposed to being returned to the young falconer, flew away, unfettered and free above their heads.

"Oh, dear."

They called to the bird for several minutes until the boy from the mews assured them the merlin was no great loss. His father had no luck training it thus far, so it would not be missed.

After insisting he would personally explain the matter to the elder falconer anyway, Roarke sent the boy home, an extra coin tucked into the bag at his waist.

Leaving Roarke and Ariana alone.

"Hungry?" His hand rested on the saddlebag that carried the wine, hard cheese and bread he'd packed before they left.

"Famished."

She followed his lead through the quiet French countryside, content to explore her surroundings. She had not seen much of the landscape since her arrival, as the English troops had kept her in the middle of their long lines of mounted knights. The men were so tall, especially in their helmets and armor with full weaponry at their sides, that she could see little other than the sea of warriors around her.

But now she was able to appreciate the subtle differ-

ences from her homeland. It was not half so green as
Wales, but then it was not as uncomfortably damp, either. And it was more temperate than Glamorgan would
be in late November.

"*Addien.*" She breathed the word softly to herself.

"Pardon?"

"*Addien,*" she repeated. "It means 'beautiful.' As
much as I have spoken your English tongue these last
weeks, I still think in Welsh, you know."

"France is not nearly as beautiful as England, and not
half so fair as your own Wales."

"You truly like Wales, my lord?"

"Aye. I found it immensely to my liking. I cannot imagine a more lushly fertile land."

Ariana smiled her approval. "Many foreigners find
it too wet and foggy. I am pleased you appreciate the
happier side of rain and mist."

He paused to hold a low tree branch for her, guiding
her into a small clearing. It had the soft look of a resting place for deer, covered in green needles and warmed
with dappled patches of sunlight. The crisp, cool air
blew fragrant breezes from the pines. And though, upon
first glance, Ariana thought they were hidden from all
the world in their secluded niche, when she dismounted
she caught a glimpse of the keep down several long hills
below them, and noted the spot Roarke chose had a
clear view of the road to the main gate.

"Fertile land is the foremost requirement for a man
with dreams of a prosperous holding. I will never govern profitable properties if I ignore the benefits of wet
weather."

"It is a blessing if it comes at the right time. It is the

bane of our land when it comes too early or too late, or in too great an amount—"

Roarke gently covered her lips with a quieting finger. "You cannot dissuade me, lady. My hope of the peaceful life has pulled me through more years at Henry's side than I care to count. I hope to see for myself the corresponding hardships of such an existence in the near future."

Her mouth trembled where he had touched her. Did he not feel any of the same longings she did?

He passed her the wineskin and went about breaking the bread and cutting the cheese. Ariana sipped the delicious vintage appreciatively. "The greenest land in the world cannot produce such a fine wine, I am afraid."

"I prefer English ale."

Noting his preference did not diminish his taste for the vintage, she said nothing. They sat in companionable silence some moments, and Ariana thought of possible topics for conversation. She wanted to know so many things about him, but did not wish to pry.

"Roarke?"

He did not turn to look upon her or even answer in words, but lifted a curious brow as he peered down the hill to study the keep below.

"Tell me about your family."

"I am a bastard." The sternness of his voice was meant to intimidate.

Undaunted, she forged ahead. "But you still have family, whether they be recognized by the law or not. What of your mother?"

"Dead."

"I am sorry—"

"It's been over ten years."

"It has been that long since my own mother died, but I do not think that makes the loss any less keen."

Roarke shrugged, apparently satisfied to let the subject drop.

Ariana was not. "What of your father? Your brothers and sisters?"

"My father is an important man in England. An earl with numerous holdings, great power and plenty of money. He also happens to be cruel, vindictive and ruthlessly driven to continually add to his wealth."

She did not miss the fire that fueled his words. "Did you spend much time with your father when you were young, my lord?"

"Thankfully, no."

Frustrated, she changed tactics. "Roarke, tomorrow we leave for Wales so that I might be returned in disgrace to my father. And while I realize that I have brought this upon my own head by deceiving you, I never anticipated being returned to Glamorgan with a questionable reputation. My father will install me in a nunnery as I cannot marry.

"In a few short weeks, I will be as good as imprisoned for the rest of my days, with naught to do but pray and repent my mistakes." She toyed with the worn lace at her sleeve. The fine gown showing signs of wear after her time spent among the English knights. "Is it so much to ask then, considering I may very well never have the chance to speak to any man save a priest for the rest of my life, that you share a bit of yourself with me, talk to me, allow me to feel like I have befriended you?"

The back of her eyes burned, and she feared the tears that threatened. She did not mean to become so impassioned in her speech, but there was an excellent chance that she painted an accurate picture of what would happen when she returned.

She did not know how she could bear it.

"Your father will see you do not belong in the cloister."

"He will have no choice, Roarke. No man will have me."

Roarke's eyes darkened as they swept her form, lingering on every curve. "Nay. Many a man would have you, Ariana."

Keen awareness tripped through her. Her body tingled with the memory of his touch as her skin shivered with anticipation of that touch again.

Roarke saw the want in Ariana's eyes. A want he was sorely tempted to answer once and for all. But he knew he could never give her what she needed. Would never be the man who could heal the hurt inside her.

So he looked away and dragged out the story of his past to keep himself from touching her. "I only learned the facts of my birth shortly before my mother died. Apparently she felt the need to unburden herself in her final hours, so she told me the truth. My father, Fulke Kendall, deceived my mother into sleeping with him after her husband failed to return from the Crusades. Assuring my mother that Lord Barret had been killed on the battlefield, he comforted her in her grief. Shortly thereafter, when her husband returned home as hale and hearty as ever, she told me she was devastated. Disillusioned."

He hadn't wanted to hear her story. And at the time, he'd barely understood her half-conscious ramblings as she relayed the tale over the course of days and hours, sometimes out of sequence. But he'd made sense of it since then. Had gone on a quest to seek out his real father in the hope that Fulke Kendall had some reason for his behavior or that he'd loved his mother deeply. Roarke had been every bit as devastated as his mother claimed to have been since Kendall seemed to possess no conscience and even less heart.

"How horrible." Ariana poured him the rest of the wine from the skin. "But since you carry the Barret name, her husband must have forgiven her?"

"Aye. He died when I was but a child, so I have little memory of them together, but his acceptance of me was such that I never would have guessed my heritage had my mother not confessed her transgression." He'd often wished she'd taken her secrets to the grave. But since leaving Barret Keep he had realized that perhaps she spoiled him too much in an attempt to relieve her own guilt. Roarke was far more proud of the man he'd become since leaving his protected corner of the world to seek his own fortune, even if the path had not been easy.

"He must have loved your mother very much." She tore off a bit of bread and tossed it to a bold young crow perched nearby. Or perhaps she meant to feed a squirrel who gathered fallen nuts.

He found himself drawn to her gentle healer spirit that doled out food to wild creatures and strange herbs to his fellow knights if they so much as sneezed in her presence.

"Perhaps. Or maybe his pride was less injured if he simply embraced me as his own son." He'd wondered on the matter more than once over the last ten years, but it was something that would never be solved.

"What of your other family? Do you have brothers? Sisters?"

"I only count my Barret kin as family now." He had no desire to talk of his conniving half brothers on the Kendall side. "My mother's other son, Lucian Barret, has a keep in Northumbria along with a wife he adores and a slew of children. Three orphans they took in long ago who have surely made their own way in the world by now. Three babes of their own in the last ten years. Thankfully, my brother has brought prosperity to his home and his people despite my long-ago attempts to wrest his keep away from him."

"You?" She sounded as if she didn't believe him.

"Aye. At a time in my life I am not proud of." He didn't wish to speak of his family—or his failings—any longer. He was more interested in watching her speak, savoring the way her lips moved as she formed every word.

"No matter. One day, you will bring prosperity to your lands, as well." Ariana finished the last of her meal and folded the scrap of linen she'd used as a plate. "I do not need the sight in this matter to know you will provide peace and contentment to your people at Llandervey."

Her words warmed him, making him realize how much he'd come to value her opinion. Her intelligence. She would make a fair and generous lady to govern any household.

She frowned now, however, her brow furrowing in thought. "But what of your Kendall kin?"

Roarke held up a warning hand, cutting her off. "Enough. I have told you my story, and I will dig through the past no more. I prefer to think on the future."

"What future?" She turned her lips to a halfhearted pout. "Your marriage to my cousin?"

"Nay." He grinned as he reached into the cheesecloth containing their lunch, and pulled out a handful of sugared fruits. "Dessert."

He recalled the last time he shared such a confection with her, that first night at Glamorgan when they'd sat beside one another for the meal. He had fed her from his fingers, felt the tug of her lips along his skin.

"Ladies first."

She almost reached a small cluster of three grapes when he plucked them up for her.

"Allow me." Pulling the first grape from its stem, he fed her with his thumb and forefinger.

Ariana took it carefully from him, as if trying to delicately avoid his fingers against her lips. The first time she managed a credible job; his thumb barely brushed her mouth as he fed her.

The second time he held the fruit a bit longer than necessary, startling Ariana with the presence of his finger in her mouth as she took the grape. He knew better than to do this to himself. Yet he could not find the will to resist.

Just one more kiss. If he could steal just one final taste of her, perhaps then he could give her up.

"They are to your liking, I hope?"

Ariana nodded, not trusting her voice as the warmth of his presence stole over her like a cup of mulled wine on a cold winter's night.

She saw the third grape in his fingers and dutifully parted her lips to receive it, but in its trip from his hand to her mouth, Roarke must have hidden it, because the only thing that touched her tongue and lower lip was the callous-roughened pad of one fingertip.

He smoothed the fullness of her lower lip as her gaze flew to his. His eyes traveled as boldly as his wayward finger, following its path over her mouth.

Her heart increased its rhythm, speeding up the closer Roarke came. And he was most certainly coming closer. His hands were suddenly upon her, seizing her gently, his lips looming above hers. She watched him in fascination, willing him nearer, eager for his touch after so many, many weeks without it.

His eyes remained fixed upon her mouth until the last second, when he finally returned her gaze. *"Mor-for-wyn."*

Like the final blow a conquering knight delivers his enemy, Roarke's one word was her devastation. Her eyes closed in abandon, and her body ceased to be her own, falling into his waiting hands.

He kissed her hungrily, pulling the lower lip he teased into his mouth to soothe it lovingly with his tongue. Ariana curled her arms around him, pulling him closer until they were both upon the ground, the full length of their bodies pressed together.

And the feeling was like nothing Ariana had ever experienced.

Where his fingers trailed, fires blazed. Where his lips

touched, she melted. She could not get enough of the warm, hard, muscular feel of him; the pine, leather scent of him; the vintage grape taste of him. He filled her senses to overflowing.

And still she wanted more. Seeking to be ever closer, she arched more deeply into him, drawing an anguished growl from Roarke. He pushed her back to the ground, cradling her head in his hand, and allowed her to feel the weight of him against her. Still she arched and sighed, seeking fulfillment long denied her.

"Ariana." Her name was a strangled plea on his lips as he ceased his hungry kiss. She reached up to stroke his face, reveling in the male hardness, the sharp angles.

His eyes closed at her touch, as if he were under her spell, completely in her thrall.

And he unleashed the power of his hands.

They were everywhere, no longer restricted to cradling her head from the ground. They sought under her hair to the softness of her neck and found the warm pulse of her throat. They edged beneath the bodice of her gown to cup her breasts, testing their weight, gently squeezing, then danced over the tautness of their peaks.

His thigh pushed between hers as he bared one breast to his gaze and lips. Taking the crest into his mouth, he suckled her while his hands slid up the length of her leg.

Ariana could think of nothing but Roarke. She craved his touch, his mouth, the joining that came between man and woman. Heat swirled in her belly. Her fingers moved restlessly over his body until she found the ties for his tunic and pulled. Roarke removed his hauberk and tunic with lightening speed, leaving her for only the briefest of moments.

Her reward was the heat of his chest, the soft whorls of dark hair against her breasts. He loosened her gown even farther, allowing his fingers to play over her belly.

In the recesses of her mind, Ariana felt the wind pick up, but she ignored it. The cold breeze against her skin only made the heat within her burn more brightly.

Then, far above them, came the cry of the merlin.

Ariana stilled, gripped by a sudden sense of foreboding. Roarke paused, pulling her gown over her breasts before he looked heavenward to find the source of the sound.

The bird circled overhead a moment longer, then tucked its wings for a rapid descent. The wings extended again just in time to slow him to a graceful landing on a tree branch near Ariana's head.

In its talons he grasped a red swatch of cloth stitched with a small piece of golden braid.

Roarke shook his head as if to clear his thoughts and squinted hard at the newcomer.

And was on his feet instantly.

"The cloth of the French King's Guard. Troops must be on their way."

He yanked Ariana to her feet so fast her head spun, but she knew what his terse words meant. The French king was on his way to make war with the English. She was barely recovered and dressed when he was mounted and ready to ride.

"I must go ahead. The keep is poorly defended because of last night's celebrations. You may come down the hills, but remain in the shelter of the forest and wait for me. I will come back for you when the keep is secured."

She wanted to remain at his side. She had barely managed to emerge from the sensual haze of a few moments ago. How had Roarke regained control so quickly? Hadn't he been as affected by their intimacies as she had been?

When she mounted her horse to follow him, however, Roarke pulled a short knife from his belt and thrust the handle toward her.

"Keep this near just in case, but I will watch the edge of the forest, as well. It is too dangerous for you to come forward if there is battle."

Reluctantly, she accepted the weapon. And before she could protest further, he silenced her with his lips, kissing her swiftly.

With that, he disappeared, galloping through the wooded hills at a dangerous pace.

Chapter Twelve

Ariana watched the small skirmish from the camouflage of the forest with Griffin—her new merlin—beside her. They had moved as close to the battle as they dared.

"You are marvelously clever to deliver that piece of cloth to Roarke." Chattering to the bird without thought, she peered over the keep grounds from the protection of a stalwart walnut tree, glad of Griffin's company to soothe her nerves. "Though it hardly looks as if the French army is on its way."

The skirmish involved about sixty men, several of whom wore the uniform of the King's Guard, but many who did not. Perhaps the additional French knights came from a nearby keep that owed loyalty to this one. But Ariana was confident the English would carry the day.

Roarke fought at the forefront of the melee. She panicked the first few times she had witnessed him exchange blows eight weeks ago, but by now she felt assured of his prowess. Whether it stemmed from her ability with the sight, or merely confidence in a great warrior, she could not guess, but Ariana knew instinctively Roarke Barret would not die in hand-to-hand combat.

"Things already seem well in hand." She stroked Griffin's smooth brown-and-white feathers as she watched Roarke spin around for his next opponent. When no new fight was forthcoming, he hurried to Edgar Hughes's side to relieve the knight of one of his two opponents.

Just after Roarke engaged the French knight, Ariana noticed a man circling about the perimeter of the skirmish, as if gauging a method of attack. Oddly, there was no one to attack. The battle neared a close, and the English were clearly the victors.

Yet the man persisted his careful watch of the battle, and, although Ariana could not see him clearly, it appeared as if his glance settled most frequently upon Roarke. A warning pricked through Ariana; cold fear mixed with a strong need to protect. Griffin shifted anxiously on his tree branch, feathers rising and ruffling.

Leaving the forest's edge to get a better view of the proceedings, Ariana stood as close to the fight as possible without being seen. Everything about the furtive watcher—his posture, his gait, his manner—reminded her of the man who had stalked the English tents on the dark French seacoast and would have struck at Roarke.

It was the same man.

Only now, in the soft autumn sunlight, she could better discern his features with his helm raised. The man seemed to need his visor lifted to get a better view of the field. When he lowered it again, he stealthily entered the fray.

In the confusion of the skirmish, it seemed none of the English realized the newcomer slipped into the battle with no opponent. He merely danced about the clanking swords, ducking blows from other fights in progress, and positioned himself near Roarke.

Roarke.

She read the stranger's intent and recalled her vision of Roarke's death in the same instant. Her dream came to life before her eyes.

The traitor had one hand on his sword, ready to take the opponent that Roarke fought, and in his other hand, a short knife flashed down low. If he killed Roarke quickly, he could slay the knight Roarke battled and the English would blame Roarke's death on the Frenchman.

Ariana watched the traitor's eyes as he scanned the battle one last time, sweeping the field for anyone who might notice him in the act. Apparently satisfied there was no one, he flipped the short blade forward at a deadly angle to Roarke's unprotected side.

As if sensing her tension, Griffin launched into action the same moment she did. A scream tore from her throat as she called Roarke's name. Between the bird's cry and her shout, Roarke must have heard something. Spinning around, sword drawn, he knocked the treacherous knight to the ground with the blunt edge of his blade.

While her heart lodged in her throat, she watched Roarke turn back to battle the French knight as if the treachery at his back had been no more than a nuisance. A fly to be swatted. Indeed, the English knight he'd hit scrambled out of the fray and back toward the keep with all due haste.

In the meantime, her blood boiled so hot she could barely stand still. If she were a man—nay, even if she possessed a bigger blade than the small knife Roarke had given her—she would have mounted to ride after the traitor herself.

But she was determined to do as Roarke had asked of her. She waited at the edge of the forest with her horse until the skirmish ended and the English knights carried the day.

The sun was nearly set by the time he returned for her.

"You waited." He rode to a hand's length in front of her before he slid off his horse.

"You sound surprised." She wanted to throw her arms around him and tell him she was happy he was alive, but he was different from this morning. Restrained. Smeared with other men's blood.

"I am not accustomed to your doing the sensible thing, Ariana." He untied her horse to lead them back toward the keep. "And I fear I, too, do not always do the sensible thing where you are concerned."

"You're frighteningly levelheaded as far as I can see." She thought of the way he'd plucked off his opponents today with a cool head and an impressive swing. He did not bring passion to the battlefield, but wits.

"I can only apologize for what happened earlier today," he continued. "I have sworn to bring you back to your father, yet today I put your innocence in danger because of my lack of restraint." He spoke to her as if she were a child, leading her out of the forest and toward the shelter of the keep.

She wanted to shake him. "You need not apologize. I know how dearly you hold your honor."

"The keep is secure, but I want you to stay close to me until we can leave tomorrow morning."

"What of the knight who crept up behind you?" She still shook with indignation and fear for Roarke. Seeing a knife at his back had made her realize how important he'd become to her these last few weeks. She could not bear to see anything happen to him, even if he would never be her husband. "I am certain he was the same man who sought to kill you inside your tent eight weeks ago. He might even be the same man who poisoned our wine."

"You recognized him from the scuffle outside my tent?" He paused as they walked, turning on her with narrowed eyes. "Recall how dark it was that night."

"It was him. I recognized his walk, his manner, the way he held his weapon. Did you not recognize him as one of Henry's knights when you knocked him down?"

"Perhaps." He seemed to hedge, as if unwilling to confront his assailant. "You are prepared to accuse a man of trying to murder me?"

"Aye. I would gladly point out this man in front of your king. Unless you wish to seek your own justice?" She would not blame him for it.

"Nay." He looked down at his hauberk and shook his head ruefully. "I seem to have accrued too much blood on my hands already. But I do possess the man's blade from his first attempt."

Reaching beneath his tunic, he withdrew the small knife he'd found outside his tent. "I wear it to remind myself an enemy lurks near."

"Then between the two of us, my lord, we can surely convince your king."

Hellfire, but his Welsh bride was most determined in this matter.

Roarke rode into the courtyard of the French keep and plucked Ariana neatly off her saddle. He had not expected such loyalty from a woman who had married him for reasons as selfish as his own. He'd been able to forgive her deception during their wedding by reminding himself he had married her strictly to achieve his own ends. Why should he blame her for having ambitions of her own?

But ever since she'd confessed her ruse, she'd been steadfast in her loyalty to him, proving a gentle champion when he least expected it.

He had not been certain of his attacker's identity on the battlefield thanks to a light helm covering a portion of the man's head. Still, Roarke had definite suspicions. He was eager to see if Ariana's description confirmed his guess.

They reached the perimeter of the great hall where Henry held informal court with his trusted advisors. A fire roared in the huge grate, filling the hall with warmth despite the growing chill of the night. Men drank and milled about, reliving their battles with comrades and discussing possibilities for the king's next move. Some of the knights with more strategic wisdom urged Henry to forsake his Norman territory to ensure peace at home. Younger men with need of lands and keeps urged him to continue his wars.

While Roarke measured the mood of the hall, Ariana whispered instructions to a knight who nursed a wounded arm.

Roarke hauled her away from the lad, bringing her deeper into the chamber. "Is it any of these men?"

She shook her head.

"Barret, your absence has been noted." The king paused in his proceedings to both welcome and chastise Roarke.

He bowed to the king to signal the formality of his coming request. "Your Highness, I ask you leave to gather the men. Treachery is among us, and I wish to ferret out a traitor."

A rumble of oaths and murmurs rolled over the assembly until the king stood to greet the charge.

"What proof have you?" Henry demanded, his round face pink with the heat of the room and perhaps a bit of temper at having to address such a charge.

"The knife with which the cowardly knave would have stabbed me in the back."

Henry cocked an eyebrow, looking skeptically over Roarke and Ariana. Roarke gave him a level look in return, unwilling to let Henry intimidate Ariana. The king was responsible for her long presence at court, after all.

"Very well then." He nodded to his guards, wordlessly extending the order for his men to assemble. "I trust there is a reason Lady Ceara is among us for these proceedings?"

"If you will recall sir, she was present on the coast the night an attempt was made."

The king nodded, his gaze still hard and unwavering upon Ariana.

"And you still wish to return Lady Ceara to Wales tomorrow?"

"Aye. Assuming you will allow me to see this new matter through to its conclusion."

"Of course." Henry's glance swung back to Roarke. "The crown does not tolerate treachery, Barret."

Soon the hall was filled with knights and their squires, while servants lit every available torch to brighten the room.

One of the guards announced that all of the men were accounted for with the exception of four sentries still at their posts. Ariana was already engrossed in her task. She studied each face in the first two rows, her gaze moving quickly over each man.

When she reached the third row she paused. Exactly where Roarke had expected she might. The man she studied was young, clean-shaven and blond. His classic looks and cool blue eyes were undermined by a profusely sweating upper lip.

"That is him," she murmured to Roarke, pointing to the uneasy knight in the middle of the group.

"Six from the left?" Roarke had hoped his suspicions would not be confirmed, but now he saw no choice but to follow through with his accusation and worry about the consequences later.

"Aye." She seemed to recoil as she stared at him.

"Are you certain?" he pressed, his anger mounting at the treachery he faced.

"Yes, but—"

"By your leave, my lord?" He shouted the words to be sure the whole assembly could hear his words. By God, he would see his assailant brought low.

The king nodded almost imperceptibly.

"Then I would announce that treachery has befallen us. And I would appeal to the traitor who seeks my death to redeem himself in small measure by claiming this."

He held the knife out for all to see. It was unremarkable. And very likely unidentifiable. But Roarke was appealing to the knights' sense of honor and nobility. Henry's court was notorious for its commitment to the code of chivalry, even if they weren't successful in retaining Henry's Norman lands. Though an attempted murderer might not care about such ethical codes in private, he would not wish to blatantly break the code of morality before his king and fellow knights.

"'Twould be better to admit ownership than be dragged from the ranks to be accused." Roarke's eyes narrowed as he waited. He searched the courtyard, as if looking for the traitorous knight, yet allowing his gaze to return most frequently to the spot where the culprit stood, willing the cur to admit his guilt.

It worked.

The clean-shaven blond man stepped forward.

"It is my knife, Your Highness." The traitor appealed to the king, his eyes skipping over Roarke's head toward King Henry. "I throw myself upon your mercy, and respectfully ask to explain myself to the man I have wronged."

The packed hall stood in silence to hear Henry's reply. Roarke hoped the king knew better than to leave him alone with this sweating whelp. It had taken all of his restraint not to seek out the man when Ariana suggested she would understand if he sought his own justice. But in order to atone for his own past wrongs, he preferred to act as honorably as he knew how in his life now.

To speak with this man face-to-face would be asking more of Roarke than he could withstand.

"If Barret requests you meet him on the field, I am powerless to deny him that right," Henry warned.

"Aye, my lord. I only ask that you demand he hear my explanation first." The young knight looked beseechingly to his liege and Roarke recalled the knave wasn't much older than Ariana.

"Very well then," the king agreed, obviously growing weary of the drama by the way he waved his hand impatiently. "Come forward, Roarke. You will hear what your brother has to say."

Brother?

Ariana's heart stopped midbeat. Roarke's brother had tried to kill him? And worse, what if Roarke was forced to raise arms against his own flesh and blood on a field of honor?

King Henry bade Roarke and his brother enter an adjoining chamber before they went any further, and as the two men departed the room, the warriors all around her broke into discussion of the matter. Although she was curious enough to wonder about their hushed references to an old feud and the insolence of youth, she forced herself to wait for Roarke's explanation. She knew well how whispers and rumors could distort the truth.

She had guessed Roarke's past had been troubled, but now it looked as if his problems reached forward through time to plague him.

"Come, Ceara. They will settle this." The king appeared at her elbow and gestured toward the door where Roarke had disappeared.

"Let us hope they can do so without bloodshed." She had no wish to enter Roarke's private affairs without his invitation, but what choice did she have but to follow where the king led?

"Niall Kendall is too young and stupid for Roarke to hold these offenses against him." One of Henry's guards opened the door as the sovereign approached.

"Treachery and near murder are serious offenses, my lord." Though she prayed the king was correct.

Niall Kendall's raised voice resonated through the nearly empty room. Ariana suspected the former French lord of Rennes had hidden away his treasures before the English took his keep, leaving this chamber hollow and echoing.

"I did not truly wish you dead, Roarke." Niall shrugged as if wielding a knife at his kin was but a small offense. "I thought if I could succeed in injuring you, Father would see that you were not as invincible as he thinks."

Suddenly self-conscious about her presence in the room, Ariana halted at the entrance.

As if reading her thoughts, Roarke crossed the floor and drew her forward. "You have witnessed my brother's actions, Ceara." He called her by the name the king recognized. "I want you here." Nodding tersely in the direction of his brother, he ran a restless hand through his hair. "This is my half brother, Niall, by the way, who has explained he attempted to stab me to prove to his sire that I am not indestructible."

Ariana shifted nervously, feeling out of place and

awkward in the midst of the confrontation. Finally settling upon a narrow bench, she cast her eyes to the floor, hoping they would all forget she was there.

"That is not all there is to it, Roarke." Niall's voice wavered. "Miles is dead."

Curiosity made her raise her eyes to gauge Roarke's reaction. His supreme stillness forced her out of her seat. Although frightened of his reaction, she wanted to offer some measure of comfort if Miles proved to be anyone he cared about.

"How?" If Roarke noticed her nearness, he did not reveal it.

"Poison."

For a moment, Ariana forgot all about Niall's attempt to kill Roarke. As if she had arrived at a dramatic performance a little late in the story, her mind raced with scenarios to put the odd bits of news together to make sense.

"Do you know who did it?" Roarke noticed her then. And though he did not display any sign that he was pleased for her proximity, he picked up a lone lock of hair from her shoulder and smoothed the long strand with the rest behind her back. Warmth curled through her at his touch.

"Nay. But it has the mark of a woman, does it not?"

When Roarke did not respond, Ariana took the moment to voice a question. She cleared her throat awkwardly. "Why do you say that?"

"A woman resorts to slow killers like poisons because she has not the strength to murder by sword or knife or strangulation," Roarke explained. "And poison is usually given in food and beverage, which are largely prepared and presented by women."

"I would think it would be a good way for anyone to commit murder if they did not wish to be discovered." She could not help but think of Roarke's last encounter with poison the night of their wedding. Did yet another enemy lurk nearby?

"Has Father looked into the matter?" Roarke was calm now, betraying no sign of rage at his brother. His attention seemed fixed on the matter of Miles.

"Who was Miles, my lord?" Ariana had to know.

"My father's oldest legitimate issue. Niall's full brother. I can only assume Niall foolishly believes there is a chance Father will choose me as his heir now that Miles is dead, and he sought to kill me before such a thing could come to pass." He glared at his brother as if daring him to deny it.

"He will choose you, Roarke, now that you have the king's ear." Niall smiled apologetically to Henry. "Father reminds me daily that I have made no name for myself in spite of every advantage in life, while you have made tremendous strides in the world when you have been given nothing."

The king's mouth flattened into a cold, hard line and Ariana thought she detected a shadow of sadness within his eyes. "Yet we are all given certain mantles at birth that cannot be dislodged, young Niall. You would do your house credit to wear yours with more pride and less suspicion."

Beside her, Ariana could feel the tension emanating from Roarke. His jaw flexed. His hands clenched and unclenched. "You must be aware, Niall, that I would not take a thing from our father now."

Niall's eyes narrowed. He was quite handsome

though his eyes were cold and cruel. "You would snub your nose at Southvale for some godforsaken keep in western Wales? How gullible do you think I am?"

"I think you are quite gullible if you allow our father to taunt you into thinking I covet Southvale. I swear I will have naught from Fulke Kendall. I needed his name and money long ago and he would not give it. If he should ever give it now, I assure you, I will not have it." Roarke turned to the king. "I am satisfied with this explanation, my lord."

"Your wishes will not prevent him from naming you his heir," Niall raised his voice, to strident tones.

Ignoring Niall, the king responded to Roarke. "Yet I am not satisfied in the least." He gestured to Niall to come closer. "Your actions are unbecoming for a knight of my court. Now that Miles Kendall is dead you should strive to become a worthy heir to one of England's largest estates. Instead you would commit a vile crime against your own kin."

Niall bowed his head, but not before Ariana caught a glimpse of his unrepentant gaze.

"Therefore I am banishing you from my court and my troops for one year. You are to return home and give an accounting of yourself to your father. Roarke will escort you to be sure the deed is done."

Both Roarke and Niall moved to speak, but the king interrupted them both. "My decision is final. Roarke, you wished to leave France to escort Ceara home anyway. It is not so far out of your way to stop at Southvale first. I trust you to keep Niall in line and address whatever trouble brews in your father's household."

Roarke bowed formally to the king, indicating his

acceptance of his mission, though the rigid lines of his body revealed opposition to the plan. Ariana regretted Roarke's unhappiness, but could not help feeling a moment of relief that she would be able to stay with him a little longer while he escorted Niall to England. Maybe it would be the time she needed to change his mind about their marriage.

"Niall, you will return to court one year from today for my judgment upon you. If you are to be lord of Southvale, you will need to master honor and loyalty. You would do well to learn from Roarke rather than begrudge him his success."

Niall raised his eyes and also made a formal bow. "Yes, my lord." His tone—too falsely earnest—grated on Ariana's nerves.

The king rose, indicating an end to the discussion.

"Then I wish Godspeed—and good luck—to all of you."

Chapter Thirteen

Reining in the horses north of London shortly before sunset two days later, Roarke retrieved the sack that carried food he had purchased early that morning. Their tense party spoke little to one another. He could tell from Ariana's withdrawn manner that Niall made her uncomfortable.

Not that Roarke liked the knave better. If anything, he thought it rather lenient that Niall had been excused from the king's service and given safe passage home as punishment for attempting to kill his own flesh and blood. Although Roarke had accepted his brother's accounting for his crime, he did not agree with the king's sentence for Niall. The journey seemed more a penalty for Roarke, who was now burdened with the safekeeping of a witless fool he detested.

But the journey granted him more time with Ariana, for which he was grateful. Although he knew he did the honorable thing to return her to her father and take Ceara Llywen for his bride, the plan held no appeal for him. He watched Ariana now as she stroked her horse's nose and slipped the mare some morsel she must have hidden away earlier in the day. Struck anew by the generosity of her spirit, he could not fathom how he would ever give her up.

And for the first time, he realized how devastating it must have been for his half brother Lucian ten years ago when he had fallen in love with the woman Roarke planned to marry. Lucian had given up someone who he'd grown to care about out of a sense of honor. Duty. Two qualities he'd never lacked.

The difference between Lucian's dilemma back then and Roarke's quandary now was that Roarke had not fallen in love. Nor would he. He simply felt protective of his Welsh wife and did not wish to see her hurt. Not by him, and not by anyone else, either. For that reason he could never keep Ariana for his own, no matter how much she tempted him.

She still had a chance to find the love and fulfillment her father had always withheld from her.

"Are we almost there?" She appeared before him as they prepared to eat, her face pale and drawn as she helped unwrap the bread and apples that would serve as their supper.

"Aye," Niall interrupted, lazily strolling about the area as if surveying his property instead of helping set up camp. "We have only to pass through a few more holdings 'til we arrive. Now we are almost on Radborne lands, where Roarke spent some time courting his last bridal prospect, if memory serves."

Roarke had wondered when Niall would dangle news of Marie Radborne in front of Ariana. Ariana paused in her humming, a sure sign the words had found their mark. She continued to pass around the small store of food they shared, however, as if she possessed no interest in the women of Roarke's past.

While Roarke silently applauded her cool aloofness, Niall leaned against the trunk of a gnarled old oak tree and turned his malevolent gaze on his half brother. "Perhaps you had not heard, Roarke, that Marie has pledged herself to me since our brother Miles's untimely death."

"Since Marie Radborne seems to have her sights set on Southvale, I cannot say that surprises me." Roarke had seen past young Marie's open flirtation and coy manners soon after he'd visited her at her father's keep. But then, he had courted her in the days when he suffered under the delusion he might still form an alliance with his Kendall kin. Marie had quickly made her preference for Miles known, engaging herself to the Southvale heir two years later.

Ariana dropped down to a flat rock near the bush where they'd tied their horses. She concentrated on her food as if each bite was worth far more of her time and attention than the conversation about Roarke's past.

Niall's gaze seemed fixed on Ariana, too. His eyes followed her as she ate in silence, though he continued to direct his words to Roarke. "It's a pity you were forced to wed such an unassuming maid after courting a legendary English beauty. But I suppose the Welsh do not breed women of Marie Radborne's caliber."

Griffin, who had attached himself to Ariana since the day they went hawking, cried his displeasure and ruffled his feathers from his perch on Ariana's saddle. Ariana's cheeks flushed pink, though she did not react otherwise. Roarke's temper simmered for her sake, but would not allow Niall the satisfaction of seeing it.

"You are blind."

Ariana smiled up at him, her pleasure at his rebuff radiating.

And just like that, she took his breath away. Roarke couldn't say when she'd come to have such power over him, but there it was—strong and undeniable and making him question how he could ever give her back to her father. Selfishly, he hated the idea he'd been so certain was the only solution to their false marriage.

Niall seemed to lose interest in them, declining his share of bread to take a walk about the small glade of pines. As if sensing the removal of a threat, Griffin flew off on his own, unerringly able to find his way back to his new mistress time and again.

"I apologize for my brother." Moving closer to Ariana, Roarke thought it might help her understand Niall if he confided in her. "He is a victim of my father's cruel sense of humor and lifelong preference for his older son, Miles. Though it does not excuse Niall, it may help you comprehend him more." He studied her face. "And detest him less."

Her hands flew to her cheeks in simultaneous guilt and denial. "I do not detest him!"

"Aye. You do." Roarke grinned broadly. "But I can hardly hold it against you."

The meal was soon finished and they worked side by side in easy rhythm to prepare a shelter against the cold winds of early winter. Ariana gathered wood without him asking, her ease in the outdoors obvious despite her highborn upbringing.

"Will we spend much time at Southvale, my lord?" she asked between treks to gather wood. Settling herself near him as he scrubbed a flint to strike a blaze, she huffed her warm breath over her fingers to ward off the chill.

"Nay." He peered around to check Niall's whereabouts and spied his half brother cleaning his sword to a sheen that glinted even in the falling twilight. Roarke kept his voice low as he confided his plan. "I will take Niall home as Henry requested, but I will not dance attendance on my father who will only ignore my words and use my presence as a chance to provoke his youngest son. Perhaps I will send a letter to Southvale through someone I trust so that I can tell Henry in good faith that I did communicate with Fulke."

"And then we will proceed to Glamorgan?" Her voice seemed closer somehow, as if she had moved even nearer to him.

Or perhaps he was just frighteningly aware of her every move and sigh. Memories of her underneath him just two days ago came back to taunt him. Tempt him.

For once he thanked God that Niall remained nearby, providing a strong reminder why he couldn't touch her tonight.

"Aye." He succeeded in coaxing a blaze to life just then, the warm firelight illuminating Ariana's face a mere arm's length from his.

Her soft lips looked full and inviting as he stared at her across the small fire he'd started. Her mouth glistened with a hint of moisture as if she'd just been kissed. Or as if she'd just licked her lip in anticipation.

"Then perhaps once we are alone, we will have time to resolve what lies between us." She extended her hands to warm them over the flames.

He didn't have to ask what needed resolving. His desire for her was so thick it clogged his throat. Itched his palms with the need to touch her.

"It should only take two days." He'd make certain it didn't take a moment longer.

"And two nights?"

He told himself that her throaty question could not have been issued to provoke him. It was an innocent query. Intended only to gather information and not to rouse his already simmering passion.

"One night only." But even as he said it, he knew it would take longer than that under the best of circumstances. Heaven help him, he'd never keep his hands off her for that long.

"I fear that won't be nearly long enough. I have many things to say to you before you cast me aside, Roarke Barret." She rose to her feet, brushing the dust from her skirt before meeting his gaze again. "For now, I will content myself with letting you know that I need to excuse myself and bathe away the dirt from the road before I retire. *Nos da,* my lord. Good night."

Roarke watched her walk away, knowing he would never sleep tonight with thoughts of her bathing by moonlight plaguing him every time he closed his eyes. He did not need her gift of sight to envision clear stream water cascading over every curve and hollow of her beautiful body.

Hellfire, but this would be a long night.

* * *

She didn't know where she found her nerve, but Ariana was exceedingly thankful for its timely return as she trudged through the cold, dark woods toward the sound of running water, the memory of hunger in Roarke's eyes warming her all the way.

For too many weeks she'd been plagued with guilt about deceiving him, unwilling to push him any further after he'd vowed she would have to return to her father. But what of her wants? Her wishes?

The time had come to remind him she would not go home quietly. She desired this marriage to work for so many reasons, not the least of which was that Roarke Barret needed her, whether he realized it or not. She had vowed to help him, to make herself indispensable to him at Llandervey so that he might never regret wedding her. And while Ceara possessed all the skills becoming to a noblewoman, she would never owe as much loyalty to Roarke as Ariana already did. If anything, she would resent being pulled into a marriage she did not want.

Ariana was running out of time to make Roarke change his mind about returning her to her father. Why not use every weapon at her disposal to convince him otherwise? And although she had not fully understood the simmering pull of desire between them when they first met, by now she was accustomed to the heated attraction that drew their eyes to one another time and again.

And she knew he felt it, too.

If that passion could help her sway Roarke, then she had every intention of calling upon it over the two days they traveled to Glamorgan. Her attempts to entice him might appear rather artless to a man of the world like Roarke, but as long as he continued to follow her with his eyes, she would be content.

She found the stream she sought nearby but she did not linger as the water was frigid. Wearing her tunic just in case anyone came along, she did little more than splash herself with the water, but she was numb and shivering when she finished. Griffin joined her for a few moments before flying off again, his blue eyes almost ghostly in the dark. She scrubbed her scalp and soaped her hair in an effort to finish with all haste.

When she returned to the camp, there was no sign of Roarke or Niall. Guessing they sought small game for a meal or fatter logs to keep the fire burning through the night, Ariana combed her hair and gazed into the leaping flames. She had almost drifted to sleep when a vision in the fire startled her into wakefulness. Blinking rapidly, she hoped the sight would vanish, but it remained.

There, in the midst of the warm blaze, the wise-woman Eleanor of Bohemia materialized, wraithlike and shadowed.

"Eleanor!" She whispered the name hoarsely as fascination held her there, transfixed.

"Do not be afraid, child. I send you only my spirit, not my ghost. While my body rests contentedly by the fire in my Cymru cottage, my spirit seeks you out, answering your call for comfort and aid."

Ariana knew she must be dreaming, yet the vision and the voice comforted her as her old nurse's presence always had.

"You are so real, your voice, your appearance...." Ariana noted every detail about the old woman, down to a small tear at the hem of her gown, probably acquired on an herb-gathering mission that morning. "Why have you sought me out?"

"Your heart calls to me, Ariana, telling me you have not found happiness."

Ariana peered slowly around the stream and surrounding trees, assuring herself she would not be caught talking to a campfire. "'Tis true. Roarke seeks to bring me back to Father so he might wed Ceara. I thought I could make him change his mind, but he is so committed to what he thinks is right, he cannot be swayed."

"He cannot?" Eleanor's eyebrows arched surprise. "Have you so changed these last few moons, Ariana, that you are ready to admit defeat? What of your noble mission to save your nieces? What of your promise to your mother to shatter the myth of the curse?"

"There is little more I can do." Save use her womanly wiles, limited though they may be.

"Does he love another?" The vision faded a bit and Ariana rubbed her eyes, clinging to sleep and the comfort of her dreams.

"Nay..." Although she had not forgotten Niall's hint that Roarke had courted an Englishwoman before he'd been forced to choose a Welsh wife. "At least, I don't think so. He merely seems intent on pursuing the most honorable course of action."

"Follow your heart, Ariana, and you will not be led astray."

But what if her heart was as confused as the rest of

her? She was about to ask Eleanor that very question when the image before her wavered. Her vision of her old friend and mentor became more and more shadowed until only a voice whispered through the trees.

"Love can overcome all obstacles…."

Ariana could not be sure if the words came from Eleanor's wise lips or from the wistfulness of her own heart.

Roarke slept as little as possible on the road with Niall nearby.

An intelligent decision in light of his brother's treachery, but an idle-headed mistake given that it meant Roarke had naught to do but keep watch over Ariana's slumbering form for hours at a time.

He gazed at her shortly before first light, fascinated by the way she flung her arms wide in sleep, as bold and brazen in her dreams as she was while awake. The fire had burned to naught but warm embers by now, and though he did not want to stir up a blaze since they would ride out shortly, he did not want his Welsh *morforwyn* to catch a chill. Or perhaps he only wanted to justify his need to touch her as he reached for her woolen blanket and pulled it higher over her soft breasts.

She turned to her side. Toward him. Her hair fell over her neck, a dark contrast to her pale, creamy skin. The temptation to run his fingers through those silky locks proved too strong to ignore. He leaned to skim away the dark tresses, exposing the slender column of her throat to his avid gaze.

So beautiful.

He could not fathom how the blind lads of Wales could have overlooked this fey creature for so long. And even if her superstitious countrymen feared the legend surrounding her family, what man in his right mind wouldn't be called to test its truth with such a woman as his prize?

Hunger for her besieged him. An ache for her that he could never fill yawned wide in his very soul. His hand reached for her again, desirous of one more touch.

Until a voice called to him from the other side of the fire.

"You look like a man who has lost his heart as well as his wits, Barret." Niall watched him while laying still in his bedroll, his eyes keenly focused on Roarke's hand above Ariana's sleeping form.

Roarke's fingers clenched slowly into a fist, angry with himself far more than his milk-livered brother. Roarke knew better than to allow a woman to distract him. Sliding farther away from Ariana, he cast his half brother a level look.

"What heart? I have Kendall blood in my veins, the same as you. I think the birthright precludes any warmth of feeling." Whatever his sentiments toward Ariana, they did not—could not—include anything more than sensual attraction.

"Then perhaps you cannot see what is before your very eyes, brother." Niall's mouth flattened into a hard line. "You appear plenty warm for the Welsh wench from where I'm sitting."

Shoving to his feet, Niall walked away from the fire and out of the camp leaving Roarke alone with the woman who was slowly tearing down every defense he had ever established.

"You're not a Kendall," a soft voice reminded him.

Turning, he found Ariana awake and studying him every bit as keenly as Niall had been earlier. Roarke had been too absorbed in his own thoughts to sense either of them awakening. Perhaps his brother had the right of it that he was losing his wits after all.

"Calling myself a Barret does not change my heritage, much as I would wish otherwise." Roarke's gaze could not help but fall upon the slight gape in the neckline of her gown as she lay propped on her elbow. Her position allowed for only a sliver of skin to be made visible, but that did not stop him from a more thorough disrobing in his mind.

"You are not bound by your father's cruel legacy." She stared up at him with her clear amber eyes, as if she could see those parts he had never revealed to another. "Your mercy in the face of your brother's perfidy proves you are already a far better man than he could ever hope to be."

Her words soothed him even as he told himself she had no way of knowing as much. Somehow this gentle healer with her seer's eyes could chase away the darkness in his soul with no more than soft words.

Hellfire, but he could not afford to allow her to see inside him. She threatened him more with her siren's body and kind heart than Niall's duplicitous blade.

Rising to his feet in the cold air of early morning, Roarke tore his gaze from the temptation of Ariana.

"That does not mean I will not one day succumb to my father's wicked ways. It only suggests I have forestalled my downfall another day."

Chapter Fourteen

Ariana welcomed the faster pace later that day as they neared Southvale. Although she had not seen any visions concerning Niall or the father he shared with Roarke, she could not shake the sense of foreboding that overcame her as they rode for Kendall lands through patches of dense pine forests and wide-open fields stripped of the fall harvest.

She had grown up in rather ominous surroundings herself considering her father's willingness to let his keep fall into disrepair while he ruminated his days away. But she feared Southvale housed deeper ills than misery. Fulke Kendall sounded like a greedy man and a cruel one at that.

He'd pitted his children against one another for his own amusement, and he'd swayed Roarke's mother into unknowing adultery with his lies. And those things aside, she disliked him already simply because he had never embraced Roarke as a son.

Thus, she was ready to dispense with Niall once and

for all, and to put Southvale far behind them. Not even singing had helped to ease her worries about the day's outcome.

Roarke slowed his pace as they neared the top of a rise. Niall continued ahead, trotting out of sight on the other side of the hill.

"My father's keep lies just ahead," Roarke called over his shoulder while her mount caught up with his. "Just over there."

He pointed to the north and with only a few more steps, a spectacular rectangle structure came into view. Surrounded by water with one long bridge spanning the moat, Southvale was at least twice the size of Llandervey and made Glamorgan look like a peasant's accommodation. She did not recognize the dark, reddish stone the builders had used for walls and assumed it must not be a stone native to her part of Wales.

"No wonder the king concerns himself with who will be heir here." Ariana's sense of unease increased, her belly fluttering with anxiety.

"I do not plan to enter." He reached to stroke her horse's neck, and somehow, watching him soothe the horse soothed her, as well. "At most I will call out to my father. If he cannot stir himself to come hear the king's message for him, then I will simply wait to see that Niall enters the keep and we'll be on our way."

"I have no wish to tarry near this father of yours, my lord. He sounds far more wretched than mine." Her grip tightened on the reins as she shifted uneasily in her saddle. "You do not think there will be a confrontation?"

She had no liking for harsh words of any kind, and

had always preferred to spend time with Eleanor, visit the mews or sing to herself in the forest rather than risk possible confrontations with her father at home. She'd spent much of her life avoiding conflicts of any kind and telling herself things weren't so bad with her father.

"Not with you beside me. Henry does not expect me to put my bride at risk for the sake of settling matters at Southvale." His gaze connected with hers for a long moment, making her yearn to be his bride in every sense of the word.

Once they had put Fulke Kendall behind them, she would begin her quest to capture Roarke's attention. Just the notion of having him all to herself strengthened her resolve.

"Very well then." She nodded, tearing her gaze away from Roarke to settle on the intimidating keep some two leagues distant. "Let us ride."

They did not catch up with Niall until they reached the drawbridge. Roarke's brother waited for them there, a bored expression upon a face that would have been handsome if not for his cold eyes.

A small gatehouse nestled at one end of the expansive bridge while an imposing outwork stood at the other. After the outwork, another bridge awaited at a right angle to the first, making entry to Southvale a complex proposition for any invader.

"Father is not home," Niall informed them before Roarke could approach one of the men-at-arms outside the gatehouse. "You may come inside while we await his return."

Roarke made no answer, but spoke to one of the guards—a portly young man who looked as though he had an aversion to bathing. "Is my father home, Randall?"

"Aye." He stood up straighter as Niall cursed him for telling the truth, but Randall kept his gaze on Roarke. "I've already sent word to him that you're here, my lord."

"You're a good man." Roarke clapped him on the shoulder and—Ariana suspected—passed him a coin of some sort. "Thank you."

Indeed, no sooner had Randall opened his mouth to reply when a booming voice shouted across the drawbridge.

"Welcome home, son! Do not stand at my gate awaiting entrance like a stranger. Come in."

Ariana squinted to see an immaculately dressed nobleman on horseback on the other side of the bridge, a full head of lustrous gray hair touching his broad shoulders and a sleek white hound at his horse's feet. A tall man with a commanding presence, the lord of Southvale was dressed in elaborate finery of rich blues and velvets.

Because it was not a festival day, Ariana guessed Lord Kendall placed a great deal of importance on outward appearances.

But even more fascinating than this imposing newcomer was the willowy young woman seated on horseback beside him. As elegantly attired as Roarke's father, the fair-haired woman sat draped across a snowy-white palfrey outfitted to match her sky-blue gown. Hair bound in an elegant knot atop her head, she wore a tiny silver circlet to secure gossamer thin veils that draped over her shoulders.

Roarke sat rigid and unmoving beside Ariana.

"Nay. I told you once I would never again enter your keep, my lord, and I have not changed my mind. I bring you your son and a message from your king." Roarke's words carried easily across the narrow strip of water, his voice as deep and resonant as his sire's.

As one, Roarke's father and the young woman rode out across the bridge to greet them. Niall hung back as if waiting to see what happened before greeting Fulke.

Lord Kendall rode the length of the drawbridge, the echoing clomp of his horse's hooves growing louder until he loomed a few feet away. "I scarce believed my ears when I learned you were here. We so hoped you would return when you heard of Miles's death. This has been a difficult time for us…."

In spite of Fulke's treatment of his other sons, it was apparent he'd loved his eldest a great deal. If not for the comforting hand the blond woman gave the older man, Ariana half expected to see him weep.

"I am sorry for your loss," Roarke offered, waiting a moment before he forged ahead. "But that is not why I'm here. Henry has commanded me to escort Niall home for reasons he can share with you. My only message from the king is that you need to settle your differences with Niall with all due haste so that Henry can be certain of the security of your keep."

"And Henry worries like an old woman." Fulke waved the matter away with the careless swipe of one large palm. "But I would be glad to discuss the future with you, if you would come in and join Marie and I for a few days." He gestured toward the soaring towers behind him. "We have much to settle between us—"

"Such as who inherits the keys to the kingdom?" Niall moved closer, his uneasy stance belying the boldness of his words.

"Diplomatic as always, Niall." Fulke had no embrace for his youngest. "Welcome home."

Fulke's young companion edged her horse forward, her gaze falling on Ariana.

"My lord, have you asked Roarke about his Welsh bride?" The woman—Marie Radborne, if Ariana did not miss her guess—distracted Fulke from glaring at his legitimate son by turning him toward Ariana.

She did not find the woman's tone warm or welcoming, but a lifelong habit of common courtesy made her nod before the Earl of Southvale.

"Ceara Llywen, my lord." Ariana introduced herself with her cousin's name, the name she had used throughout her time with the English knights abroad. "It is a pleasure to meet you."

"The wife foisted on my son by our illustrious king?" Fulke frowned while his tall hound sniffed Ariana's feet. "I did not expect you to travel at Roarke's side. Who oversees your household in your absence?"

Trepidation shivered through her at his cold stare and Ariana wished she could be anywhere but here, awaiting this man's certain condemnation.

"Our steward, my lord." Ariana nudged the dog's intrusive nose away with the toe of her shoe.

"You left a steward to oversee a woman's domain?" Turning to Roarke, he narrowed his gaze. "Roarke, you have grossly underestimated your worth to King Henry if you think this little Welsh wench and a godforsaken keep are all you are entitled to. Why would you accept such a miserly hand-out when—"

"When he could have all of Southvale at his disposal?" Niall interrupted.

"Enough!" Roarke's command bit the air with its viciousness, though he never raised his voice. "Fulke, if you think to insult my wife again, our discussion will go no further."

The elder Kendall smiled. "Ah! I am not surprised my son possesses a large dose of backbone. You would not have come so far if you did not. Perhaps it would be most prudent if we conducted our business in private, without the whining backdrop of Niall's complaints."

Niall's face mottled.

"Nay." Roarke and his father continued to speak while Niall sidled nearer to Ariana and the fair-haired woman accompanying Fulke.

Not wishing to be separated from Roarke, Ariana attempted to stay close to him while Niall greeted Marie Radborne with an enthusiastic kiss. No easy task when Fulke Kendall slid off his horse to take a seat on the crenellated edge of the outwork while waving Roarke over to do the same.

Fulke grumbled while Roarke followed suit. "You would have me believe you are prepared to turn down a noble title, holdings worth a substantial fortune and power second only to the King of England, because you will take nothing from me?" A purple vein stood out in dark contrast to Fulke Kendall's red face. "No son of mine could be so pigheaded."

Their conversation carrying easily on the cold winds

of late autumn, Ariana could not help but hear their words. She tightened her cloak about her shoulders, eager to leave this place behind her to be alone with Roarke.

"You are precisely right," Roarke said to his father, seeming to forget Ariana's presence. "I have never been, nor will I ever be your son in any meaningful way, and I will not be thrown into your political machinations because you are desperate for an heir."

"You are my heir!"

Ariana could not decide whether to join Roarke in what seemed more and more like a private discussion, or if she should simply remain upon her horse near Marie and Niall. Neither option appealed. What happened to Roarke's plan to relay a simple message to his father and leave?

"Niall is your rightful heir now." Roarke was saying as he paced the outwork. "I will not cheat him of his inheritance. I come to you at King Henry's command to settle this matter, so it would be in your best interest to give me your word you will name Niall as your heir and be done with it."

"You are worth ten of Niall."

"And, according to your mysterious calculations, Miles was worth twenty of me." He raised his voice, frustration written in every line of his countenance. "Perhaps Niall is causing trouble because he has been made to feel worthless since the day he was born. You are fortunate he is not more of a wastrel."

"It is all my fault, then?"

"You have been warned, Fulke. The king will not tolerate trouble at Southvale. 'Tis too important to him."

Niall's horse edged Ariana's farther away from Roarke, away from the tense conversation between father and his illegitimate son. Although she had no wish to spend any more time in the young Kendall's presence, at least he provided a distraction from the raised voices on the other side of the low tower connected to the drawbridge.

"Lady Ceara, you have not met your husband's former love," Niall offered, grinning that cold, vacant smile of his. "This is Marie Radborne who will one day be my wife."

The blond woman held her hand out to Niall to be kissed and scarcely spared a glance for Ariana.

Not that Ariana particularly cared. She longed to depart this unhappy family reunion as quickly as possible.

"Your father is in one of his dangerous moods today." Marie took his arm and guided him to a small clearing, her voice low and soothing.

"Dangerous enough to cheat me out of my rightful inheritance?" He swiped a nervous hand through his golden hair, making chaos of his perfectly groomed locks.

"Easily. I bet he is signing over the lands to Roarke right now." Marie glanced in Ariana's direction and smiled as if letting her in on a joke.

Niall sneered at his father, but Roarke and Fulke continued their discussion, unaware of him.

Ariana knew Lady Radborne played some sort of game, but curiosity drew her to listen. She knew so little about Roarke and his family intrigue. Perhaps if she understood his Kendall relations better, she would understand Roarke better, a notion with definite appeal. Besides, Roarke was still exchanging heated words with his father.

Marie studied the wealth of rings on her pale fingers for a long moment before returning her glance to Ariana. "Fulke Kendall is one of the most powerful earls in England. If Roarke inherits his title, you will be an extremely wealthy woman."

"I have no care for more wealth than that which I already possess," Ariana returned. "And frankly, I prefer Wales to your England."

"Yet you are so valuable to Roarke, my dear. You are a symbol of his good relations with the king; a sign of how well he has done for himself." Marie's smile was as lopsided as it was insincere. "Roarke would be devastated should anything happen to you."

What in the name of Arianrhod did that mean?

"What are you suggesting?" Niall pounced on Marie's words.

"Only that Ceara would be a wonderful bargaining tool to make Roarke sign over to you whatever you might want."

Blood froze in Ariana's veins.

"What?"

Ariana barely heard Niall's question as she tugged her horse's reins, ready to back out of this conversation. Niall, however, blocked her path. He sat his horse like a rock, oblivious to Ariana's maneuverings as he gaped at Marie.

Ariana did not wish to startle Roarke, but the turn of the conversation unnerved her. Marie could not seriously be suggesting Niall swipe Ariana right out from under Roarke's nose. Ariana glanced at the network of drawbridges and towers that could easily separate Southvale Keep from the rest of the world.

A dangerous design if one happened to be on the wrong side of those bridges.

Marie's gaze narrowed, her blue eyes full of treacherous intelligence and greed. "If you held Ceara," she pressed, "Roarke would do anything for you, settle the estate with you, make some kind of reparation to you...."

Scarcely a heartbeat passed before Niall wrenched Ariana off her horse and kicked his horse into motion. Niall's arms clamped around her so tightly she could not breathe, her voice providing her with only a squeak when she desperately needed to scream.

They raced across the bridge at breakneck pace. For one moment, Ariana caught a brief glimpse of Roarke as he quit his pacing. Confusion seemed to hold him still for an instant before fury twisted his features and he vaulted atop his horse.

But already, Niall was wrenching back the mechanism to lift the drawbridge between them. The great barrier rose, trapping them inside.

She struggled away, prepared to cast herself in the muck of the moat before she allowed Niall to use her as a way to torment Roarke.

"You would be wise to hold still." Niall poked Ariana in the ribs with a short knife, putting a quick end to her struggles. "Marie will be all too glad if I have to kill you."

Ariana had sensed the potential for evil in Niall the first moment she saw him. She did not doubt for a moment he would use his blade on her.

"Welcome to Southvale, Ceara," he shouted as they galloped through the southern entrance of the keep. "Enjoy your time here, my lady, because you and your bastard lord will never be returning."

"Your son is a dead man."

Roarke made the pledge easily, more than ready to do harm to Niall Kendall for endangering Ariana. Roarke had not cared so much about Niall skulking around his tent at night and trying to nick him with his blade. But this, he could not bear.

"He must know that as Lord of Southvale, I command the gates here." Fulke stared up at his own keep, not seeming in the least distressed about Niall locking him out along with Roarke. "I can get back in the keep. The question remains, however—can you?"

Silently cursing every vile oath he could conjure, Roarke forced himself to remain patient with his father's games. To lose control with the elder Kendall would be a strategic mistake when Roarke needed his aid.

Marie Radborne urged her mount near them, her sky-blue skirts spread neatly over her horse. "Perhaps Niall possesses more backbone than you suspected, Lord Kendall."

Fulke snorted. "My son is a fool to think he accomplishes anything with this ploy. Roarke brings us word that we must cease our infighting and settle the matter of Southvale's future heir. I do not think his rash act is a step in the right direction."

Wondering why Marie's cheeks flushed so pink at Fulke's words, Roarke studied the soaring keep to hunt for possible points of entry when a dark blue swath of cloth waved out a narrow window in the southeast tower. As he stared at the soft material that matched the hue of Ariana's dress, Roarke spied Niall leaning out the small opening.

"You wanted your bastard son under your roof again, Father," he shouted from his perch high above them. "And I've found a way to get him here." Pulling the blue cloth back into the window, Roarke realized the material did indeed originate from Ariana's gown. Fear knifing straight to his gut, his fingers flexed about his sword that was useless against an enemy walled within a keep.

God help Niall if he harmed her. No keep would be safe for his half brother.

"I do not think this is the sort of hospitality that will sway your brother to our cause," Fulke called back, his silvery-haired hound howling in empathy with his shouting master. "I have no choice but to allow Roarke inside."

Niall cursed and Roarke could have sworn he heard Ariana cry out somewhere within the tower.

Hellfire, but he'd had enough of his family's games. He turned on his father, rage coursing through him.

"Open the gate now or consider yourself my enemy." He held himself utterly still while he waited for his father to declare himself. No matter how much Roarke disliked his father, he had never wanted to cross swords with him.

But Ariana had been more devoted to him than any of his Kendall clan ever had, making him realize that family wasn't just about bloodlines and heritage. It was about honor and loyalty.

"Very well then. I will open the gate, but understand this." Fulke lowered his voice, no doubt forcing every man-at-arms guarding his tower to strain their ears to hear the rest. "If I do this for you, you owe me your allegiance."

Roarke stared back into his father's eyes and wondered what to do. Forsake his hard-won honor by forswearing himself? Because he would never, ever willingly give his father his allegiance.

Yet, if he did not lie, he would be forced to lay siege to Southvale. A fool's proposition even in midsummer, but a death wish as winter loomed and food supplies became scarce.

"Very well then, Father." He sought the words that would be least damning, knowing he could make no promise to his treacherous sire. "Open the gate and I will endeavor not to kill your son."

Chapter Fifteen

Ariana followed Niall Kendall up endless narrow staircases as they ascended another tower. She'd lost track of which part of the keep they climbed since Niall had dragged her down one tower and up another, hauling her along behind him through countless dark passages and hidden doors.

She squinted into the slim shafts of sunlight every time they passed an arrow slit in the rock, but her captor always pulled her past them too quickly for her to see anything outside. She lost her bearings in no time.

Niall had seemed to take great delight in taunting Roarke out of one of the windows earlier. Infused with new vigor after waving a torn portion of Ariana's skirt out the window, Niall had run through the keep like a wild man, as if he had some vital destination in mind.

"This is it." Now he stopped suddenly in front of a small wooden door that looked to be built for dwarves.

Ariana stared at the absurdly small opening as Niall pushed it open to reveal a small chamber. Or what looked to be a small chamber. One would have to nearly stand on one's head to be certain what lay behind the barricade.

Gesturing grandly toward the opening, Niall motioned for her to enter.

"I cannot fit through there." The door was no higher than her waist.

"Would you like me to put you inside, Lady Ceara?" His question was gratingly polite while he stared at her with his soulless blue eyes, his small blade still flashing dully in the darkened corridor.

She would have been angry if she weren't thoroughly frightened. It had been bad enough stowing away in a cramped crate to make a sea crossing when she had followed Roarke. How would she manage to fit inside this tiny space with a crazed man hell-bent on hurting Roarke?

Then again, he presented her with little choice.

Dropping to her knees to crawl inside the chamber, she tried not to think about Roarke outside, frustrated as he wondered about her fate.

"You made a grave error taking me." She hadn't meant to speak the words aloud, but they seemed to jump out of their own volition.

Once she was inside the chamber, she realized it wasn't so small a space. The tiny door led to a normal-size room furnished with naught but a few heavy rocks and a pile of arrows. Weapons for defending the keep, she realized, her eye lifting to the lone arrow slit within the chamber while Niall crawled inside.

If she'd thought more quickly, she could have hit him with a rock. But he was in the room in no time, barricading the door behind them with an iron bar.

"Perhaps I have made a mistake, Ceara," he seemed to mutter to himself more than her as he hefted a few of the heavy stones in front of the small door for good measure. "I keep asking myself why on earth would Roarke come for you, when your permanent absence would allow him to choose another bride? Now that he's wed you like a dutiful subject to his king, he would be free to select another woman, mayhap even an English-woman."

Unwilling to converse on the subject, Ariana rubbed her hands along her arms, certain she must have cobwebs clinging to her gown after crawling through the short door.

More relaxed now that he had fortified their hiding place, Niall took the time to study her. "Surely he was drunk when he chose you for a bride. I have heard you do not even have a dowry."

Ariana stiffened—offended and frightened, too. Her ability to convince him Roarke valued her could be the difference between life and death.

"Then you have been misled, my lord. Possibly Roarke does not wish to jeopardize further grants from King Henry by admitting he wed a great heiress, but I assure you, my husband has every reason in the world to ensure my well-being." She twisted the truth to suit her purpose, since she possessed a dowry but it had been as small as her father could possibly make it.

Niall seemed to weigh the lie then laughed bitterly. "Now why doesn't that surprise me? Roarke is nothing if not a strategist. No matter what setbacks he encounters, my brother somehow makes them work to his advantage."

Ariana said nothing more. If Niall believed her and thought Roarke would indeed bargain for her, no harm would come to her.

"When Roarke first came to Southvale to introduce himself to my father," he rattled on, moving toward the arrow slit to peer outside the keep. "Miles proposed a fishing contest for a diversion while he stayed with us. While Roarke gathered wood to start the fire that would cook the fruits of our labor, Miles sneaked over and cut Roarke's fishing line to bits, just to see what he would do. Do you know that bastard tied the bits into a net and caught more fish that afternoon than Miles and I combined?"

Ariana shivered from the hatred in Niall's voice even as she applauded Roarke's resourcefulness. Would he be able to salvage this latest wayward act of his brother's and somehow extract her from the obscure tower room where Niall had installed her?

She said nothing, determined not to anger a man who seemed so unstable. And vengeful.

"He should have died by my hand a fortnight ago in France. Instead, he is alive and well and almost certainly in line to inherit my father's title." Niall turned away from the window and reached over to Ariana to lift a drooping black curl of her hair. "So it comes as no surprise that he was forced to wed a dreary little Welsh girl and turns around with a fortune."

Holding her tongue proved very difficult with a man whose vision of Roarke was so twisted. So unfair. Her skin crawled from his touch even though he had barely grazed her hair. "How can you begrudge Roarke his success when your father deliberately slighted him his whole life?"

"Hah!" He continued to toy with her hair, smoothing a lock between his fingers as he spoke. "Some would argue it was to Roarke's advantage not to be brought up at Southvale with Fulke judging him at every turn."

Ariana saw his point, but she was unwilling to concede it while his unwanted touch was upon her. She turned out of his reach, striding boldly toward the arrow slit so that she might look out the high window for herself, hoping maybe Roarke would see her. Find her. Save her.

A bird flew close to the keep, too fast to distinguish, but she couldn't help but wonder if it might be Griffin, who seemed to have appointed himself her stalwart companion.

Holding herself very still, she hoped Niall would content himself with anything but touching her again. Her heart slammed in her chest, sensing the danger just beneath Niall's perfectly groomed surface.

"And now we wait." His words seemed closer than they should be. As if he had moved closer.

She scanned the courtyard below for signs of Roarke but saw no one other than the men-at-arms milling about, staring toward the drawbridge that was…down?

Hope tingled in her chest. For all she knew, she stared at a different drawbridge than the one she and Niall had entered. But still, an entrance yawned wide open to the keep.

Assuring her Roarke would be inside. Looking for her.

A song resonated inside her; a soothing companion for her fears.

Then Niall's hands landed on her shoulders. She jumped, a cry springing to her lips although he had not touched her roughly.

"Since we have nothing else to do while we await a standoff with my father and his favored son, perhaps you would like to lie down?"

She'd sooner crawl naked through the chamber's cobwebs than lay anywhere near Niall Kendall. Her throat going dry with fear, she wrapped her arms around herself in a physical shield. "I am comfortable, thank you."

"I, however, am not." Without warning, he grabbed her around the waist and yanked her toward him. "Besides stealing Roarke's wife, I can think of only one other act that would taunt my half brother who can do no wrong in our father's eyes."

He backed her into a wall, her spine colliding with rough stone since her surcoat and tunic provided little protection.

No. A wave of fear rolled through her, filling her throat and making her go silent for one horrible moment. Her mouth moved, but no words came out. No sound.

He could not mean to do this.

"Nay!" Her voice returned in a hoarse splutter. She shoved at his arms even as he reached for her skirt. Kicking at his legs, she struggled to put space between them. Any space. He was suffocating her with his weight, his sweaty smell, his vengeful lust.

But although Niall was far more slender than Roarke, his strength easily overcame her. His mouth bruised hers in a punishing kiss.

Turning her head away, she vowed next time she would bite him. She kept clinging to the hope he would change his mind and not do this horrible thing.

"At last, I have thought of a way to slay that damnable pride of his." Niall smirked.

Squirming as much to the side as she could manage, she took advantage of his comment to fight back with logic. "He will kill you, Niall. And he will be well within his rights."

"Luckily, Roarke has far too much damnable honor to kill his own brother, lady. You have learned nothing about your husband if you do not realize that yet."

Laughing, he ran his hand leisurely up the curve of her body, resting appreciatively on her breast.

Through with the reasonable approach, Ariana spat in his face. As he raised his arm to strike her, she used her free hand to gouge her fingers into his eyes.

His scream mingled with the far-above cry of a merlin.

Chapter Sixteen

$\sim\!\!\sim\!\!\sim\!\!\sim$

Darkness closed around Roarke as he descended another one of Southvale's endless staircases, the last rays
of daylight too pale to penetrate the scant arrow slits
scattered along the outer walls. His father had given the
order for the drawbridge to be lowered and then
promptly disappeared within his mammoth keep, leaving Roarke on his own to locate Niall and Ariana.

After scavenging an extra blade and a small axe,
Roarke had taken off on foot to search the keep, comforted somewhat by the thought that if Niall sought to
use Ariana as a tool to bargain for Southvale, he would
be smart enough to keep her alive and well. Yet, no matter how many times he told himself that, a little voice
in his head kept reminding him Niall had tried to kill
his own flesh and blood—not once, but twice.

Heaven help his half brother, did he harm Ariana.

The thought of her with Niall, being subjected to his
anger and vengeful hatred… Hellfire, but he could not
think on it. Instead he forced his steps to be as quiet as

possible along the cold stone passageways, his ears straining for any sounds that might lead him to his wife.

His *wife,* damn it.

He'd never known such possessiveness as she had inspired in him. By God, when he found her, he would claim her for his own. For the first time in the ten years since he'd left his sins behind at Barret Keep to seek his own fortune, Roarke was willing to sacrifice the most honorable course of action for the selfish one. Keeping Ariana might not fill her need to be loved, but he would safeguard her always. Ensure that no other man ever touched her again.

Vowing not to squander away any more time with her once he got her back, Roarke wanted only to see her again. To hear her sing and hum as she rode along beside him, or whistling to her ridiculous bird—

Griffin.

Tightening his grip on the axe, he quickened his pace to the next narrow opening in the south tower wall. He wondered what had become of her ill-bred bird after Niall had stolen her. The thing had a skill for returning to her no matter where she wandered.

Peering out the window, he saw nothing. Heard nothing.

Plucking a torch from the wall as he reached the main floor of the keep again, he hastened to another tower. As he moved through one darkened passage after another, his thoughts wandered to the day he'd spent hawking with Ariana before the whole mess with Niall began. She had been softly warm and welcoming despite her innocence. Roarke had glimpsed heaven that day before her confounded bird delivered news of the French Guard.

He could no longer deny that he had come to care for Ariana Glamorgan.

Not only did he admire her courage, he was continually surprised at her clever mind and generous spirit when she dispensed her healing wisdom. A peculiar tightening in his chest came over him whenever she came near.

Ascending the next tower, he wondered how long it would take to find her. Indeed, he could not even tell if he moved in the right direction in the vast keep.

Until he heard the fearsome cry of a bird of prey.

Ariana's merlin.

Tearing through the shadows to the next arrow slit in the stone wall, Roarke paused. Leaned out the narrow opening as far as he could to see, hoping to hear Ariana's winged protector again. The cry he heard was not one of a bird, but the far-off shout of a man's rage.

The southwest tower. Adjusting his path toward the sounds, Roarke sprinted through the keep in the dark, still carrying the torch to illuminate the narrow passageways winding around the tall tower. He prayed the ill-begotten brancher would call out again, provide Roarke with some sign of Ariana's whereabouts.

He would torture Niall slowly before he gutted him. God's blood, but there could be no other answer. No other way to keep her safe.

Fresh air wafted toward him and Roarke paused his running long enough to peer out another window. Heart slamming wildly in his chest, he waited for two critical seconds, hoping for another clue. He heard nothing. Was just about to move away when a huge dark shadow swooped past him.

The bird.

As his vision struggled to adjust to the darkness of the night sky and the stone tower against it, he found the tell-tale movements he sought. A bird's wings flapping nearby. Circling a window just a little further up the tower.

His target found, Roarke scaled the steps. Sought an opening along the inky blackness of the stairwell. He nearly missed the low door in his haste. But then his brother shouted a torrent of cruel words that drew Roarke's eye to the small entryway with an iron cross-bar glinting dully in the light of his torch.

Stopping short, he prayed the bird would distract Niall. The small door was built to ensure defenders of the keep would have a jump on their opponents. Any-one seeking to enter such a room would be greeted with a rock to the head or an arrow in the back before they could shove their way inside.

Not that rocks or arrows could halt him now.

Hefting the axe high and aiming low, Roarke cleaved the doorway neatly in two on his first hack. Tossing the torch into the hidden chamber ahead of him, he chopped at the iron reinforcement bar. Bent it enough so he could squeeze through. And as he was sliding his way inside, he heard Ariana scream within.

That sound was all he needed to propel him the rest of the way through a rock barricade and into the room.

Once inside, it took a moment for his eyes to com-prehend what he was seeing, even with the help of the torch that had landed on the floor. His half brother was atop his wife, hands wrapped around her throat. Dress torn and shoulders covered in blood, Ariana struggled with the brute for only a split second before Roarke tossed him off of her with an inhuman cry that he scarcely recognized as his own. His rage filled his ears and blinded him to all but Niall, who had apparently failed to arm himself in his quest to injure a gentlewoman.

Not waiting for explanations, Roarke landed one blow after another to Niall's body.

"Roarke!"

Ariana called to him from a long way off, bringing him back from an unspeakably dark ledge. The control he had prided himself on for the last ten years had snapped, rendering him as dangerous and battle-hungry as ever his father had been.

"Roarke, I am fine." That soft, musical voice continued to appeal to him, blurring his focus on Niall's motionless form.

He looked up to find Ariana standing over him, bathed in blood. Smeared across her face, it stained the torn surcoat and tunic she wore.

Forgetting his brother, he rose on unsteady knees.

"Your face." He saw his hand shake as he brushed her hair from her sticky cheek where some of the red stain was beginning to dry. Fear delivered a blow that could not compare to any he had ever received in battle. "There is so much blood."

"It is not mine." She spoke soothingly. "At least most of it isn't."

Roarke thought it odd that she would try to comfort him when she had nearly been killed or heaven knows what else. Forcing himself to set aside his anger long enough to think about her, he lay his hands on her shoulders. Absorbed the soft feel of her. Alive. Warm. "What did he do to you?"

"He thought to injure you by forcing himself upon me." She shuddered. "But he did not succeed because you stopped him. And now that he is no longer a threat, you mustn't hurt him anymore."

Hellfire, but he would be the judge of that. He looked to Niall lying on the floor, his eyes closed in unconsciousness. "Sweet Mary, Ariana. He could have killed you."

"You are here now." Squeezing his hands for emphasis, she looked calmer than he felt. "I am fine."

Niall's groan interrupted their words. Roarke moved to go to him, but she held him back.

"Do not hurt him. It would be better for your king to punish him."

He nodded, knowing that if he killed Niall now, Fulke could easily twist the tale to Henry to make Roarke appear at fault. He did not trust his father's loyalties or his recent overtures. Though Roarke did not feel his half brother had suffered nearly enough for his actions, he contented himself with prodding Niall's still form with the toe of one mud-covered boot.

"I cannot move, Roarke." Niall's voice rasped thickly in the echoing, empty room.

"You have taken worse beatings in French brothels. If you have a care for your life, you will stay away from my wife for the remainder of your days. You can hole up here at your precious Southvale and horde all your father's wealth for comfort."

Niall's breath came out as a shuddered sigh, but still

he managed to glare at Roarke. "I will not let you steal it from me."

"I have not taken it. But seeing what you really are makes me reconsider why I should not. Southvale is too important to the king to be given into the keeping of someone so wicked."

Niall rose on one arm, his face bleeding profusely under one eye. "You did not arrange to take over Father's title?"

"Nay." Roarke nudged Ariana toward the door and backed away from his half brother. "You can dream about all your inheritance while we leave." Peering over his shoulder to be certain Ariana had safely left the room, Roarke indulged in one last swing of his fist, connecting soundly with Niall's jaw. "Sweet dreams, brother."

Ariana had never guessed it could be so sweetly satisfying to travel in the rain and dark.

At Roarke's side, however, she felt safe in the middle of a dark forest, the tall pine trees blocking out the little sliver of moon that loomed somewhere high above them. The horse's hooves fell more softly here on the bed of pine needles, the easy rhythm lulling her eyes closed until Roarke called for them to halt.

Blinking herself alert, she peered around to see the spot he'd chosen for them to camp now that they'd put Southvale many leagues behind them. Thank God. A meager cottage took shape in the darkness, possibly an abandoned hunter's dwelling or an outbuilding for a larger manor home somewhere nearby. Either way, the dilapidated structure looked like heaven to her tired eyes.

Her body sore from being dragged behind Niall up and down countless steps, she was grateful when Roarke held out his arms to help her from her horse. She slid down gingerly, her healer instincts warning her to be careful.

In no time, Roarke had a small fire burning in the narrow fireplace and blankets laid before the warmth of the blaze. While he went outside to collect fresh water from a nearby creek, she couldn't help but wonder what it would be like to lay in the warmth of his arms, as well. She changed quickly in his absence, casting aside her torn surcoat for a clean garment to sleep in.

Their shelter for the night was drafty and devoid of furnishings, but despite its vacancy, the place still held a pleasant scent of pine thanks to being nestled within a dense evergreen forest.

Settling herself into the blankets, Ariana's gaze moved over Roarke as he returned to the cottage, a wineskin filled with water for each of them. She drank greedily before running a damp linen over her face, her skin heating as she watched Roarke stalk about the one room hut, his big shoulders attracting her gaze.

When he could find no more chores he needed to accomplish, he lowered himself onto the blankets near where she had settled. Her heart thudded hungrily to be so close to him. Awareness of his every movement, his every breath, awakened her tired body.

Roarke took away the soiled linen she'd laid aside, then nudged a clean blanket toward her. "I'm sorry we ever set foot on Kendall lands, Ariana. And I swear to you that it's a mistake I will not ever repeat." He lifted a hand to her face, stroked the pad of his thumb across her cheek. "Do you want to tell me what happened back there?"

The warmth of his touch soothed her as no herb or potion ever could. She closed her eyes for a long moment, absorbing the feel of his skin on hers. Finally, she forced herself to share the details of her brief time with Niall, knowing that Roarke hurt for her, too. "At first, he was merely determined to use me as a means to negotiate the return of his father's lands since he was convinced you would steal his inheritance. But after he barricaded us into that hidden chamber, things spun out of control. He decided it would wound you more if he...defiled me before he returned me to you."

The muscles in Roarke's jaw flexed. In the warm glow of firelight, she discerned the flare of rage in his eyes that had not been abated by the beating he'd given his brother. "How did you stop him?"

"*You* stopped him, my lord. I could not have held him off a moment longer."

"But he was bleeding and hurt even before I arrived." The words faded away under his surcoat as he pulled the wet garment over his head, revealing more of his fine male form clad in only a damp tunic.

"I scratched one of his eyes." Her skills as a healer and knowledge of the body's most vulnerable areas had helped her know where to strike. "It slowed his advance, but not by much. He bled all over, but he didn't stop coming toward me."

"I never thought he would go this far." Roarke's dark brow furrowed, the anger in his gaze dissolving into something that looked more like tender concern.

"But perhaps I should have. Seeing him on top of you that way made me wonder again about what happened between Fulke and my mother. She never suggested that Fulke might have attacked her, but I have always known the Kendalls possess a propensity for violence."

She reached to lay her hand on his arm, to offer what comfort she could.

That small touch seemed to ignite a need within him for more. He wrapped his arms around her and pulled her near, burying his face in her hair. "I am so sorry."

Warmth stole through her. Comfort, too. Yet the tingling heat just beneath her skin was more than that. She cradled his face, savoring the rough feel of his bristly jaw in her palm. "You could not have known the lengths he would go to."

"We will put this behind us tomorrow." His green eyes locked on her as he settled her across his lap, her hip nestled against his thigh. "We ride for Glamorgan in the morning and need never think on this again."

Glamorgan.

Merciful heaven, but she'd almost managed to forget his need to return her to her father.

"Home." Her hand slid away from his face as she thought of facing her father. Of facing Ceara, who would fear Roarke and resent her cousin for consigning her to fate as his wife. "Of course."

"Unless…"

Her heart stopped, hanging on the word.

"Yes?"

"Unless you meant it when you said you would consider legalizing our vows in your own name."

Unblinking, she stared at him. Would he tease her so cruelly? His face was inscrutable.

"Do not toy with me, Roarke. You hold my fate and my cousin's in your hand, and I would rather not be given false hope."

Plucking her fingers from where they rested on the blanket, he smoothed his palm over the back of her hand. Absently examining the silver ring on her finger, he seemed to notice the clasp on one side of it.

"What is this?" he asked, tugging her hand closer. Examining the ring closely, he sprang the catch before Ariana could explain. Finely ground herbs spilled out on his hand.

"Oh, no!" She swept futilely at the powder, scattered farther by Roarke's impatience.

"What is it?"

"Black wort. Hold still!"

"What does it do?"

"It is a healing agent for many afflictions, and I have a very limited supply this year." She carefully scraped the remnants off Roarke's hand, now that he was still.

"Do you always keep it hidden here?"

"Hidden? Yes, I guess so." Pouring the powder back into the small compartment behind the face of the ring, she secured the latch once again. "But it is not as if I am trying to hide the herb, I merely carry a supply with me constantly. It is a miracle herb for bleeding wounds."

"Do many women possess rings of this sort?" His brow furrowed as if he were deep in thought.

"If they know anything about healing, they might. But I am afraid it is a dying art for many women. Why?"

"Marie Radborne has a ring like this. I was unaware it held such a compartment."

The wave of jealousy she felt surprised Ariana. "Just because it looked like this does not mean it concealed a chamber."

"It is of no matter." A warm smile took the place of the furrow in his brow. "You have not answered my earlier question, Ariana. Were you serious when you said you would legalize our vows using your own name?"

Hope sprang up in her, stronger and more vibrant than the fear and confusion that grew there, too.

"You must know I was perfectly serious, Roarke. It is my greatest wish." The words discomfited her, but they were true. She needed this marriage if she were to ever dispel the Glamorgan legend for future generations. More than that, she wanted Roarke Barret with a longing rooted deep in her soul. No matter that he said he could never love her. He still demonstrated more gentle regard for her than her father ever had.

Praying she did not misunderstand his meaning, she stared down at her hands, nervousness making her fingers pluck restlessly at the woolen blanket draped around her shoulders.

"I have been thinking." Reaching out to her, he brushed his hand through her hair that was still damp from their ride through the rain. Sword-callused hands smoothed over her shoulder.

"And?" Delicious shivers coursed through her.

"And I do not believe it would be fair to take your cousin to wife when she is so adamantly opposed to marriage." Thumb pressed into her palm, he lifted her hand to his mouth and grazed his lips across her fingertips.

Heat flooded through her, the chill of the rainy day forgotten in the warmth of his touch. "You would make her miserable."

"But I would not make you miserable, *mor-forwyn?*"

Placing her palm upon his chest, Ariana could feel the steady beat through the muslin of his tunic and a wall of hard muscle.

"Nay." She barely breathed the word, yet it seemed to draw Roarke closer. His lips slanted over hers, the scent of leather and rain filling her senses.

His tongue sought hers. Teasing. Tormenting. She kissed him back with all the fervor of pent-up desire, her arms twining about his neck so that she might arch into him.

For so long she had wondered about this. Wanted this. Ached for this. Now she could not feel enough of him, could not get close enough to all that warm male strength.

He groaned beneath her touch as her fingers quested down his tunic. Shifting positions, he leaned over her, his body pressing hers gently to the woolen blanket. "Roarke?"

"Ariana." The whisper of her name on his lips made her skin tingle and tighten.

"Please, I must know…"

Slowly opening emerald eyes, he half smiled at her. "Aye?"

"Do you truly intend to marry me?"

"Are you proposing?" His tongue darted out to lick the corner of her mouth, sending a sensual shiver straight through her to the juncture of her thighs.

"I have to know what your intentions are." Even

knowing the moment she had waited for nigh on three moons was at hand, Ariana found she wanted more than just for the curse to be broken. She wanted Roarke Barret.

Fingers skimmed down her neck, over her shoulder, to lie within the neckline of her tunic, where her skin met soft white linen.

"I intend to claim you for my own tonight, Ariana Glamorgan." He kissed the skin exposed above the linen. "Then I intend to stop at the first chapel I see in the morning and beg whatever holy man we find to wed us with all haste to uphold King Henry's chivalric code." With his thumb, he smoothed the place he'd kissed, breathing his words into her skin. "Then, when you are my wife in every way before man and God, we will return to Glamorgan Keep to ask your father's forgiveness."

"What of Marie?" It pained her to bring up the object of her jealousy, but she would know where he stood with the woman before she gave herself to him.

"I think I only courted her because my father wished it. And I'll admit that when I first met him, I was of a mind to please him." He paused in his kisses to answer her question with as much seriousness as it was proffered. "My eyes have since been opened with regard to both Marie and my father."

It was enough. Relief swept through her and she nodded, unable to speak for the lump in her throat.

"You are all I see, Ariana."

His lips touched hers, igniting the spark he started within her so many weeks ago. She moved against him, asking for more than he had given, wanting to be as close to him as she could be. She thought to ask him what had changed his mind, but half feared that more discussion might sway him to recant his decision. Besides, at last he was touching her, kissing her…thinking became too difficult.

The low groan in his throat held an animal note that vibrated right through her. He pressed her to the floor as he deepened his kiss, his tongue sliding along hers with a sensuality that left her dizzy. Hungry. Her hands sought the hem of his tunic to slide up his bare chest. He tore off the garment in a heartbeat, scarcely breaking his kiss. His body loomed above hers, as perfect as she remembered. Hewn of solid muscle and sprinkled with dark hair, his chest was a magnificent thing to behold. And even better to touch.

She ran her fingers over every ripple and hard plane, savoring everything about this man. She tugged him closer to her, silently urging him to let her feel more of his weight against her. His thigh nudged between hers, with only the fabric of her long tunic to shield her from him. Ribbons of pleasure fluttered up her thighs and snaked around her belly. Her womb. Her breasts tightened and ached from the press of his chest.

He kissed her until she cried out for more of his touch. Only then did he untie the laces of her tunic. Each lace trailed slowly across the skin between her breasts as he undid them until Ariana shivered with desire. The taut peaks of her breasts rose to meet his touch when he separated the halves of her garment with his hands.

Watching him stare at her in the firelight, Ariana warmed at his gaze.

"Perfect."

Her mind barely registered the word before his mouth was upon her, drawing circles around one tight crown with his tongue. The kiss left her breathless, her hips twitching helplessly at that intimate contact.

He growled with a primitive hunger as she slid her fingers into the dark silkiness of his hair. Urgent hands stripped off her tunic, rendering her deliciously naked against him. Shedding his own clothes in haste, Roarke covered her body before she had a chance to feel the chill of the night air on her skin.

And as much as she appreciated his thoughtfulness, she wouldn't have minded just a little longer to look at him. What she had spied both fascinated and scared her. A small amount of the hunger that filled her seeped away in newfound apprehension.

"Roarke. I am not sure…."

She could see the twinkle of humor in his eyes. "It is too late now, *mor-forwyn*. You should not have been so quick to goad me into action this night."

"But I wonder if—"

"Do not." He breathed the words across her lips before kissing her, his tongue mating with hers in a rhythm both primal and new.

Fear falling away by degrees, she relaxed against him. Unaware of how long he held her, kissed her and stroked her body, she only knew the hunger grew within her once again, erasing any misgivings she might have had. His clever tongue twirled around the peaks of her breasts, before moving lower.

Her breath caught in her throat as her fingers skimmed over his shoulders. And then he moved lower still until his whiskers chaffed along her thigh. A low gasp wrenched from her throat as he kissed the place where she burned for him most.

Heat swirled in her belly, flourishing still further when his fingers sought the womanly center of her, eliciting her cry for release.

"Please." The plea was breathy and ragged, dragged out of her by the sudden provocative invasion of his fingers.

"Ariana." He raised himself above her, his eyes meeting hers in the flickering firelight as he poised to take her. "You are mine."

He sheathed himself to the hilt, his whispered words and tender kisses dulling any pain she might have felt.

And as tears streaked down her cheeks unnoticed, Roarke filled her with greater pleasure than she ever guessed existed. His possession of her was so thorough, so complete, she could not even remember what it felt like to have his half brother's unwanted hands upon her.

Whether she'd broken the one-hundred-year-old Glamorgan hex, she could not be sure. But as she saw stars even with her eyes tightly closed, Ariana knew she had never felt so fulfilled, so happy—so full of pure magic.

Chapter Seventeen

Traveling with Ariana across his lap two days later made for slow progress over the frozen bogs of western England, but Roarke was loath to give her up. She fit neatly in the crook of his arm, the top of her head resting below his chin so that an occasional raven strand of silken hair caught on his unshaven jaw.

He traversed the densely wooded road in silence, reveling in his good fortune. Long accustomed to fighting with every bit of strength he possessed to obtain what he wanted, it amazed him that Ariana Glamorgan had fallen into his hands. Too blind to see her worth at first, Roarke thanked God his eyes were opened before he lost Ariana forever.

"Are we truly wed?" Ariana asked softly.

Though Roarke could not see her face, he knew she was staring at the wedding ring he placed around her finger for the second time this morning. "Think you the priest performed the ceremony in jest?"

"Think you he really was a priest?"

"I think the document we signed looks authentic enough." And that was good enough for him. No matter what any church said, Ariana Glamorgan would forever be his wife. He'd felt it clear through his soul the night he'd claimed her for his own.

He still couldn't think about it without wanting her again.

They'd seen no churches on their journey the previous day, but this morning they'd come across a collared man headed south, prayer book in hand. He had wed Roarke and Ariana amid much grumbling and protest, claiming he was in too great a hurry to see to the needs of those outside his personal flock. The holy man would not have performed the sacrament at all if not for Roarke's ridiculously generous donation.

"I've seen better manners on wild boars," she grumbled.

Roarke kissed the top of her head, savoring the rose scent of her hair. "Nevertheless you are well pleased at our marriage?"

She turned to look up at him, her cheeks flushed but a hint of mischief lurked in her amber eyes. "Very."

He knew she was thinking of the previous night. The weather had been cold but clear their second night on the road and they had slept pressed against one another for warmth. When they were not sleeping, they pressed closer still....

Blocking out the memories that assailed his senses, Roarke sat straighter in the saddle, determined to see Glamorgan before the end of the day. His Welsh wife posed a formidable threat to his control, a distraction he could not afford when he needed to be vigilant about keeping her safe. Now that he understood the full extent of Niall Kendall's desperation, Roarke planned to reinforce his keep, hire extra retainers and if need be, bankrupt his own coffers to do everything necessary to safeguard his wife.

Aware that Ariana would not appreciate the extent of his plans, he had delayed sharing them with her just yet. These two days alone with her had brought him both peace and pleasure he had never before known. He would not forsake their harmonious accord just yet.

"Glamorgan is not far off now." He peered around the landscape, recognizing a few landmarks from his trip to Wales two months ago. "If we ride separately, we will be there by the vespers hour."

When she did not answer, he looked down at her. A shadow clouded her face.

"Unless you prefer we wait until morning?" Despite his need to fortify Llandervey at once, it would be no hardship to spend another night alone with her.

"No," she whispered, though the throaty regret in her voice told Roarke she did not look forward to her reunion with her father.

"Do not worry, *mor-forwyn*. He will understand." Halting the horses, he punctuated the statement with a kiss, wanting to erase the fear from her eyes. "And even if he does not, there's naught he can do to you now that you are under my protection."

Sliding his lips over hers, he pulled her against him, twining his hand through the long black skein of hair that draped her slender form. Her tongue greeted his with the knowing caress of a long-time lover, welcoming him and heating him throughout.

She looked sufficiently dazed when he released her, but no more so than he felt. Settling her atop her own mare, he allowed his fingers to stray beneath her cloak and gown for the briefest of moments, his hands hungry for the feel of her long legs.

"Roarke!" Her flushed surprise at his touch erased all remnants of the fear in her eyes.

Smoothing her gown back into place, he remounted, eager to have the confrontation at Glamorgan Keep behind them. He knew he could make Ariana's father appreciate the need to keep her safe at Glamorgan until he could strengthen Llandervey's defenses.

But he was not at all sure his Welsh wife would understand.

"I am amazed it took you this long to come back."

The Lord of Glamorgan did not appear surprised to see them. Roarke thought the elderly man looked older than a mere three moons ago. Glamorgan's awkwardly crafted seeing glass scrunched into place with a hard squint.

Ariana knelt by her father's hearthside seat, worry etched in her brow along with a liberal dose of guilt. "I am so sorry to have worried you, Father."

"You did what you thought was right."

Glamorgan's behavior puzzled Roarke. Ariana's father should have been furious with both of them. Indeed Roarke had never understood why Glamorgan had not sent his men after Ariana once he realized her deception on their wedding day. Did he care so little for her? The man paid scarce attention to Roarke, and seemed even more deeply morose than the last time Roarke had visited.

Something was wrong.

A feminine shriek interrupted his musings.

"Ariana!" A fair creature with voluptuous curves and short cinnamon ringlets stood framed in the portal.

"Ceara!" Ariana gasped, smiling for the first time since they'd arrived.

Hurrying to one another, the cousins embraced, laughing and teary-eyed at the same time.

"You look so beautiful!" The exclamation came from both of them simultaneously, calling forth more laughter and hugs.

Anxious to explain their visit to Ariana's family, Roarke introduced himself to Ceara, earning a frankly reproving look from Ariana's young cousin. At a loss to understand the strange undercurrents at work in the hall, he launched forward with his story. "I am sure you are wondering why we are here today, unannounced, in the early days of winter."

"I am only surprised it took you this long to return my daughter to me," Glamorgan muttered again, talking more to himself than to anyone else in the hall.

"I originally intended to return Ariana to you so I might wed the woman you truly offered me, Lord Thomas—your niece Ceara."

He ignored Ceara's dramatic intake of breath, thanking the merciful heavens he would not be taking Ariana's convent-bound cousin to wife.

"When I discovered the truth of my bride," he continued, hoping to smooth things over with Ariana's father. "I was incensed at her deception and felt disloyal to you and your generosity by keeping Ariana."

"But you are not returning her?" Thomas leaned forward in his chair, his voice hopeful for the first time since their arrival.

"No. I came here to extend my apologies and to tell you that I have remarried your daughter using her real name."

Glamorgan and Ceara both stared at Ariana, as if waiting for her to speak, perhaps expecting her to confirm his statement.

"Does that mean…?" Glamorgan rose slowly from his chair, his gaze shifting from Ariana to Roarke. "Have you already…?"

Roarke waited for him to finish his sentence, certain Glamorgan could not possibly be asking the question Roarke thought he was asking in front of his innocent niece and his own daughter.

"You are truly wed then?"

"We crossed paths with a preacher bound for London this morning. We were married again using Ariana's real name."

Glamorgan shook his head impatiently. "No, no. I mean is the marriage consummated?"

Ariana's cheeks burned bright red, her gaze never wavered from Roarke's.

"Yes, but I really do not think—"

His words were drowned out by the Lord of Glamorgan's loud whoop.

"Merciful saints, you did it." The old man rose slowly, a broad grin upon his weathered face as he moved to embrace his daughter. "Your mother always said you would show all of Wales that the house of Glamorgan would be strong again. I am sorry I did not have more faith in you, daughter."

Roarke watched his wife's eyes fill with tears even as she smiled, knowing how much she must savor her sire's approval, even though it had been ridiculously late in arriving. Glamorgan's acceptance boded well for Roarke's other plans.

The plans he had not yet shared with his wife.

He hoped she would forgive him for what he needed to do, but truly, he had little choice.

Ceara turned to Roarke while Ariana dried her eyes. "You will be staying with us for a few days, my lord? Ariana's people have missed her in her absence and I'm sure they will all join us in celebrating your marriage anew."

His gaze met Ariana's and he reveled in the warmth of her amber eyes for a few final moments before he delivered the news she would not want to hear.

"Alas, I must return to Llandervey in all haste to make fortifications to my new keep." Turning to Lord Glamorgan, Roarke could not meet his wife's eyes any longer. "But I had hoped that you would welcome Ariana to stay with you for the winter while I strengthen my defenses. It seems I have made an enemy of my half brother and I would not bring her back to my keep until I can be certain it is fit to keep her safe."

Niall would never think to look for Ariana here considering he did not even know her real name.

Ariana's sharp intake of breath came as no surprise, but he had not expected her disappointment to hurt him so deeply.

Glamorgan cleared his throat as if to answer, but his

daughter interrupted him. "My lord, I have every faith in your sword arm as well as your stalwart keep. I would feel safest at your side."

She moved into his field of vision so that he was forced to look at her. See her dismay. The answering ache within him reminded him exactly why he needed some time apart from her. Not only did he need to secure his keep. He would be wise to fortify his heart, as well. Caring for her was costing him dearly.

"My best knight, Collin, is still in France with Henry." He brushed his hand down along her arm, feeling the tension radiating through her slender body. "Without his help to oversee training the new men-at-arms, I will be burdened night and day all winter long, and I will not install you anywhere that compromises your safety."

Her cheeks flushed darkly as her cousin moved closer to wrap a comforting arm around Ariana. But Ariana, it seemed, did not wish to be comforted. She shook off Ceara's arm and stepped closer to him, pointing a slender finger in his face.

"Very well then, my lord. If you are in such a hurry to leave my presence then I wish you Godspeed. I will not keep you if you want to go." Her voice trembled with anger. Hurt.

And although her lone finger made a more effective weapon than many a blade he'd battled in his day, he could not regret his decision when it would ensure her protection.

Thomas Glamorgan cleared his throat again, straightening long-stooped shoulders. "I would be honored to safeguard my daughter for you until you can return for her. I vow she will come to no harm under my care."

Roarke nodded gratefully even though he could feel the rebuke in Ariana's eyes clear down to his toes. Hell-fire, he had not expected this to be so difficult. Still, even if he'd earned his wife's anger, he had at least given her father a chance to reclaim his honor and right an old wrong.

It would be small comfort over the cold months ahead.

Ariana had waited and waited to speak to Roarke alone that night. But he'd found much to do about Glamorgan, searching the town for able-bodied men to help him make repairs at Llandervey. She suspected he was also avoiding her, the same way his eyes had avoided hers when he delivered his devastating news in front of her father.

Now she'd given in and laid down to sleep, her pillow damp with tears. She wanted a chance to confront him. To demand her right to be at his side. But she could hardly do so if he never came to her bed.

Of course, she *had* told him to go ahead and leave, allowing her temper to get the better of her. She could not believe she had spoken so boldly to him. Her father had hurt her many times with his cold actions and cutting words. But she had never decried his behavior.

Then again, she'd never felt as at ease with her father as she had become with Roarke over the last three months. Up until tonight, he had always seemed to care for her welfare, even if he did not hold her in tender regard. Perhaps his solicitous concern had given her a false sense of comfort with him.

Or maybe it had been the intimate way he'd treasured her body when they lay together that had her believing he felt more for her than he did. The last two nights on the road had given her a glimpse into what marriage could be like. And now that she'd had a taste of those sensual joys and teasing conversations that marked her time alone with Roarke, she did not want to give them up.

So why should she?

Rising to a sitting position in her bed, she peered into the flames that danced in her hearth, recalling the way Eleanor had given her a charm to make that first night she'd had dinner with Roarke. The wisewoman had encouraged her to put all her hopes and wishes into those useless herbs she had mixed, convincing Ariana that somehow that potion would give her all the magic she needed to make Roarke truly see her.

Ariana had since decided that the only thing valuable about that harmless charm was the way it had gathered her courage and allowed her to be free of her own fears. What if she could be so daring now, without the herb mixing and the chanting? What if she simply focused all her determination on making her wishes come true?

She was not the same woman she'd been three months ago. She'd stowed away on a royal ship. Tamed a merlin that no one else could train. Faced down Niall Kendall and had managed to hold him off until help arrived. Surely she could make Roarke Barret see reason.

Sniffling, she dried her cheeks and flipped over her

pillow, vowing to fight for her husband. If she could overcome the legendary power of the Glamorgan hex, could she not overcome the stubborn resistance of one man?

He could not resist saying goodbye.

Roarke gathered his things and moved silently through the keep the next morning, knowing he couldn't leave without seeing Ariana once more. He held his food rations from the kitchens in one hand, his bag in the other as he strode through the darkened corridor toward the main door. All was in readiness for his trip to Llandervey except a few final words to his wife.

He had not slept at all after she'd bade him good riddance, preferring to gather men and supplies for his household rather than face her anger. Or admit his own hurt. But he could not put off a visit to her chamber any longer, his need to kiss her one last time too strong to ignore.

Prying open the heavy door to the courtyard, Roarke stepped out into the first rays of morning and promptly spied Ariana. Not tucked in her warm bed, but dressed and mounted on her horse, ready to ride.

Hellfire.

"Good morning, my lord," she called across the stony courtyard, smiling at him in spite of the soft snowflakes quietly blanketing the ground. "A lovely morning for a ride, is it not?"

A stable boy brought out his horse and led it beside hers while the townspeople he'd hired the night before began gathering nearby with their small sacks of belongings to make the trek to Llandervey.

"Ariana." He nodded a cool greeting, unwilling to argue with her in front of her people. "You must wait to go riding until after your father is awake and can send someone with you."

"But I am not taking any idle ride, my lord." She gestured airily to her packed bag attached to her saddle. "I am ready to return home with you." Lowering her voice, she reached down to stroke her mare's neck, in effect leaning closer to him, as well. "I'm eager to speak to my maid about the matter of the poisoned wine on our wedding night since I did not have time to discuss it with her before I followed you to France."

"All the more reason it is unsafe for you to return with me now. I will not endanger you further by bringing you into an unstable household." He checked over his horse and loaded his supplies for the trip in an effort not to look at her.

Never had his wife appeared more beautiful. She'd left Glamorgan last time dressed in another woman's clothes. Now she seemed to have delved into her own finery for the lavish red tunic she wore and the dark blue cape emblazoned with fanciful Celtic creatures. A silver clasp held the cape about her shoulders while the hood sloped over her face to frame pink cheeks and bright amber eyes.

Hadn't he been trying *not* to stare at her? Frustrated, Roarke took his seat atop his horse and hoped he did not have to carry her back into the keep himself. Surely he could make her see reason.

"You endanger me far more by leaving me here," she returned, head held high. "Although I am grateful to have made some small measure of peace with my father, you must know that he has never treated me with kindness. Would you honestly prefer I spend this winter here as I have spent every other winter of my life—abandoning the keep on a daily basis? I cannot abide the somber tone of his company for long, my lord, and will surely need to visit the mews or seek out my former nurse who was long ago banished because she could not meet my father's approval."

She could not have seized a more effective weapon with which to convince him. He did not approve of the way her father had treated her in the past. No man would ever again tell his wife she was unworthy in any way. "Things will be different with your father now."

He had to believe that.

"Maybe. But how could you think I would want to spend weeks with the man I fought so hard to escape? And moreover, why should I trust that my father will come to care for me now when he had no use for me the last nineteen years?" She stared at him as a veil of snow fell between them, a chilly barrier where once there had been warm accord.

"But you will be safer here." And he would be safer if she was here, damn it.

"Can you be so sure of that? If Niall were to show up here tomorrow threatening retribution, what's to stop my father from simply bewailing his fate and thinking he continues to be accursed? And why would he go out of his way to protect me when his lands have always come before me? His shadows run deep, Roarke, and although our nuptials have cheered him, I promise you that no amount of happy news in his life will ever heal him fully."

Roarke recalled Glamorgan's morose state on his

last visit, acknowledging that Ariana might have more insight into her father's dark moods than Roarke could.

And recognized that he had no choice but to bring her with him.

"Very well then, Ariana. You may join us today." Frustration gnawed at him when he had too many things on his mind, too many potential enemies to guard against. "But know this if you choose to come to Llandervey. I will not take unnecessary risks where you're concerned. For your own safety, you will be little better than imprisoned to a secure section of the keep."

She blinked. Nodded. "Fine. But in turn, may you know this. I have never met a prison that has succeeded in holding me for very long."

Chapter Eighteen

Her husband did not prove to be pleasing company on their ride to Llandervey, but even so, Ariana remained content with her small victory. Though she had no wish to be locked within protected walls for months on end, her habit of thinking cheerful thoughts in spite of her circumstances kept insisting that she could change his mind.

They had arrived at Roarke's keep well before nightfall, the smoke from a hundred small cottages surrounding Llandervey's walls wreathing the village in a gray fog as snow mounted at every doorstep. A few brave souls ran out to greet the returning lord, mostly children, but also a few young men who perhaps hoped to seek favor and find work at the keep.

Ariana's heart caught at the thought that these people would look to her and Roarke for their welfare and their security. She had brought all her herbs with her three months ago on her first trip to her new home by the sea. But she had left so quickly that she had not been able to visit the villagers to see if anyone needed healing. A fact she would quickly remedy just as soon as she could make Roarke see reason.

He barely spoke to her as they entered the keep. After he dispatched orders to one of his men to guard Ariana, he closeted himself in a private chamber with his steward. Roarke had left Ariana alone and under the watchful eye of a surly looking man-at-arms who had been told to contain her to the northwest tower. A huge prison, all things considered. But it would hardly help her plans for meeting the villein.

Having already won her victory for the day, she retired to the northwest tower where all her belongings lay in wait for her. Although she wondered if Roarke would ever come to her again in his anger with her, she soon lost track of time as she organized her things and reacquainted herself with her healing supplies. She only realized she'd missed supper when a knock sounded at her door. Her fire growing cold in a room full of shadows, she thought the hour must be late.

She bade the newcomer enter, fully expecting to see Emlyn with a tray for her.

Roarke entered the room instead, his dark surcoat strapped about his hips, his sword still lashed to his side. Snow clung to his dark hair as if he'd just come in from outside. In fact, he brought the scent of cold wind and pine into the chamber with him.

He also seemed to bring a bit of temper.

"You are not so much of a prisoner that you cannot attend your meals." He blasted into his speech without prelude, his voice slightly elevated. "Confound it, Ariana, I would not have brought you with me if I thought you would create more difficulties."

Setting aside a small store of herbs she needed for a tincture she planned to make, Ariana rose to face him. "It was not my intention to create any difficulties. I simply lost track of the time."

They stood gazing at one another in the dim light from the dying fire, and she couldn't help but think what activities they'd been engaged in the two nights before he'd taken her back to Glamorgan. By the time the moon had risen this high in the sky, they had been well entwined around one another, their bodies fitting together in the most delicious ways. As her fingers itched with the need to touch him now, she couldn't help but wonder if Roarke's thoughts mirrored her own.

"Then perhaps you should go eat now." Some of the tension seemed to slide out of his rigid shoulders. "'Twould not be wise to have you waste away from weakness when I endeavor to strengthen the whole of Llandervey by spring."

She couldn't help but smile at the image. "Then perhaps I will join your men in the practice yard some morn, my lord. I have always wondered what it would be like to wield a sword."

Recalling the way it felt to have his hands upon her, she reached to touch him, her fingers trailing over the dense muscle of one thick arm. "It certainly seems to have given you plenty of strength."

A spark flared in his eyes as he stilled her fingers in his own, halting the progress of her questing hand. "Aye. But not enough where you're concerned."

He smoothed his palm over her cheek with slow deliberation, then sifted his fingers through her hair.

Her heart jumped at the thought she could sway this

strong warrior. Still, any methods of persuasion she possessed paled in comparison to the weight of his words. His rules. She would be his captive here until he said otherwise. "Any strength I have is nothing compared to yours."

"I disagree. You seem to have a knack for wielding power, wife." Whatever anger Roarke had felt toward her, he seemed to transmute it into a physical hunger he could ill disguise. "Yet I wonder if you are prepared to contend with what you have wrought tonight?"

Ariana gazed up at him, so intense and so close. The dancing hearth blaze lit him from behind, creating a fiery glow all about him. "Had I known I possessed the power to make you touch me, Roarke, I would have employed it weeks ago."

His lips crushed hers in a kiss that gave no quarter. Massive hands bound her to him in a fierce embrace as Ariana forgot all about herbs and tinctures and organizing her belongings. She only wanted Roarke. Here. Now.

She did not care if he still harbored resentment toward her for maneuvering her way into staying by his side. The kiss he gave her was fraught with as much desperation and hunger as she had felt last night alone in her bed.

And for now, that was enough.

Roarke watched Ariana's eyes close in sensual abandon and knew she yearned to be with him as much as he longed for her. *Thank God.* He didn't know how he would have found the strength to pull away if she had protested, but he would have forced himself to manage it.

Although part of him had been furious to see her mounted and ready to ride to Llandervey this morning, he had also admired her boldness. And now that she was here under his roof and she was his wife in every way, there was no longer any reason to deny himself the pleasure her body offered him. For that matter, he hadn't lain with her since the priest had married them two mornings ago. Tonight, he would enjoy her knowing that she would remain his forever.

A small sigh escaped her lips as he rained kisses down her throat. He licked and tasted, the warmth of his breath intensifying the lavender scent of her skin. Tugging at her tunic, he freed the silken fabric just enough to expose the tops of her breasts and the enticing hollow that lay between them. He was ready for her now, his body hard and hungry after their night spent apart. But he would not take her on the floor of her solar.

Lifting her into his arms, Roarke marveled at her trust as she sagged against him, her arms twining easily about his neck. Didn't she know he meant to ravish her senseless? Shoving the door to her bedchamber open with his boot, Roarke squeezed her against him. After weeks of denying himself, he could not wait to touch and taste her, to wring cries of pleasure from her lips.

He fell into the mattress with her, their combined weight plummeting them into a soft sea of linen-covered feathers. In the low light from the hearth fire, Roarke could see her hair fanned out around her, blanketing the pristine sheets with silky dark locks. And he was overwhelmed by the way she gave herself to him even though she surely hadn't forgiven him for attempting to leave her behind.

All his life he'd struggled to find something to call his own—first as a second son in the shadow of his brother Lucian, later as a bastard—yet the reward of his own keep didn't awe him the way Ariana did. She had chosen him even before he chose her. And she belonged to him in ways a pile of stones and mortar never would.

She shifted against him, her twitching thighs calling him to take her. Claim her again and again. Unable to deny himself any longer, he tore through the rest of the long laces of her tunic to expose all of her creamy pale skin.

He could not resist the feast her body presented. She seemed uniquely made for him, a treasure he would hoard to himself for the rest of his life.

"Ariana." Her name rasped in his throat and sighed over her damp flesh as he fed upon her breasts, circling the taut peaks of her nipples with his tongue until she whimpered with need.

Ah, but he needed her so much more. Spending last night away from her had been torture, and thinking of spending months away from her had been even more painful. Now, he couldn't get enough of her delicate scent, her soft skin against his.

Hands roaming over her shoulder and belly, hips and thighs he found soft curves and warm willingness, her broken cries urged him to shove aside the voluminous folds of her skirts. To seek the center of her heat.

Her thighs parted at the slightest brush of his fingertips. He sought the soft curls at the summit of her thighs, finding her slick with readiness for him. Hunger surged through him, almost painful in its sharp ache. He yanked his tunic over his head and shed his braies, needing her around him. All over him.

When he finally eased between her thighs, Ariana whimpered with need. Triumph surged through him along with desire. Steadying her curved hips with his hands, he edged his way inside her. Her fingers scratched lightly at his back, her leg twining about his to urge him closer. Deeper.

He stared down at her flushed cheeks, her teeth biting into her lower lip and the wanton image of his sensual wife emblazoned itself in his mind. He'd always held himself back just a little before, unwilling to lose the hard-won control he'd prided himself on these last ten years. But she'd seen him at his worst with Niall. And she'd given herself to Roarke anyway. If anything, she'd fought to be at his side.

And still she urged him farther, her hips lifting to meet his every thrust. Both legs twining about him now until he could not hold back anything. Heat radiated through him along with a fierceness he had not expected. He clamped her hips to his and took her again and again. Possessed her more fully than ever.

As the first blinding waves of his release rolled over him, Roarke knew that at last she was truly and completely his. And God help him, he would never let her go.

Chapter Nineteen

Snow blanketed all of Llandervey the following week, coating the landscape in winter white. Roarke had commanded fortifications for the keep, but he had also dispatched workers to make repairs on numerous homes in the village after seeing the sorry state of living conditions throughout the small town. He had spent the greater part of the day in the village and then visited a few outlying homes built farther from the city walls.

As he rode back toward the keep, he began noting all the news he needed to relay to Ariana. She'd been frustrated at not being allowed to ride out with him today, but he did not want her outside Llandervey's sturdy walls.

They'd settled into an uneasy truce since returning home. Although she remained frustrated at not being given freedom to move about the town at her leisure, she had accompanied him twice to visit the village to provide her healing aid to families in need of her skills. And she had welcomed him to her bed each night, always greeting him with wordless kisses and heated caresses, driving him to depths of passion he had not known existed.

But he wondered if those sizzling nights they shared would be enough for her. Indeed, they spoke to one another less in the whole last week then they had in those mere two days on the road between Southvale and Glamorgan. Ariana might be willing to share her body with him, but she seemed to have retreated from him in every other way.

And, strangely, he missed her.

Clearing the last rise to the east of his keep, Roarke vowed to speak to her about it. Even ten years after leaving Barret Keep he remembered the way Lucian had treated his wife Melissande. Roarke could not imagine his elder half brother allowing his mate to brood quietly when something was wrong. Surely Roarke could approach Ariana and figure out a way to alleviate whatever unhappiness kept her from speaking to him openly.

To demonstrate concern for her did not mean he had fallen in love.

He'd just hit the top of the hill when he heard shouting. Peering down from the small hill outside the city walls, he spied a long, dark line of men on horseback snaking from the north down to Llandervey. The men at the front of the line were already at his gate. The back of the line trailed into the dense forest behind them. At least one hundred and fifty men marched to the keep, battle-ready and bearing a blue-and-gold standard.

The crest of Lucian Barret flew above them.

The half brother he'd grown up with had come all the way to Wales to see him.

Pride filled him at the thought of welcoming the brother he'd long admired into his own keep now that he'd made his own way in the world. Taking stock of the situation before moving to greet his guests, Roarke could see down into the outer ward from his vantage point. It seemed the keep's occupants scurried about making rudimentary preparations for a possible siege. Because Roarke no longer bore the same standard as his Barret brother, the people of Llandervey had no way of knowing whether the new arrivals were friend or foe. Supplies were being brought into the inner bailey. Water was being pumped and carried within at a furious rate. The few men-at-arms Roarke had begun training were gathering weaponry to haul up on the parapets for use on the enemy.

In the midst of it all, was Ariana.

A spot of rich, royal blue amid a sea of drab stone, she stood on the outer wall with a man, probably his steward. As she pointed down the length of the wall, Roarke was pleased to see the man hurry to where she indicated with his arm full of arrows.

Although it made him proud to know Ariana would be concerned enough to circulate among the household in his absence, he couldn't help but wonder where the hell was her guard charged with making sure she did not leave the northwest tower.

But he would settle the matter later. Right now he needed to inform Llandervey's people that there would be no siege today.

Riding down the hills to the keep, he plowed through the gold-and-blue line to his gates, and spied the broad-shouldered man lounging alongside his mount at the front of the assembly. And although it made Roarke's heart glad to see his Barret kin, he could not deny a twinge of guilt, too. He'd never forgiven himself for the selfish acts of his youth that had nearly cost Lucian his keep.

"You are a long way from home, brother," Roarke called to Lucian before he slid from his horse to greet him.

"And it seems you are home at last, Roarke." Lucian embraced him, thumping his back too hard in the same manner they had as boys. "Congratulations on a fine keep."

"Do you ride to France to take your turn abroad?" Roarke knew Henry had returned to England until after winter, but he needed men in Normandy to hold his lands.

"Aye. We make for the coast tomorrow, but I thought to see Llandervey for myself first. Can you house us for the night?"

"It would be our pleasure." Roarke was already giving the signal to his guards for the gates to be lowered. "You can meet my wife."

Lucian grinned. "Melissande threatened to turn me out if I did not meet the newest member of the Barret clan. I look forward to meeting Lady Ceara."

Dozens of mounted knights and men-at-arms rode past them into the keep's walls, the ground rumbling with the force of one hundred sets of hooves.

"Actually, she is Lady Ariana." Roarke had sent word to Henry of his bride's identity when he informed his king about Niall's crimes. Although he had not heard back from his sovereign as of yet, he'd hoped the matter would not present a problem. "'Tis a long story that requires a few rounds of ale for the telling. Will you join us for supper this eve?"

Lucian could not hide his surprise. "Ariana? God's blood, Roarke. You have more trouble holding on to a bride than any man I have ever met. I will gladly join you for the meal and meet this wife of yours."

As they strode into the keep together leading their horses behind them, Roarke enjoyed standing beside his brother again, remembering that his roots were not so tainted after all. No matter that he was the son of a Kendall father, Roarke still possessed the honor of his Barret blood.

"She is a healer," Roarke explained, pointing out Ariana on the parapets. "And a bit of a warrior, it seems, when it comes to protecting our home."

"I have no doubt of her strength if she hauled you to the altar at last." Lucian's dark eyes followed Ariana's progress on the wall until she disappeared behind a high crenellated fortification. "Perhaps she was fated for you all this time."

Roarke could not credit the thought. If anything, Ariana should have belonged to a man who could have given her his whole heart. But he said nothing, instead leading Lucian into the inner bailey and pointing out his chamber.

Lucian took a few steps toward his rooms and then stopped. "However you came to wed this woman, Roarke. I want you to know that Melissande and I are both very happy for you."

His words echoed in Roarke's mind for a long moment as he took in Lucian's somber expression. In all of ten years, it had never occurred to Roarke that his brother might still bear some guilt at having fallen in love with the woman Roarke had chosen first.

"If Ariana was fated for me, I assure you Melissande was long destined to be yours. It seemed everything happened for a reason." Roarke edged backward to find his wife and leave his brother to wash for the meal, his heart lighter than it had been in a long while. "You are most welcome brother, and I look forward to drinking you under the table at dinner. You have not tasted ale until you've tried the Welsh variety."

Ignoring Lucian's scoffing protests, Roarke hastened outside to speak with the woman fate had chosen for him.

After meeting Niall Kendall, Ariana had never expected a visit from one of Roarke's brothers to be such a happy occasion. But as she watched Roarke and Lucian Barret share laughter and trade accounts of their adventures growing up, she had to admit the visit had been very good for her husband.

As the brothers dined on fresh fowl provided in large part thanks to Griffin's efforts, Ariana sipped her mulled wine and observed the similarities between the two men who shared the high table in the great hall with her. The chatter of conversation and clank of serving platters faded from her mind as she focused on naught but the brothers. Lucian loomed even broader than Roarke, but Roarke rose slightly taller. They both shared dark hair, with Roarke's being a shade lighter. And where Lucian's dark eyes were fathomless and deep, her husband's emerald gaze was more subject to his moods, changing from the color of fresh spring grass to the deep hue of a churning sea when angered.

Despite the minor differences, Roarke and Lucian shared much more in common than Roarke had with Niall Kendall. Lucian's dark eyes went warm with love when he spoke of his wife and children. Well-spoken and articulate, he had been exceedingly diplomatic throughout Roarke's explanation of how he'd married both Ceara Llywen and Ariana Glamorgan. For that alone, he earned Ariana's respect.

But more than anything else, Lucian seemed to hold his younger half brother in high regard, a fact which touched her healer's heart and made her hope that Roarke would come to peace with himself one day. From Roarke's stories of his past, she gathered that he felt guilty about the wrongs he'd done to this brother in the past. Yet it was clear to her that Lucian had not only forgiven him; he embraced him as an honored equal.

She rose as the hour grew late, thinking to leave the great hall to the men. They were on their feet in an instant, nearly knocking over a bench in their haste.

"Please, do not rise on my account. I would retire now, my lords, but I invite you to make merry long into the night." She backed away from the table, her feet moving quietly over the stone floor. "Lord Barret, I am glad to have you at Llandervey and I wish you would extend our hospitality to your lady wife and family if ever you should care to visit."

While Lucian sketched a low bow and spoke his thanks, Roarke cleaned his eating knife and tucked it into his belt before moving toward her.

"I would join you, my lady." Her husband's gaze had taken on that dark green hue, but she didn't think he was angry tonight.

Wrapping an arm about her possessively, Roarke gave her no chance to escape quietly. Nor, in truth, did she want to. Even if their days had fallen into a pattern of cool distance, their nights together had her sighing dreamily all day long, wishing she could break those last barriers between them.

After bidding Lucian good-night and safe journey on the morrow, Ariana sought the corridor that would lead to her tower. Roarke's footsteps echoed behind her for a moment, then settled into pace beside her.

"I did not mean to interrupt your company." She walked along beside him, wondering what it would be like to incline her head to rest on his broad shoulder.

"Nay. Lucian should have retired long ago." Roarke plucked a torch from the wall of the drafty corridor as they neared the staircase to her chamber. "I will awake with him at first light so we might say farewell."

As they reached her door, Roarke reached for the key that hung from a slender chain about her waist. The brief warmth of his hand against her thigh set tremors of anticipation shooting through her.

Unlocking the wooden entryway, he escorted her in and flung himself into a chair before the fire to gaze into its flames.

Was he staying?

His presence dominated the room. The magnificent furnishings and the intricate stained glass could not compete with Roarke Barret. Every line, every sinew of his body bespoke its strength. He was a knight exemplified, hewn to perfection, imbued with a warrior's grace.

Ariana could see why Ceara had feared him. No doubt the man stirred fear in the hearts of many formidable knights on a battlefield, too. But when Ariana looked at him, she saw wisdom and compassion in his eyes, as she had from the moment she first spied him in Glamorgan's great hall.

Roarke laughed as she went to fill their cups with wine, jarring her out of her pleasurable contemplation of his masculine form.

"What is it?" Ariana had not witnessed his laughter in much too long.

"That is a sound I have not heard in quite some time."

"What sound?" She balanced two bone cups and a flask before handing one to him.

"You're singing."

"Was I?"

"Are you unaware of it?" Draining the cup, he studied her. "When you are happy, you are always singing or humming some light, cheerful tune. It is like having a minstrel forever at my side."

"Do you mind it, overmuch?" Turning her gaze to his, she willed him to say "no," to find some redeeming characteristic in her. To care for her just a little.

"I did not realize until this moment how much I have missed it." His eyes beckoned her.

Like one in a dream, Ariana walked to his chair. Sword-worn hands wrapped around her waist, pulling her on top of him.

"Your song calls to me, *mor-forwyn*." Tracing a line

from temple to chin with his thumb, he wrapped his hand about her neck beneath the wave of midnight hair. "Siren. You work magic on me."

Lulled by his voice, she found herself mesmerized by his touch. "Nay. 'Tis no more than you use on me."

Drawing his thumb across the fullness of her lower lip, the sensual swirl began in the pit of her belly. It seemed forever since he had touched her like this, with infinite tenderness. Their nights together of late had been filled with fire and sparks, but she found she had craved this gentleness, as well. How easy it would be to get caught up in the play of the senses, the pleasure wrought by his touch. But she had realized sometime tonight as she gazed at Roarke Barret in the great hall that she had fallen in love with him.

A grave mistake perhaps, considering he had as good as promised her he could never love her in return. Yet there could be no help for the matter. She simply found herself drawn to him. She admired his commitment to honor—a characteristic she especially appreciated after growing up with her miserly father.

And she had found surprising glimpses of masculine charm underneath Roarke's dark moods and determined efforts to fortify his keep. She'd seen it that day they'd gone hawking together in Normandy, had spied it again tonight at supper. Even more surprising, she had heard strains of a lute being played from within his chamber earlier in the week.

Now, as he tempted her to forget her worries and simply let him touch her, she found she had questions to ask him, answers that could only be sought in the privacy of her darkened chamber and not in the cold light of day.

Closing her eyes in an attempt to ward off the sensual onslaught he provided just by being close to her, Ariana found her voice.

"Have you healed matters with your brother, my lord?" Maybe some part of her wished that if he could come to terms with his past, he would have more room in his heart for their future. For her. She realized now that she'd been foolish to think simple marriage vows would be enough to heal her heart after a lifetime of being overlooked. She wanted—nay, needed—so much more from Roarke.

Sweeping aside the veil of her hair, he found the sensitive hollow of her neck and breathed hot kisses along her skin. She shivered with need as pleasure floated through her, making her skin tighten and quiver.

"He has never blamed me for all that happened between us, and yet I sensed a new level of accord between us." He trailed kisses over her closed eyes. Tugged at the laces of her surcoat and tunic until the garments fell wantonly about her shoulders.

In their other nights together since returning to Llandervey, an air of fierce possession had marked Roarke's visits to her bed. Although her husband had always given her exquisite sensual fulfillment, he had never taken such care to unveil her body by slow degrees, seeming to savor every spot of skin he uncovered.

She quivered as his head dipped to the hollow between her breasts, his breath fanning provocative fires just beneath her skin. His fingers flexed into her hip as he pulled her closer on his lap, settling her against the hard length of him.

Her back arched as he freed her breasts, her body instinctively seeking the lush feel of his lips on her. He drew on one taut peak as he cradled the soft weight of her in his palm.

"Look at me, Ariana."

With an effort, she pried open her eyes. Saw him studying her in a way that had her heart jumping within her chest.

Growing less gentle as his touch trailed over one hip, Roarke scooped her from the chair and into his arms, carrying her to the bed. Sliding one hand beneath the hem of her gown and up the agonizing length of one thigh, he kissed her until her head fell back in abandon. "You will sing more sweetly than ever for me tonight, *mor-forwyn.*"

True to his word, Roarke wrung kisses and promises and undying devotion from her lips before the sun rose, but even at its most passionate, the night never presented Ariana with the words of love she longed to hear.

Chapter Twenty

Shortly after his dawn farewells with his brother, Roarke returned to Ariana's bed only to have her wrap herself around him more snugly than woolen braies after a rainstorm. She clung to him in sleep with an urgency she would never display while awake.

Somehow, in spite of everything, she cared for him.

The knowledge still amazed him. Although he had been wary of her after the way she'd initially deceived him in marriage, he had to admit that she continued to be loyal and unswervingly devoted to him ever since he'd discovered her true identity.

Roarke had threatened to marry her cousin, had put her in the worst danger of her life and later locked her away in her own keep. Yet still she had sweetly welcomed him into her bed at night, while during the day she spent her time healing the sick and visiting the elderly villagers.

Roarke stroked his wife's raven locks, draping the smooth strands over him like a silken blanket. Despite his efforts to distance himself from her, he knew he was in danger of losing his heart to her.

Smoothing his hand along her sleep-warm body, he caressed the curve of her flat belly. What would she look like when she grew round with his child? She could carry a babe even now. All the more reason why she should confine herself to the secure section of the keep until he'd finished fortifying Llandervey.

Was she eating well? Resting enough? He would have to watch how much time she spent working in the village. No child of his would ever have cause to wonder if his parents cared for him. Roarke would make sure his children were well cared for. As would their healer mother.

Uneasy with the depth of tenderness the thoughts spurred in him, Roarke disentangled himself from her and dressed quietly. He could not give Ariana the love she deserved, but he could at least protect her and care for her. Starting today, in fact. He would retrieve a small feast from the kitchen for her so he could see for himself that she was eating well.

He had almost reached the great hall, feeling his way through the still darkened corridors, when a painful thud in the back of the head knocked him to his knees.

His last thought was for Ariana before his world faded to naught but shadow.

She was not surprised to wake up alone.

Roarke had mentioned meeting his brother at first light, and it was long since past the break of day when Ariana rolled from her bed, her bare body still sensitive from their night together. She had rather hoped he might come back to her bed after bidding farewell to Lucian, but her chamber remained empty. Quiet.

However disappointing Roarke's disappearance might be, Ariana was grateful to have some warmth restored to her marriage, even if there was not yet love. She dressed quickly, hoping to convince Roarke to take her to the village to administer a few salves to the workers whose hands blistered from the new form of labor this winter's building projects offered.

Hurrying from her chamber, she wound her way from her tower to the corner of the keep which housed the great hall, surprised at how silent the corridors remained.

Until she heard a gentle tapping sound.

She paused in the passageway, not sure at first why the soft reverberation made her uneasy. But as the noise grew louder, closer, she realized it was the sound of footsteps. Not a man's because of the light footfall. Not a servant's because whoever approached around the next bend in the corridor wore delicately made shoes with a small wooden heel.

And Ariana could not imagine why any other noblewoman would be inside her keep.

Barely stifling the urge to flee, she edged backward in the passageway. Colliding with the solid form of a big, male body.

Her scream was smothered by a sweaty hand from behind her. Strong arms banded her hands to her sides. And just as Ariana realized Niall Kendall had entered the keep, his ladylove Marie Radborne turned the corner of the passageway wearing an elegant red tunic, and quite probably, small wooden heels beneath it.

Confusion and fear warred within Ariana as she struggled to make sense of what happened. How had these interlopers gotten inside Llandervey? And more importantly, where was Roarke?

"You need not look so pathetically frightened," Marie crooned to her in a whisper as a disconcertingly beautiful smile called dimples from her cheeks. "Niall will not get out of control today since his father should be arriving at Llandervey shortly. He's going to be a very good son this time." She cast a stern look in her lover's direction.

Ariana moved to bite Niall's finger, but Marie moved forward to slap her with a blow that left her dizzy.

"Bring her this way," she heard Marie hiss before Ariana was dragged into a small chamber off the passageway, Niall's chain mail biting right through the back of her tunic into her skin.

As soon as the door had been locked behind them, Niall slammed Ariana into a chair near the hearth and quickly replaced his stifling hand with a length of linen Marie tore from the bed. Together, they tied Ariana's hands to the chair and secured her mouth with a gag that threatened to suffocate her.

"I will not waste time pretending to be grieved your husband is gone, Lady Ceara." Marie seated herself on the hearth to stare straight into Ariana's eyes. "Or should I call you Ariana now? Not that it matters. I'm sure you've guessed Roarke's disappearance is no accident."

She turned a winning smile on Niall who paced the small guest bedchamber like a trapped animal.

Ariana felt the blood drain from her face at the thought of anything happening to Roarke. Where was he?

Marie plucked at the lush fabric of her fitted crimson surcoat. "Niall, perhaps you should see if your father's troops are at the gates. He will need your help to enter."

At her words, Niall departed the chamber, his quiet, sullen manner quite different from the crazed way he'd behaved the last time she had seen him. But then, her healer instincts told her something was very unbalanced within Roarke's younger half brother.

She forgot about him as Marie edged closer on the hearth, as if they were best friends sharing confidences and Ariana was not choking on the folded linen stuffed in her mouth.

"You know, it was all Niall's idea to hide himself among Lord Barret's troops yesterday to gain entrance to Llandervey." Marie smiled as she lifted a strand of Ariana's hair from her eyes. "He really is smarter than he appears. And now it's the talk all over English garrisons in Wales that Niall came here to halt a Welsh uprising in your ineffectual husband's absence. King Henry will be grateful when he learns of the Kendall clan's generous assistance in this matter."

Uprising? Ariana was horrified at the lengths to which Roarke's Kendall relations were willing to go to cause him harm. Her skin still crawled where Marie had touched her.

"We have planted the notion all across your godforsaken little country on our way here. And Fulke should be joining us any moment." Ariana's blue-eyed tormentor folded her arms in satisfaction. "King Henry is fortunate Lord Kendall happened along to put an end to Welsh resistance here."

Ariana's vision swam. Roarke would refute such a claim. But what if they planned to kill him?

As if called by the hateful she-demon, Fulke Kendall shoved his way into the chamber, his son behind him along with a group of retainers clad in the crimson-and-black colors of his standard. His gray hair perfectly groomed, scarlet robes draped carelessly about his shoulders, he took command of the small guest chamber with his sleek hound padding along beside him.

"Good morning, daughter." He stood to pull out the chair beside him. "I am afraid we have had some unfortunate news this morn. I am glad to see you are seated."

Ariana stilled, profound fear chilling her blood. Niall and Marie were to be feared, but they were only two souls. Fulke Kendall commanded many men, his value to the king without question.

Sweet Arianrhod, where was Roarke?

Fulke waved forward a boy from within the midst of his retainers—a lad of about ten summers whom Ariana recognized from her trips into the village. While one of Fulke's guards brought the youngster before her, Marie gestured to Niall to untie Ariana.

"Geoffrey? How are you?" Ariana leaned closer to the boy, but he showed little enthusiasm at her greeting, hanging back in the shadows of the room.

"Go ahead, lad," Fulke encouraged him. "This is the Lady of Llandervey, Lady…Ariana." Fulke turned thoughtful eyes to her, as if he had already discovered all her secrets.

Although Ariana no longer sought to hide her own

name, Fulke made it sound as if she had committed
some nefarious deed by the level of contempt in his
voice.

Awkwardly, the boy bowed. His mouth opened, but
no words came out.

"Yes?" Ariana prodded.

"I am so sorry, my lady, to be the one to bring you
this news."

Ariana stared at him, willing him to say anything but
that which she dreaded most.

"It's your husband, lady. I bring you word he was
murdered this morning just outside Glamorgan keep.
My father saw the whole thing with his own eyes. The
English lord was out riding and was beset by thieves.
My da says they stabbed him more than once."

Ariana was vaguely aware of Niall clearing his
throat. Marie tossed her blond curls impatiently as if
they'd spent far too much time discussing her husband's
death.

Turning to Fulke, she blinked back the tears that sprang
to her eyes. It couldn't be true. She still felt the warmth
of his hands upon her body. Her skin bore the whisker
burns from where he had kissed her the night before.

"This is some sort of trick you have devised." Her
words sounded more certain than she felt.

"No. Do you not recognize this lad from your own
lands?"

Unable to respond, unable even to think clearly, she
stared blankly around the room, noting Marie's bland
expression, Niall's remote, careless attitude, Fulke's
healthy color and perfectly groomed person despite the
news of his son's death.

They all sickened her.

When Ariana made no reply Fulke asked, "Would you prefer to speak with the boy in private?"

Ariana stared at Geoffrey, the messenger. An orphan raised by the local blacksmith's family, Ariana trusted the lad well enough. She could see in his eyes that he did not lie.

Or at least he *thought* he did not.

"I would know it in my heart if Roarke were dead. I have the sight." She turned a level gaze on Fulke, assuring herself that if she showed enough conviction that Roarke yet lived, it would somehow be the truth. "And I do not feel any such knowledge in my heart, despite the young man's message."

"Are you calling the messenger a liar, my lady? I have a policy of dealing with false messengers very harshly."

Geoffrey looked faint as his color went several shades paler.

"Nay," Ariana said quietly, knowing Fulke worked her to the center of his elaborate web with the skilled efficiency of a predatory spider trapping a fly.

"Then you trust in the truth of the message—that your husband is dead?"

"Aye," she agreed, knowing she could do nothing else if she wished to spare an innocent life.

The spider had the gall to smile. "Then you admit to being a widow, Lady Ariana, and fair game for a worthy suitor."

"I admit nothing of the sort, Kendall. I will have no suitor until I discuss this development with my husband's overlord, King Henry."

"We both know I am your overlord now, Lady Ariana, and as such, I command you to wed your dead husband's brother in the king's best interest, to protect his lands from Welsh rebellion."

Ariana's gaze swept from Fulke to Marie. Would Niall's lover stand idly by while Niall wed Ariana? 'Twas preposterous. Yet Marie smiled at her sweetly as if such a marriage was no concern of hers, then gazed down at her hands where she adjusted her ring.

The ring bearing a secret compartment for herbs that Roarke had said looked so much like Ariana's.

And with that telling gesture, the Kendalls' grand scheme fell into place in her mind. They would kill her—perhaps poison her—shortly after any wedding to Niall. They merely sought to solidify their claims to Roarke's lands.

No wonder Marie didn't seem to mind if Niall married Ariana. The woman would be only too glad to step into Ariana's shoes as mistress of Llandervey.

Reeling with the sting of so much treachery, Ariana fought to find some way to delay Fulke's plans.

"It is barbaric to give a wife no time to grieve. Your king defends the chivalric code, my lord. He will not be pleased with your cold-hearted refusal to listen to my preference." She struggled to keep her wits about her when she only wanted to know what had happened to Roarke. Even if he still lived—and her heart refused to accept the alternative—she knew something horrible must have happened to him or he would be here now. Beside her.

But despite the fear and pain burning through her, she needed to contain those feelings so she might think. Plan.

"The king will do whatever is necessary to secure his lands, whether it be chivalric or not." Fulke's gaze turned venomous as he reached for a stray strand of raven hair. Ariana did not move, though her skin crawled at his proximity.

"You will be brought low, Kendall."

"Not before you are, Ariana." He turned to his son. "What say you, Niall? A wedding tonight?"

Marie hovered behind the youngest Kendall, and Ariana wondered how Fulke would separate Marie from his son long enough to see him wed another woman.

Nodding, Niall did not so much as glance in his bride's direction.

"Then prepare yourself, my dear." Fulke oozed false charm as he took his seat in the position of power once again. "My son will be your salvation so you might keep your seat as Lady of Llandervey. I will see you joined in marriage this eve."

Roarke prepared for bloodshed this eve. In truth, he could not wait for the fight and longed to launch all of his fury in the direction of Niall and whoever helped him in this godforsaken scheme of his.

Crawling through the maze of hidden passageways that connected all the chambers of Llandervey, Roarke kept his movements quiet so that he might better hear any sounds emanating from the rooms around him. Ever vigilant for signs of Ariana, his ears strained to listen for any hint of her voice while he gripped a candle and scuttled through the darkness. Sometimes he'd been able to stand upright in the secret tunnels and corridors, at other times he was forced to slide on his belly. He'd discovered the passageways earlier in the week but hadn't found time to fully explore them.

Now they would lead him straight to the source of this treachery. His anger reigned and honed, he would not allow any misguided sense of honor to slow him this time.

He could move faster if he didn't carry half the keep's arsenal on his person. He'd strapped a knife to his thigh, his back and his arm. And he'd been tempted to clamp one between his teeth, as well, after he'd awoken in his own dungeon a few hours earlier, but he'd chosen to carry the small candle instead.

He'd been confused about what had happened when he first awoke, but the guard Niall had assigned to kill him had filled him in on the Kendalls' plans quickly enough. Roarke may have been lacking a knife after he'd been dragged to the bowels of the keep to be tossed into the sea, but the belt around his waist had made an easy tool to loop about his would-be killer's neck.

With a deft tug of the leather, Roarke had learned Niall had hidden himself and two others within Lucian's troops the previous day. They'd explored the keep by night while Roarke had slept, helping Marie and her guard into Llandervey by dawn and eventually admitting a troop of Fulke's men.

After killing the man who'd held him, Roarke had hidden himself within the secret corridors of his keep to reclaim his wife as well as his lands.

Having no luck in the passageways on the first floor, Roarke ascended a series of iron rungs built into one wall of the passage and ascended to the next level of

Llandervey. Whoever had built the keep had obviously been no stranger to treachery if the elaborate web of secret passages was any indication. With such a network of tunnels in place, the lord of the keep could spy on his guests at any time.

Or rescue the woman he loved from a backstabbing, soulless half brother who did not deserve to walk the same earth as Ariana Glamorgan.

Dodging a family of mice nesting in the corridor as he jogged through a wide section of the tunnel, Roarke knew he could no longer deny his love for his wife. He'd been foolish to think he could ever protect himself from the spell she'd woven around him since that very first day he'd laid eyes upon her.

Whatever enchantment she had used, it had naught to do with the fanciful charm she'd admitted to using before that fateful first meeting. In truth, he had been spellbound by Ariana before she'd disguised herself as her cousin Ceara.

Nay, his fascination with his Welsh wife had naught to do with sorcery and everything to do with her keen mind and generous spirit. His love for her had grown when she followed him all the way to France to help ensure his safety. Her rash act had demonstrated a kind of loyalty that no one outside his family had ever given him. In fact, she'd shown him far more loyalty than most of his family ever had.

Eyes burning as he thought of anything happening to her at the hands of the man she'd begged Roarke not to kill a fortnight ago, Roarke refused to allow her tender heart to cause her any harm. He would find her before anything happened to her.

And this time his justice would be swift and merciless.

He'd already dispatched Ariana's merlin to the south in the direction his brother Lucian rode. Roarke had no idea if the bird understood his wishes when he'd nudged Griffin out of the keep with the Barret medallion clamped in its talons, but the bird had never forsaken its mistress before. It seemed to possess an uncanny ability for helping Ariana.

No matter. Whether Lucian rode back to Llandervey to assist him this night or not, Roarke had no doubt as to the outcome. He meant to free Ariana from Kendall's clutches.

Slowing as he neared the doorway to a guest chamber, Roarke paused when he heard a chorus of low voices calling out "Amen."

The prayerful supplication was a far cry from the fearful screams he had half anticipated on his trek, but the mumble of holy words emanating from the other side of the wall were incongruous enough to draw his attention.

Who had time for peaceful prayer while the keep was being overrun with villains? Roarke could well understand bargains made with God while under fire, but the rhythm of the voices on the other side of this hidden doorway sounded more like a ceremonial mass or holy ritual.

Dropping his candle to the stone floor, Roarke pressed his ear to the small door which was probably tucked behind a fireplace or a heavy furnishing. The only words that came through the stone barrier were "man" and "wife."

The proceedings on the other side of the wall were not part of any sacred ritual. Rather, an unholy union took place in his own keep.

A wedding of fortunes to satisfy the Kendall greed.

A wedding Roarke would never sanction as long as he drew breath.

The fury inside him did not compel reckless action, however. If anything, his anger lent him the ability to reason through the best course of action despite the way his fingers itched to strangle Niall with his bare hands.

With slow stealth, Roarke cracked open the hidden doorway to discover a fire burning in the grate beyond. Just as he suspected, the passage would lead him into the room through the hearth, requiring him to pass through the flames. He used the blaze to heat two of his knives, laying the blades at the base of the fire. While he waited for his weapons to take on an even deadlier potency, he surveyed the layout of the room.

Ariana stood beside Niall in a sham of a wedding ceremony that she would have never willingly consented to. Her head held high, Roarke might not have suspected she was afraid if not for the way she clenched and unclenched her fingers at her side. Almost as if she was hiding something in the folds of her gown.

What if she thought to raise arms against Niall? Recalling the risks Ariana had taken since Roarke had known her, he suspected she would not submit to him without a fight.

He needed to hurry before she brought harm upon herself.

His blades roasted bright red, Roarke plucked up one of them using the corner of his tunic. From the relative safety of his hiding place, he let one blade fly through the air, end over end, until it came to rest in Fulke Kendall's shoulder.

And before his lying, conniving father even hit the floor, Roarke launched the second blade in like manner. He took out the man-at-arms guarding the door just as Fulke crumbled to the floor with a thud.

Intoning a few prayers of his own as he walked through fire to save his wife, Roarke joined the ceremony as the room erupted in chaos.

Chapter Twenty-One

Ariana did not know what had happened to make the heathen priest stop his farce of a wedding, but she was most grateful for the reprieve, no matter how short.

It wasn't until Niall flung her aside, sending her stumbling into Marie Radborne, that she understood something drastic had happened. She followed Marie's gaze to Fulke Kendall lying in his own blood, a knife protruding from his shoulder.

Sensing her chance to escape, Ariana struggled to her feet only to halt in her tracks at the vision of a man emerging from the hearth blaze.

Roarke.

Her heart rejoiced to see him. He was doused with water and slightly blackened from his walk through the flames, but otherwise unharmed.

And most of all, alive.

Relief flooded through her, and so much love she could scarce contain it. Roarke lived. And she would never again withhold the words of love that bubbled to her lips now. She would tell him every day until he believed her. Until he risked nothing to love her in return.

Niall flew at him with his sword, but Roarke stepped aside and caught him in the gut with his own knife, neatly killing the man who had sought to destroy them. Another guard lunged forward, blade drawn. Roarke held him off with his sword until he pinned the man to a wooden wardrobe.

He leaned close to the man, speaking loudly enough that all the room could hear his words.

"If you value your life, I advise you to deliver my message to the rest of the Kendall knights. Your lord is either bound for the grave or King Henry's gallows." Roarke twisted his sword in the man's tunic, bringing the unfortunate knight that much closer to the edge of the blade. "I invite any man into my protection who lays down his arms to join forces with me. All others would be wise to leave before I gather my forces and seek my vengeance."

The chamber went utterly silent in the aftermath of his declaration. Ariana could hear her breathing echo in her ears for a long moment until the Kendall guard nodded and Roarke let him go.

Ariana held her breath as the only other knight in the room laid down his sword.

She moved toward Roarke, her feet closing the gap between them even before she made a conscious decision to go to him. She fell into the strength of his strong arms, and even though she knew wily Marie still remained at her back, she also knew that Roarke would protect her. Nothing would ever hurt her while her warrior husband was at her side.

Inhaling the smoky scent of him, she searched his body for any signs of burns, but he seemed well enough. His hair still dripped with whatever water he had found to douse himself with before stepping into the flames, a few droplets trickling down onto her skin.

"Thank you." She breathed the words over and over against his chest, so grateful to see him. To hold him. She closed her eyes and allowed herself to absorb the feel of him for a long moment before Collin Baldwin, Roarke's old friend, burst into the room.

His face muddied and blood streaked, his sword still at a defensive angle across his body, his gaze went straight to Roarke. "Your brother sent me ahead but he rides shortly behind me, Barret. He bid me tell you that his troops are yours for as long as you need them."

Ariana did not need to see her husband's face to know what those words meant to him. She could almost feel the new sense of peace flow over him. His grip tightened about her waist as he nodded to Collin.

"Your assistance comes when it is most needed. I would have you take my father to the dungeon and then find a secure place to install Lady Radborne until I can send her home to her father." Roarke then pointed at the holy man still cowering in a corner with his good book propped atop his head. "The priest needs an escort outside of Wales, too, so perhaps he can tend to the souls in need of salvation at Radborne Keep."

Collin dragged Fulke over the stones, then hoisted him over his shoulder while Marie followed, tears clouding her blue eyes.

Roarke bent to kiss Ariana. "I must go now. But we

have much to speak of, wife. And I will return to you as soon as I am certain the keep is secure."

Nodding, Ariana watched him go. Although she admired his dedication to Llandervey and his people, in her heart she was already counting the moments until he came back.

Later, ensconced in the privacy of her solar, Ariana greeted him with open arms.

She'd watched from the safety of her tower as he'd raised his own standard over the keep once again. Now, she could not keep her hands from him another minute as she drew him toward her bed. Tugged him down to sit beside her.

"I am sorry about your father, Roarke," Ariana ventured, knowing the day had to have been filled with mixed emotions for him. She hoped to offer him whatever comfort she could when his whole Kendall family had proved faithless.

He pulled her into a tight embrace, his arms none too steady.

"Do not be. He is to blame for this foolishness. The king will have him killed for this treachery if he lives through his wounds."

"Aye. But no man should ever have to raise arms to his own sire."

"I had to protect my family. The Barret clan—our clan—will always come first."

Warmth curled through her at the sentiment. She was grateful he would not allow Fulke's death to torment him. Staring up at Roarke, she remembered her need to profess her love for him. And she would do so just as soon as she confessed what had happened in his absence.

"They forced me to wed Niall—" she started, tears burning her throat as she recalled the sickening feeling of exchanging vows with another man, not knowing if Roarke yet lived. "They gave me no choice as they threatened one of the villagers' children. But I swear I would not have let him touch me, my lord."

"Any wedding would not have been legal." Roarke held her closer, pressing a kiss on the top of her hair, his hands squeezing her tightly to him. "I am so sorry."

He spoke the words softly, but Ariana heard the vehemence behind them.

"Whatever for?"

"What am I not sorry for? *Sweet Jesu,* Ariana. I let you stay with me in France when I knew you would be safer at home. I brought you to Southvale with me and let my anger with my father distract me from protecting you. Then upon our arrival at Llandervey, I locked you away from me so I might not be tempted to fall in love with you."

He frowned, his expression fierce. "I cannot recall one sound decision I have made since I met you."

Ariana knew it would be a mistake to smile in the face of his tirade, but the only line of his diatribe that she cared about tugged at the corners of her mouth in spite of her best efforts to conceal it.

He'd been tempted to fall in love with her.

"I do not think that falling in love is such an unwise decision." Gathering her courage, she forced herself to admit the truth she had long felt in her heart. "I have already grown to love you, Roarke Barret."

He gazed upon her for so long she feared he would cast her out for even suggesting such a thing. But then he kissed her so fiercely, pressing her whole body to his with strong, greedy hands, that she knew he was not disappointed.

"And I cherish you, Ariana. So much." He whispered the words across her lips, then broke away to stare into her eyes. "I vow I will love you to the end of my days."

Her heart seemed to fill and expand, containing more joy and hope for the future than she'd ever dreamed possible. Somewhere in that tender expanse of soft emotions she remembered Eleanor's long-ago words that if love was meant to be, all obstacles would fall away.

And at last, now that they'd each made peace with their pasts and with themselves, it seemed there was nothing left standing in their way.

"I cannot begin to say how much that pleases me," she confessed in return, her cheeks warm with pleasure at how her marriage made out of deception and desperation had turned into her greatest blessing.

"But since I am committing my heart into your keeping forever, I must confess I am curious about one thing." He twisted one of her dark curls around his finger and kissed the silky lock.

"I will answer you if I can, my lord husband." She smoothed her palm across the rough whiskers of his cheek, delighting in the hard masculine angles of this man who had saved her in so many ways.

"You suggested you would never have allowed my craven half brother to touch you after your spurious marriage, but I fail to see how one so delicate as you would have fought off a warrior of Niall's might." He traced the outline of her shoulders with his broad palms, as if wondering where she hid her strength. "Did you not need my sword prowess to come to your aid?"

"I had every need of your assistance, but since I had no intention of joining any man save you in a marriage bed, I thought it best to devise a weapon of my own." She waved her ring under his nose. "Remember how our wine was tainted on our wedding night? I imagine Niall was following you even then, planting one of Marie's poisons in our libation."

Roarke grinned, a glint of humor in his eyes as they sat together in front of the small blaze at the foot of her bed. "You planned to repay the favor with your new groom?"

"Let's just say I would not want to use the contents of my ring in *your* wine tonight." She twined her arms around Roarke's neck, drawing him close.

"I don't think any potion you could craft would keep me from your bed tonight, but thank you just the same." Roarke placed a kiss upon her palm, his tongue darting out to warm the valley between her fingers. "You are a clever woman, Ariana Barret."

Pleasure flowed through her at the thought of lying beside her husband with naught but love between them.

"Clever? Perhaps." She savored the secret she'd been carrying for the last few days, grateful she had waited to share it with him until their happy future together was assured. "But mostly I was concerned about protecting your babe."

Roarke's eyes widened for one silent moment. And

then he howled with pleasure like a wolf in the glow of a full moon.

He hugged her. Kissed her. Held her apart from him so that he could gaze into her eyes. "I can think of no happier news to celebrate our future."

"Do you forgive me for deceiving you when we first met?" She had long craved this assurance from him, and could not resist asking on this day of so many happy beginnings.

"I admire your strength, Ariana. I am so grateful you did not allow yourself to waste away in your father's care. And I'm even more grateful I was your unsuspecting groom." He kissed her nose, her lips. "Thank you."

Warmth curled through her, and it had naught to do with the toasty fire at her feet. Happy contentment mingled with rising desire as he allowed his hands to roam over her belly.

"We must have made the babe that first night," he told her, sliding his hands beneath her tunic to touch her skin.

"Aye. It happened so quickly I cannot help but think this babe will be the first of many for us." She shivered at the warmth of his palm upon her bare waist.

"Mor-forwyn." He cupped her breasts, already grown tender and full. "You are too tempting by half."

He captured her mouth with his own and with one kiss, he answered all her questions; put to rest any doubts.

"The babe pleases you," Ariana observed, holding on to him another moment. She knew she would have to give him up soon to greet his brother's troops and clear the keep of any knights loyal to Fulke. But she had waited so long for this moment, she planned to keep him all to herself a little longer.

"Aye. She does."

"She?"

"Do you not have the sight, wife?" He laughed, sliding her tunic back into place as he kissed her cheek. "She will be another Welsh *mor-forwyn*, like her mother. Full of song and mischief."

"Mayhap our child will be a strong and stubborn little lad, with a head full of dark hair and lofty dreams."

"Nay. We broke the curse of Glamorgan with this child. She will be a girl—living proof of the strength of Glamorgan women."

"We will see."

"Aye." Roarke curved his fingers about her neck and tilted her chin to look up at him. "You will."

Savor the breathtaking
romances and thrilling adventures
of Harlequin Historicals

On sale September 2004

THE KNIGHT'S REDEMPTION by Joanne Rock

A young Welshwoman tricks Roarke Barret into marriage
in order to break her family's curse—of spinsterhood.
But Ariana Glamorgan never expects to fall for the
handsome Englishman who is now her husband....

PRINCESS OF FORTUNE by Miranda Jarrett

Captain Lord Thomas Greaves is assigned to guard Italian
princess Isabella di Fortunaro. Sparks fly and passions flare
between the battle-weary captain and the spoiled, beautiful
lady. Can love cross all boundaries?

On sale October 2004

HIGHLAND ROGUE by Deborah Hale

To save her sister from a fortune hunter, Claire Talbot offers
herself as a more tempting target. But can she forget the
feelings she once had for Ewan Geddes, a charming
Highlander who once worked on her father's estate?

THE PENNILESS BRIDE by Nicola Cornick

Home from the Peninsula War, Rob Selbourne discovers
he must marry a chimney sweep's daughter to
fulfill his grandfather's eccentric will. Will Rob
find true happiness in the arms of
the lovely Jemima?

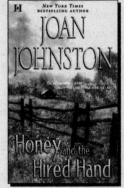

If you enjoyed what you just read,
then we've got an offer you can't resist!

Take 2 bestselling
love stories FREE!
Plus get a FREE surprise gift!

Clip this page and mail it to Harlequin Reader Service®

IN U.S.A.
3010 Walden Ave.
P.O. Box 1867
Buffalo, N.Y. 14240-1867

IN CANADA
P.O. Box 609
Fort Erie, Ontario
L2A 5X3

YES! Please send me 2 free Harlequin Historicals® novels and my free surprise gift. After receiving them, if I don't wish to receive anymore, I can return the shipping statement marked cancel. If I don't cancel, I will receive 6 brand-new novels every month, before they're available in stores! In the U.S.A., bill me at the bargain price of $4.69 plus 25¢ shipping and handling per book and applicable sales tax, if any*. In Canada, bill me at the bargain price of $5.24 plus 25¢ shipping and handling per book and applicable taxes**. That's the complete price and a savings of over 10% off the cover prices—what a great deal! I understand that accepting the 2 free books and gift places me under no obligation ever to buy any books. I can always return a shipment and cancel at any time. Even if I never buy another book from Harlequin, the 2 free books and gift are mine to keep forever.

246 HDN DZ7Q
349 HDN DZ7R

Name	(PLEASE PRINT)	
Address	Apt.#	
City	State/Prov.	Zip/Postal Code

Not valid to current Harlequin Historicals® subscribers.

Want to try two free books from another series?
Call 1-800-873-8635 or visit www.morefreebooks.com.

* Terms and prices subject to change without notice. Sales tax applicable in N.Y.
** Canadian residents will be charged applicable provincial taxes and GST.
   All orders subject to approval. Offer limited to one per household.
   ® are registered trademarks owned and used by the trademark owner and or its licensee.

HIST04R   ©2004 Harlequin Enterprises Limited